Meet Me in a Mile

Also by Elizabeth Hrib

Lightning Strikes Twice
Flirting with Disaster

Visit the Author Profile page at Harlequin.com.

meet me in a mile

ELIZABETH HRIB

ISBN-13: 978-1-335-57482-4

Meet Me in a Mile

Harlequin Enterprises ULC
22 Adelaide St. West, 41st Floor
Toronto, Ontario M5H 4E3, Canada
www.Harlequin.com

Printed in U.S.A.

Recycling programs
for this product may
not exist in your area.

One

Lydia

Lydia McKenzie wasn't usually a runner, but she sure as hell was this morning. She nabbed her jeans from the carpeted floor and shimmied into them, trying not to trip on the snaky straps of her bra that peeked out from beneath the bed. Tiptoeing around the room, she retraced last night's lust-filled haze as she finished dressing, attempting not to wake the pillow-hugging figure beneath the sheets. The sex hadn't been anything spectacular—she'd had to take care of things herself—and she really didn't feel like living through an awkward morning after.

She got down on her hands and knees, looking for her purse. *Please, don't be in the cab*, she thought miserably, scanning the underside of the bed. This had all started after a client meeting in the Financial District. Schmoozing the Wall Street types wasn't her usual style, but she'd been up for some fun, and at least Ian—or was it Ethan?—had cared enough to make small talk before blatantly inviting her back to his place.

"Kitchen," she whispered, jumping to her feet and hurrying out of the room.

Lydia stopped long enough in the kitchen to absorb the sleekness of it all. Chrome appliances. Granite countertops. It was all so sterile. There wasn't even a picture or a magnet on the fridge. She wrinkled her nose at the monotony of high condo ceilings and eggshell-colored walls. How terribly boring.

She spotted her purse next to the toaster, grabbed it, and did a cursory check—phone, wallet, keys. Then she stuffed her shoes on, threw open the door and booked it into the elevator. Her phone buzzed as she walked through the lobby a few moments later. It was a text from Ashley. Like she usually did when the occasion called for it, she'd texted her sister the address of where she was spending the night.

I'm waiting downstairs. Let me know if you need a ding, dong, ditch.

Lydia replied with an emoji of a woman running.

They often met up in the mornings for coffee before Lydia made her way to work and Ashley made her way to the gym. Ashley somehow always managed to squeeze in a yoga class before work, which she considered a necessity since she spent most of her waking hours navigating the stresses of Big Law. Conveniently, Ian or Ethan lived among the luxury buildings in NoMad, so Ashley's gym in the Flatiron District was a reasonably short walk.

As she exited the building, she was greeted by the stillness of the waking streets—nothing like the cacophony New

York City would be later in the morning when cab horns chirped, sirens wailed and bikers rang their tiny bells, fighting cars for space.

"Hey," Ashley called, walking over. She was already wearing her matching activewear set. "I come bearing gifts." She handed Lydia a large raspberry chai latte topped with vanilla cold foam and sprinkles of cinnamon.

"You are a goddess," Lydia said, taking a sip. Sugary caffeine drinks topped with fluffy cold foam were her biggest weakness. "Thanks for meeting me."

"You know, I thought I'd stop having to pick you up after wild nights out when you finished college."

Though she was only a couple years older, Ashley had crossed that threshold from late twenties to early thirties and now regarded things like one-night stands with amusement as she contemplated serious things like marriage with her equally serious fiancé, Kurt.

"Maybe I just like spending time with my favorite sister," Lydia told her, taking another sip of teeth-rotting syrupy goodness.

"I'm your only sister."

"And you secretly love it when I text you in the middle of the night with clandestine details of my love life. It keeps your week interesting."

They turned onto 6th Avenue, where short, redbrick apartment buildings rose up around them in between businesses and restaurants. As they continued, towering condos and sleek office buildings loomed overhead, casting long shadows across the street. Lydia let herself soak in the history and the colors— harsh lines from old fire escapes, the muted tones of the clay once dug from the Hudson, even the way the buildings butted up against each other—while enjoying the stark differences that announced the ending of one neighborhood and the beginning of another. In a borough as bustling as Manhattan, everyone knew there was room for more development, and her hand was itching for a drawing pencil.

"I thought you were all hung up on that guy from your work?"

"That *guy's* name is Jack. And I'm playing the long game."

"The long game requires you to actually *start* the game," Ashley pointed out.

Lydia wrinkled her nose. Jack Carson was one of the project coordinators at Poletti Architectural Studios. But despite having worked at the firm for close to three years now, Lydia still hadn't determined if Jack knew her name or if he constantly said *hey there* when they bumped elbows in the copy room because he'd actually forgotten.

"You're turning red."

"I am not." Lydia nudged her sister with her shoulder. "But I am leaving breadcrumbs for him to follow. A compliment here. A conversation there. Eventually he'll catch on."

"At least you're having fun while you're waiting for Jack to get a clue." Ashley's smile dropped from her face.

"You and Kurt still haven't settled on a venue, huh?" Lydia might still be waiting for the man of her dreams to notice her, but the man of Ashley's dreams was holding up their wedding planning. Lydia wasn't sure which one was worse.

"No," Ashley muttered darkly, crushing the empty coffee cup in her hand. "And until he does, I can't secure a date. And until there is a date, there are no invitations. And if there are no invitations, there are no guests."

Lydia almost regretted bringing it up. "Rein it in, Ash. Kurt is just trying to make you happy."

"I don't mean to be snappish. I just want to get the ball rolling. I waited years for him to propose. Is it really so inconceivable that I don't want to wait any longer?"

"Of course not," Lydia assured her. Ashley and Kurt had met in undergrad and dated through law school. When they'd graduated, Ashley was ready to settle down, but Kurt had wanted them both to climb the career ladder, to get established.

Ashley huffed, the sound not quite a laugh. "I always thought I wanted this big, extravagant white wedding. But now it can literally rain for all I care. I just want to get us down that aisle."

"I think rain's supposed to be good luck." Ashley glared at her. "Look, most brides wish their fiancés took more of an interest in this sort of stuff. If Kurt wants to be a part of it, then let him. It's less stuff you and I have to worry about in the end."

"Remind me why I made you my maid of honor again?"

"Because unfortunately for you, I am your best friend."

They slowed at Fitness Forum, a boutique gym where people paid an exorbitant amount of money to roll around getting sweaty—but not the fun kind of rolling or sweating. She followed Ashley inside, loitering at the lockers.

"You want to come to class? I can get you a guest pass for the morning."

Lydia shook her head. "No thanks. I've already done my cardio."

Ashley made a face. "Please don't launch into your sexcapades."

"I was talking about walking back from NoMad, thank you very much." She waggled her brows. "But my stories might be more fun than being stretched and contorted like spaghetti."

"That is not what happens in yoga."

"Cobra pose. Tree pose. Triangle pose. Half-seated spinal twist. Shall I continue?"

"You are so annoying," Ashley said without any real bite. "Come on. Stay. Have this transcendent experience with me."

"Yuck." Lydia checked her phone. "The only thing I'd be transcending in there is the natural curvature of my spine. I have to go shower and change before work."

"Fine. I'll call you later."

"Have fun transcending." Rolling her eyes at the pouty look on Ashley's face, Lydia turned. But instead of stepping toward the door, she walked straight into a man built like a brick wall. She sloshed her latte, thankfully just on her own shoes and not on the man—the employee—who had just walked through the door.

Lydia traced the hard lines before her. His jaw was as defined as the pectorals she'd just assessed with her face. It was unfair, really, to be that perfect. And as someone who traded in lines and curves and arches for her day job, she could appreciate perfection. She was almost tempted to reach out and touch. Then she remembered herself, stopped ogling that space where bicep met tricep, and choked out an apology instead. "I am *so* sorry."

"Are you okay?" he asked.

"You took my breath away for a second," she said, only hearing the words after they'd already left her mouth. "I mean the collision. Hitting you. Not because you're—" Lydia gestured at him vaguely. "It's not that you're not very... I mean, you are. But that's not what I—" Lydia snapped her mouth closed. For the first time since their collision, Lydia noticed the name tag pinned to the stranger's fitted black shirt: *Luke*.

"You know what?" he said, adjusting the backpack on his shoulder. "You're not the first woman to tell me that. It's been a while though, so it's nice to hear I've still got it."

He was clearly joking but Lydia's cheeks burned.

"Luke!" someone called from the front desk. "You've got a call on hold."

Luke glanced to the front desk then back to Lydia. "You're sure you're okay?"

"Yep," she squeaked. "I'm just great."

"It's First Union Bank!" they called again.

Luke hurried off to take his phone call.

"What on earth did I just witness?" Ashley asked as soon as he was out of earshot. When Lydia turned around, her sister was grinning from ear to ear.

"You really just stood there and let that happen?"

"I was too shocked to interrupt. It just kept getting worse." Ashley pitched her voice, doing a poor imitation. "You took my breath away because you're just so big and strong..."

"Oh my God," Lydia said, mortified as she bolted out the door, shutting it on Ashley's teasing.

Poletti Architectural Studios was housed on the fourteenth floor of a skyscraper that looked out over the Hudson River

with 10th Avenue at its back. Lydia had been up to the roof
once to see the view, the buildings all stacked like pieces in a
Tetris game. That was more than three years ago now. After
she'd graduated, she'd spent a couple years building her résumé, working for smaller firms before officially applying to
Poletti's. Marco Poletti had interviewed her himself and hired
her on the spot. Lydia liked to frequently remind herself that
she'd impressed the principal architect of the firm, especially
on days when her design proposals were rejected.

She found one such present on her desk as she walked into
her office, and her stomach sank. There was a familiar line of
red ink scratched across the cover page of her proposal and not
one single recommendation or note. Lydia flipped through the
whole document just to be sure, then slumped down in her
swivel chair. She wasn't in the mood for rejection this early
in the morning and contemplated seeking out her supervisor,
Erik Shaunesberg, to commiserate. Together they were considered the eco-gurus in the office, and though Poletti's wasn't
known for their green innovation like other firms, Lydia was
usually excited to sprinkle a little of her passion into projects
whenever possible. Though lately it seemed like most of her
proposals had been destined for the recycling bin.

She was still glaring at the proposal when Kirsten Watters,
the firm's administrative assistant, appeared in her doorway.
The youngest member of the team, Kirsten had the closet of a
runway model and the world-weary, no-nonsense approach of
someone twice her age. She was known for abruptly hanging
up on rude clients and leaving passive-aggressive sticky notes
on desks. She was also Lydia's favorite person in the office.

"Who red-lined your proposal?" Kirsten asked, leaning against the doorjamb.

"That is a question for the ages." Lydia dropped the proposal on her desk.

"How was last night? You left with that guy, right?"

"Nothing to write home about." Kirsten's lips twitched as Lydia said, "Now ask me what I did this morning? I walked my sister to the gym and ran face-first into one of the most attractive men I have ever seen in my life."

"Like you physically hit him?"

"Pretty sure I rebounded off his pectorals."

Kirsten plopped herself down on the corner of Lydia's desk. "Okay, rewind. How attractive are we talking? I'm trying to decide if I should start going to the gym."

Lydia laughed. No one besides Ashley knew about her little workplace crush on Jack—she'd never wanted pesky feelings to interfere with her career. Though she did enjoy talking about all the nonserious hypotheticals she encountered outside the office. "I have banned myself from going anywhere near Ashley's gym because I'm still mortified. I literally told this man he took my breath away, then retracted my statement and vaguely pointed to all his muscles."

"I don't know if I should be taking notes or getting popcorn."

"Ashley watched me do all this in real time."

"She's fired for not recording," Kirsten said. "I'm your sister now."

"Who's fired?" Lydia looked up to see Erik standing in the doorway. The man favored turtlenecks and suit jackets and the color black. His hair was buzzed short and he liked to pretend he was hard of hearing in one ear when people pestered him with questions. For some reason, he reminded Lydia of her father. Or *a* father. Erik had no children, but she'd always thought he would make a good dad. Whenever she told him that, he said he was still waiting on his prince charming.

"We're talking about Lydia's romantic fails," Kirsten said, clueing him in.

"Speaking of failures," Lydia said, shaking her proposal at Erik. "Did you know about this? There's no feedback. Again."

Erik frowned. "No, but I'll talk to the leadership team, see if I can at least get you some notes. Maybe you can make a few tweaks and resubmit. I'll try to catch them after the meeting."

"What meeting?"

"The quarterly team meeting," Kirsten said, making her way to the door. "It's this morning, remember?"

She had, in fact, not remembered. Lydia rifled through her desk for a pen and a notepad. Erik stayed, looking out her sliver of a window. Her office was a shoebox, but she'd lucked out with one instead of a cubicle because their team was small, so no one would ever catch her complaining about it. She had no problem complaining about her red-lined proposal, however. "Tell me the truth," she said. "Was my design bad?"

Erik leaned against the window, studying the street below. "I loved your proposal. That's why I told you it was ready to submit."

"Well, I'm kind of getting mixed messages here." As far as supervisors went, she couldn't have asked for someone more committed to her learning. But like any young architect, she was eager to make a name for herself and her designs. To do that, she had to actually get a proposal into the hands of a client. She wanted to know that her work was more than just good. She wanted it to be *great*. Though clearly whatever Erik saw in her work wasn't making the cut at the next level.

"We'll get it figured out," Erik promised. "C'mon, Marco's already in the building. We don't want to be late."

Lydia followed Erik down the hall to the conference room. It was a corner office stacked with floor-to-ceiling windows. She took a seat at the massive oblong table between Erik and Kirsten as the automatic shades lowered, darkening the room enough for the projector beam to show up. A tray of breakfast pastries sat in the middle of the table, along with a box of brewed coffee courtesy of Charmaine's, the boutique café on the first floor of the building. Kirsten helped herself, also pouring coffee for Lydia and Erik. She passed Lydia's cup over with a heaping handful of sugar packets.

"How is everyone this morning?" Marco asked, breezing into the room.

Though he was pushing seventy, he had the energy of someone thirty years younger, and it had been his exuberance that had originally driven Lydia to accept a position with Poletti's. She wanted to always be in love with her career the way Marco was.

He picked up the projector remote and started the slideshow. "If I can direct your attention away from the chocolate croissants to the screen, let's round up what we finished last quarter before we talk about the fun stuff."

When the slideshow eventually changed to an image of a nondescript brick building surrounded by yards of crumbling asphalt and a chain-link fence, Lydia sat up, nudging Erik. "What's that?"

"I have no idea." Erik usually gave her a heads-up when there was an interesting brief coming down the line, but he hadn't mentioned this place at all.

"This is the Manhattan Youth Center," Marco explained. "The city is sponsoring a design competition run by the Department of Buildings. A *multimillion-dollar* design competition. They want to take this crumbling youth center and rebuild it. And I want Poletti's to throw our hat in the ring. It would be excellent exposure for the firm if we win. It would also look good in a portfolio for whoever's design gets chosen."

Whispers erupted around the table.

"Competition deadline is November 1," Marco said, rubbing his peppery beard. "So, let's say proposals are due to the leadership team by the last Monday in October at the latest. They'll vet them and I'll choose the best design out of those to put forth as our submission."

A hand shot up. "Sir, do you want individual projects?"

Lydia turned to Jack. He was on the leadership team himself, though his question told Lydia that this announcement had been a surprise to the entire firm. Jack lowered his hand, sweeping it through his chestnut-brown hair. The tousled locks fell like unruly waves, parting on either side of his forehead, framing his face: Wide brow. Sharp jaw. Aquiline nose. And eyes so dark she'd always wondered if she'd find flecks of color buried within them like stars. With great effort, she dragged her eyes back across the table.

"Partner up or go solo," Marco was saying. "Whatever you want. Just bring me your best work."

Excited chatter whipped through the room like a summer breeze. It was the beginning of June. That gave them all about four and a half months before the deadline. Anticipation stirred in Lydia's gut. She'd wanted a chance to prove that she could be great, and here it was, practically falling into her lap.

Jack stood, replacing Marco at the front of the room. Lydia's heart thumped unevenly in her chest as his gaze passed around the table. He took control of the slideshow. "After all that excitement, I'm sure everyone is eager to find out what our office outreach event will be for the latter half of this year." He flipped through some slides from previous years—soup kitchens, animal rescues. "We've had a lot of really great volunteer opportunities in the past, but this year, we think we've come up with something pretty special."

Jack changed the slide to a photo of a man crossing a finish line, arms outstretched, mouth open in triumphant relief. Or excruciating pain—it was hard to tell.

"Poletti's is going to put together a team to run the New York City Marathon."

"That's what I was afraid of," Erik whispered under his breath for only Lydia to hear.

Silence followed Jack's big announcement. Lydia herself would have been unnerved by the reaction, but Jack remained perfectly composed. "I know you have questions. I can see them burning in your eyes. So fire away."

"Isn't it hard to get into the marathon?" someone piped up.

"It can be," Jack said. "But Poletti's would be entering on behalf of a charity. I was going to put the charity to a vote, but now I'm thinking we should run for one that supports the Manhattan Youth Center. I looked it up while Marco was talking. They still have charity race slots available. Seems to

me like a really good way to combine both the design competition and our outreach project."

Lydia pressed her lips together, keeping her thoughts to herself. It was a nice idea. Poletti's just wasn't exactly the kind of
firm that went running together…

"Hear me out before you say no," Jack said, ticking points
off on his fingers. "It really is for a good cause. We would
do a lot of fundraising. There are wonderful health benefits
that come with training for a marathon. And it'll be great for
team bonding."

Erik lifted his hand. "I will give you money just so I don't
have to run."

"I will double it," someone else said.

A chuckle wrapped around the table, but Jack still looked
so ridiculously hopeful standing up there with his eager smile.

"I think it's a great idea," Lydia said before she could stop
herself. Next to her, Kirsten snorted and lowered her head.

"See," Jack said excitedly. "This is what I'm talking about.
Enthusiasm. Where's that team spirit?"

"I left it in the hospital with my last knee replacement,"
someone muttered.

Jack laughed, humoring the group. "Okay, I get it. Not
everyone is going to run. Not everyone *has* to run. We'll put
together a small team of interested people. Me for starters.
Lydia, thank you for volunteering."

Erik turned to her, perplexed. "I didn't know you were a
runner."

Kirsten was practically wheezing beside her while all Lydia
could do was gape.

"Anyone that can't or doesn't want to run can help with

fundraising," Jack continued. "You can also be there to support the team on race day and you're free to join any office training sessions. I'll need to coordinate with the charity and get us registered as soon as possible, so I'll put out an email blast this afternoon to confirm details."

Marco stood, hands on his hips, grinning at them like an overeager track coach. "This is gonna be really great for Poletti's." He pointed to Kirsten. "Definitely going in the newsletter."

Kirsten gave him a thumbs-up. "You got it, boss."

Jack closed out his presentation and walked around the table to high-five Lydia. She lifted her hand on autopilot and his fingers tangled with hers. "All right, running buddy. Marathon here we come."

Lydia's pulse danced in her throat. How was this both the best and worst day of her life?

Two

Luke

Luke Townsend hadn't thought it was possible to stub both his big toes in one morning, but as he stumbled around his Hell's Kitchen apartment, cursing bedposts under his breath, he now knew better. He'd gotten distracted, that was the problem. First he'd gotten sidetracked writing up the fitness programming for the Manhattan Youth Center, where he volunteered a couple times a week. Then he'd found himself preoccupied with a blog article titled "How to Win the Boardroom," which had given him the brilliant idea to wear a navy polo shirt and slacks to his meeting at First Union Bank. But if he was wearing his slacks then he needed his good shoes. And if he was wearing his good shoes, then he needed good socks, which is how the toe stubbing came about. Now he was almost running late for, maybe, the most important appointment of his life.

Luke raced out the door. He had no intention of winning over any boardrooms, but he did hope to impress Mrs. Amisfield, the loan officer at First Union. Luckily, he didn't live far—close enough to make the dash and still arrive with a couple minutes to spare. Inside, the building was nothing but white porcelain floors and frosted office doors. A bout of jitters jumped around in Luke's gut.

"Hello, sir. Can I help you?"

A woman greeted Luke from behind her desk next to the entry. Luke ran a hand down the front of his polo, smoothing nonexistent wrinkles. "I'm Luke Townsend. I have a meeting with Mrs. Amisfield."

The woman nodded, clicking away on her keyboard. "Just have a seat over there." She gestured to a waiting area.

Luke slid into a sleek leather chair. Beyond those frosted glass doors, Luke could hear muted conversations. He wondered how many other people had walked in here today, chasing a dream. One of the doors rolled open, and Luke's pulse skipped unsteadily. A short woman in a black business suit emerged. She had curly dark hair, streaked with gray, and a pair of thick glasses perched on the end of her nose. She approached Luke and he jumped to his feet, reaching for the hand she extended. "Mrs. Amisfield?"

"Hello, Mr. Townsend." She smiled as they shook hands, then she flicked her head toward her office. "Follow me."

Luke did, sitting in his appointed chair, clasping his hands in his lap. He felt like he was back in elementary school, waiting to be delivered grades for a poorly written test. Mrs. Amisfield twisted her computer screen toward him so he could see the file she'd started with his information. "You're here to discuss a business loan?" she confirmed.

"That's right," Luke said.

"And what kind of business do you have in mind?"

Luke released a heavy breath—one that felt like it had been taking up space in his chest for years. "I'd like to open a gym."

"A gym," she repeated, typing away. "And what do you do for work now?"

"I'm a personal trainer."

The corner of her mouth curved. "A logical step then."

Her smile eased the nerves that were still dancing in Luke's gut. Some ridiculous part of his brain had expected her to throw him from the office the moment he uttered the word *gym*. He didn't know why he thought that. A gym was a reputable business. It made sense for him considering his career as a trainer. It was probably just old worries resurfacing. His family had never exactly been on board with his vision, and they'd spent a lot of time trying to talk him out of it. *Do you even know what it takes to get a business off the ground?* That had been his sister. *Why don't you try for a more stable career?* his mother always said. *You can always go back to school. Finish your master's.* Even his brother, an avid gym buff, wrinkled his nose at the thought. *Businesses come and go faster than people can think them up. And property is expensive to rent.*

Luke rolled his shoulders, forcing some of the tension free. "I know there's more to owning a gym than just showing up and working out every day, but I'd like to think that being a trainer has given me a good foundation for what works and what doesn't when trying to attract clients to a space."

Mrs. Amisfield clicked onto a new part of the online file. "Tell me about your gym."

Luke laughed. "You mean my nonexistent gym?"

She nodded. "Let's say we handed you the money today.

What does this place look like? Where is it located? How does it operate?"

"Uh… Okay, well, there's this empty building down on Eleventh Avenue. It was a warehouse at one point, but the space had been cleared out, and I think it's perfect for a gym. It's currently owned by an old friend of my father's. So, if I had the money, I'd rent the space from him. It's got a huge, industrial open floor plan, but I'd make it welcoming. I'd staff the place with hard workers, people like myself, who come from a multitude of fitness backgrounds. I'd offer a variety of fitness classes. And something I'd really like to do is provide youth programming. You know, create a safe, fun place for kids to be introduced to exercise."

Mrs. Amisfield nodded. "I like to get a sense of my client's vision before we really get started. I also like to make sure you've thought this through. That it's not just a dream, but a reality in the making. It sounds like you know what you want to accomplish here. All you need now are the funds. So what I'm going to need from you is everything you just told me but on paper." She handed him a checklist. "A solid business plan is going to be the key to being approved for a business loan with First Union."

Luke scanned the list. There were at least a dozen documents he was going to need to track down. "I don't have financial statements."

"That's for businesses that are already established. From you, the bank's going to want to see financial projections. But be realistic with your numbers," she warned. "Overly optimistic figures, especially for your first couple of years, could undermine your credibility. You don't want to make obtaining a loan any harder on yourself."

She handed Luke a pen and he scribbled her directions in the margins of his checklist.

"We'll want to know how you're going to use the money. That's where you'll provide a statement with your business description, company strategy, products and services, marketing plans. You basically want to show us why people are going to choose your gym. What makes you different? Why are you worth the investment?"

"I've heard market research can be helpful," Luke said. "Is that something I should be including?"

"Absolutely. Because you're not up and running yet, you should be outlining your market, the fitness industry, competition, trends. But focus on local market opportunities, not the big picture."

"Right," Luke said, foreseeing a lot of late nights in his future. He'd accumulated some of these things—the internet had been somewhat helpful outlining what he would need. But seeing it all on paper like this was overwhelming: Leases. Floor plans. Equipment budgets. Key employee breakdowns. Mrs. Amisfield must have noticed his wide-eyed look because she reached out to still his frantically scribbling hand.

"We'll follow up again to review your progress."

Luke let out a breath. "That would be great."

Mrs. Amisfield pulled up her calendar. "What kind of timeline are you working with?"

"Maybe we could touch base in about a month?" Luke said. That should give him enough time to get a good start on the market research.

"Sounds good." Mrs. Amisfield stood, reaching to shake Luke's hand again. "Contact my assistant to schedule another appointment."

Luke left the bank and practically bounded to the subway. He had to get to the gym for a client consultation, but he was glowing with something—pride, maybe—and he couldn't wipe the grin off his face. This was a huge first step toward something he'd been dreaming about for a long time, and while hunting down the information for his business plan was going to entail a lot of research, he was decidedly optimistic.

Luke made his way from the subway to the gym and headed straight for the front desk. Dara handed him a folder. She was a five-foot-nothing ball of attitude fresh out of high school who spent most of her downtime ragging on him instead of actually doing her job. As the youngest of three kids, Luke had no idea what having an annoying younger sibling was like, though he imagined Dara summed it up pretty perfectly. But as much as she was a pain in his backside, she was excellent with the clients— usually. He opened the folder, scanning the first document.

"You know, it helps if you actually get some information from the clients," he noted.

"I did." Dara poked at the paper. "Lydia McKenzie. Running."

"You don't even have her phone number written down."

Dara cocked her head, staring at him like he was a piece of gum stuck to a subway seat. "Am I supposed to do your whole job for you? It's a client consult. Go consult."

"Is she even here?"

"I put her in the waiting area."

"Perfect," he said, setting off. "I'll grab her on the way to my office."

"Plumbers are in your office today," Dara said. "Repairing that leaky pipe. Then the drywall guy will need to get in there to repair the hole they leave behind."

"Erg." Luke turned on the spot. "I forgot about that."

"My office is free," Jules called, coming down the hall toward them. "I'm the only spin instructor here today, so between that and yoga, I'll be in one of the studios for most of the day."

"Thank you," Luke said. He high-fived Jules as she passed, then headed to the waiting area to collect Lydia. When he drew closer, he realized it was the same woman that he'd run into earlier this week—*literally.* Arguments could be made that it was actually her fault—that maybe she'd walked into him—but his mother had raised him to be a gentleman. Plus, it probably *was* his fault. His mind had been elsewhere, and then suddenly there'd been a perfect stranger in his arms.

A stranger who currently had her head thrown back, staring at the ceiling. "Everything okay?" he asked, his own eyes lifting to see what she was looking at.

"You again?" There was a surprised hitch to her voice as she tilted her head, her long, strawberry blond ponytail swinging over her shoulder while her green eyes appraised him.

Her cheeks had a smattering of freckles, but it was her expressive eyebrows that really gave life to her face. Luke watched one brow slowly arch. From that expression alone, he might have learned a thousand things. The most obvious was that she was clearly thinking about their collision, if the sudden color in her cheeks was anything to go by.

"Me again," he said. "Guess the front desk staff figured since I took your breath away the other day we might be a good client-trainer fit."

"You let that one go right to your head," she muttered.

"I have to keep my ego inflated somehow."

"Clearly."

"I'm still not sure what we're doing staring at the ceiling."

"Oh, sorry!" She snatched her bag and climbed out of her chair. "I was just admiring the old brickwork."

Luke pursed his lips. "Can't say I've ever given it much thought, to be honest."

Lydia smiled, shaking her head. "I'm an architect, so I spend a lot of time staring at boring things like walls and ceilings. I also really appreciate exposed brickwork in early nineteenth-century buildings."

Luke laughed. "That makes so much more sense." He reached for her hand. "I'm Luke."

"Guess we should actually do this properly," Lydia said, shaking it.

"Throwing your coffee at someone isn't how you normally greet them?"

"There was no throwing of any kind," she argued as they started down the hall together.

"That's true. You mostly just poured coffee all over your shoes."

"It was actually a raspberry chai latte, which my sister kindly bought for me."

"Well, that changes things," Luke said. "Here I was thinking you were just clumsy, but now I see you were trying to find a convenient way to get rid of your drink."

"Are you calling my drink order gross?"

"If the drink sleeve fits."

Lydia gaped at him in what he thought was mock offense. "Let me guess. You're a one-cup-of-black-coffee kind of guy."

"Every morning."

"I'm not sure this partnership is going to work out. I don't trust people who drink their coffee black."

"I'm not sure I trust people who top their drinks with cold foam," Luke said. "But I'm willing to look past it if you are."

"Well, how can I say no to that?" Lydia said.

"You can't." Luke swung a door open for her. "Look, I even open doors for my clients."

"How chivalrous."

"I take my moral character very seriously. Now, if you'll just step into my office."

Lydia breezed by him. "*Is* this your office?" she asked, picking up the scrunchie on the corner of Jules's desk.

"Technically no." Luke plucked the scrunchie from her hand and returned it to the desk. "But mine's under construction, so Jules is letting us borrow hers for the consultation."

Lydia took a seat across from him as Luke booted up the computer. While he was waiting, he looked down at the file Dara had handed him. "All I've got written here from the front desk is that you want to start running."

"That's the gist of it," Lydia said.

"Any particular reason?"

"Oh, you know, I woke up one morning and thought 'today feels like a great day to develop some shin splints.'"

Luke tried not to smirk. "So, you're just looking to add some exercise to your life?"

"Absolutely not." Lydia pretended to shiver.

"What's the real reason then?"

"You'll laugh."

"I won't."

"You will."

"Try me."

"My firm is going to be running the New York City Marathon for charity, and for some ridiculous reason, that may or may not involve a workplace crush," she muttered, "I put my hand up when they were asking for volunteers."

"Workplace crush," Luke repeated, pretending to scribble the words.

"Don't write that down!"

"I'm just trying to get all the facts."

"You said you wouldn't laugh!"

"I'm not laughing!"

"You're making fun of me. In your head. I can tell."

"I'm just happy that I can be of service while you're trying to impress your workplace crush." Lydia popped out of her chair but he caught her hand. "Kidding! I'm kidding. Please." He gestured back to her chair and she sat. "However you got to this point, the New York City Marathon is a big goal. Have you ever attempted anything like it before?"

"First time." Lydia bit her lip. "You think it's a bad idea?"

"No." He sat back in his chair, tapping the pen to his chin. "I think it's bold."

"You don't think I can do it," she accused him, narrowing her eyes.

"Oh, I believe you could run this marathon. The question is how bad do you want it? This race is a huge deal. People train for months—years, even—to be able to run it. Is this something you can do? Absolutely. I'm just saying it's not gonna be easy."

"I don't need it to be easy," Lydia said.

"It's going to take work. That means early mornings. And sweat. And less cold foam."

"Okay," Lydia complained, "now you're crossing a line."

Luke laughed. "If you're serious about this, and about putting in the work, then I promise to get you across that finish line no matter what. Deal?"

A flicker of something—amusement, thrill, fear?—passed across her face. Whatever it was, she didn't back down. "Deal."

"Great." Luke passed the consultation form over for her to sign. "We can celebrate our new partnership by running a celebratory mile."

Lydia's face did melt into something he recognized then. Disappointment. "You've got to be kidding me."

"I need to see what I'm working with."

Lydia's face fell even further. "I sort of thought we'd ease into the whole running thing."

"Did Dara tell you to wear running shoes?"

"Yes."

"Then let's go break them in."

Ignoring the look of utter displeasure on her face, he led her out to the running room—a space filled with soft lights and treadmills and TVs that flicked between the weekly news and sports programming.

"We'll start slow," Luke said as Lydia climbed onto his chosen treadmill. "A walking pace to get the blood pumping."

"I can't wait," she muttered.

"Now, this isn't a test," Luke said. "I'm just trying to get a baseline so I know how to build your program. No pressure. If you need a break, we can drop it back to a walk. I'm gonna up the pace to a light jog in three, two, one…" Luke adjusted the speed, and Lydia started jogging. He kept track of her breathing and her stride, watching to make sure she wasn't falling behind the pace. The last thing he wanted was for her to tumble off the treadmill on her first day.

At just over twelve minutes, Luke dropped the speed back down to a walk, and Lydia grabbed the handrails, bracing herself. She'd finished the mile without any kind of voiced distress, so Luke figured she'd probably do well with three miles as a starting short run distance. When he told her that, her eyes widened comically.

"I didn't mean today," Luke cut in before she could really start to panic. "Though I did enjoy the look of pure horror on your face."

She sucked in a sharp breath, climbing down from the treadmill. "You're a jerk, you know that?"

"I've been called worse. Some people even say I take their breath away."

"Oh, please. How long are you going to milk that for?"

"Probably until the end of time. Come on," he said, getting back on task. "Let's do some cooldown stretches. It's a good habit to get into. Just some light, static stuff to stay injury- and pain-free."

"Somehow I think you'll be my biggest pain," Lydia said, throwing her head back to shake sticky strands of hair from her face.

Luke's lips twitched. "Let's start with a deep lunge stretch." When her eyebrow started to arch, he demonstrated, lunging forward with his right leg. "It works really well to loosen tight hip flexors, especially if you're sitting behind a desk for most of your day."

Lydia copied him, wobbling a little as she tried to find her balance. Her arm shot out and Luke steadied her as she repositioned. "This might be more torturous than running."

"It's good for you, I promise. Keep your knee bent at ninety degrees and your weight in your heel." Luke's eyes traced her form as he walked her through a quad stretch and then a standing adductor stretch. They were only holding the stretches for thirty seconds each, but it was long enough for his eyes to linger on the soft dips and curves of her body.

Startled by his obvious attraction, Luke looked away. He needed to think like a trainer, like a coach. He dragged his thoughts back into the moment, back to the next stretch. "Last one," he said. "Lie down on your back."

"People normally buy me dinner first."

"It's for a stretch," he said, shaking his head at her. Despite his best efforts, he felt his cheeks grow hot.

Lydia flopped down on her back, her green eyes looking him up and down in a way that did little to help the thoughts he'd already tried to banish from his mind.

"Keep one leg extended and bring your other knee toward your chest."

She followed his directions. "What's this stretch for?"

"It focuses on the hips and the gluteus maximus muscle."

She grinned at him playfully. "The gluteus maximus—"

"Don't," Luke said, interrupting her.

"Does this mean you're looking at my butt?"

"Oh my God," Luke muttered under his breath, feeling that sweltering heat in his cheeks reignite. He reached down to help pull Lydia to her feet.

"It's okay if you are," she said, angling toward him.

In truth, he'd tried not to look. Even now he tried to keep

his eyes firmly on her face, but he was apparently breaking all the rules today. His gaze dropped for a fraction of a second, but when he lifted his eyes to meet hers once more, instead of being offended by his wandering gaze, Lydia simply arched her brow. Teasing. She was a woman who seemed to know exactly what she had to offer.

Luke had a lot of thoughts. A lot of inappropriate thoughts, considering they were in the middle of the gym. "Don't let it go to your head," he mumbled.

Lydia's mouth fell open as if she couldn't believe he'd acknowledged this spark that neither of them were supposed to be acknowledging. Then she snapped her lips together, and his eyes were drawn there. Dammit. The warm flush spread down his neck.

"Admit it," she said, looking up at him.

"Admit what?" he asked, doing his best to ignore the curve of her mouth as her lips twisted into a not-so-innocent smile.

"That was the best static stretching you've ever seen."

Luke scoffed, but somewhere between crashing into each other in the lobby and now, this had become flirting. Brash, blushing, brazen flirting. In the middle of the gym. In the middle of a workday.

He could see now that Lydia McKenzie was going to be one of his more challenging clients.

Before he could do or say something he'd regret, he guided her to the door of the running room. "Enjoy your last day of freedom, Cold Foam. Things are about to get intense."

"I don't actually think I'm going to like you very much," she told him as she passed into the hall.

"Probably not while we're training," he called after her. "But you're gonna *love* me when you cross that finish line!"

Three

Lydia

"You didn't *actually* tell Jack you were going to run a marathon with him?" Ashley said. Lydia could hear her snickering through the phone. "You told him you were joking, right?"

"Obviously not. Why else would I be trekking out to the gym at some ungodly hour of the morning?" Lydia said, checking for traffic before darting across the street.

"You're actually serious about this?"

"So serious that I've hired Luke to make sure I don't make a fool of myself in front of the firm. Did you know a marathon is like twenty-six miles?"

"Twenty-six point two. And wait. Luke? As in the guy you walked face-first into and—"

"Told he took my breath away." Lydia resisted the urge to roll her eyes. "You both have to get over that already. This is a do-or-die situation. The whole conference room was staring at me. And Marco thought it was such a great idea. I can't disappoint the big boss."

Standing up and announcing to the whole room that she'd deliriously volunteered because she was harboring a secret office crush wasn't exactly the kind of thing that instilled confidence. If she wanted to impress Marco and the leadership team, she should probably try not to humiliate herself or Jack.

"Oh, you have it bad for this guy," Ashley said. "You're tripping over yourself to impress him."

"I wasn't trying to impress him," Lydia argued. "I was just trying to be nice. He was standing up there all alone and the room had gone silent." She couldn't even say what it was exactly that made her speak up. Jack's hopeful smile? His dimpled cheeks? The enthusiasm? Lydia ran her hand down her face, remembering the feel of Jack's hand as he high-fived her and their fingers tangled together. A hot flush crept up the side of her neck. God, Ashley was right, she did have it bad. "He called me his running buddy. I know it sounds ridiculous, but I want to be his teammate. I want to see where this leads. Maybe there'll be sparks when we cross the finish line. *And* it's for charity," she tacked on.

"You've had a whole fantasy about this, haven't you?"

"Shut up. It's for the kids."

"Yeah, sure, the kids." Ashley laughed. "I can't believe you didn't tell me about this sooner. I would have met you at the gym."

"I'm not going to the gym with you," Lydia said, horrified by the thought. "You're going to make fun of me."

"I'd be there for moral support!"

Lydia snorted.

"Hey, I've *always* been there for you and your ridiculous ideas. Remember when you gave yourself bangs? Who fixed them? Or in middle school when you needed help convincing Mom and Dad that you were going to be a professional tap dancer? And then you never went to a single class because you always conveniently had a stomachache."

Lydia's lips twisted as she remembered doing everything she could to avoid going to tap class.

"You kinda like to jump into things without thinking them all the way through."

"Hey!"

"I'm just saying. If you don't take this seriously, the only thing you're going to get to see is the back of Jack during the race as he runs away and you pass out from lack of oxygen."

"That's not funny." Preparing for this marathon was going to be work. Lydia knew that. On top of her regular nine-to-five and prepping a competition proposal for the Manhattan Youth Center, spending all of her free time for the next five months training was going to take some serious dedication. But if running this marathon would force her to step outside her comfort zone, maybe volunteering hadn't been such a bad idea. If she wanted to impress Poletti's and get proper recognition for her work—if she wanted to get Jack's attention—then she was going to have to start putting herself out there in ways she hadn't before. "I think maybe I can do this, Ash."

"You know twenty-six point two miles translates into *hours* of running, right?"

Lydia didn't think about that. She thought about Luke promising to get her across the finish line as long as she remained focused and determined. She thought about the sense of accomplishment she'd have finishing the race. She pictured the glowing smile on Jack's face as he lifted her off the ground in a tipsy, exhausted hug. They'd probably celebrate after. Marco would take them all somewhere nice for food and drinks. Maybe she'd finally tell Jack how she felt. Maybe he'd smile that dimpled smile, lean over and kiss her.

God, she wanted that.

"Are you even listening?"

Lydia threw open the door to the gym. "Yeah, hours of running. But I've got months to prepare, right? Anyway, I've gotta run. Literally."

"Let me know how it goes," Ashley said. They hung up and Lydia spotted Luke leaning against the front desk, holding a stack of papers. When he caught her eye, she straightened, wondering if he noticed her mismatched activewear—things she'd definitely raided from Ashley's closet.

"Morning!" Luke flashed her a smile. She pursed her lips in response, making him laugh. "Not a morning person?"

"Not when my first stop of the day is the gym." She glanced around at the people already sweating it out at the squat racks. "I don't know how people do this every day. Seems like a certain kind of torture."

"Torture that gives you endorphins. That energizes you," he said.

"Pretty sure endorphins are a myth created to sell fitness equipment."

"Oh, come on, tell me you're at least a little excited to get started? This is where it all begins. A few months from now you'll be running through the five boroughs—"

"More than a few," Lydia interrupted. "I've got five months to mentally prepare myself for this. Don't scare me like that." She gestured to the equipment floor. "Should I hop on a treadmill or something?"

"Actually, I thought we'd take our session outside. It's a gorgeous day. Plus, running outdoors will simulate the actual marathon environment. The sooner you get used to that, the better."

"You want me to make a fool of myself in front of other people too?"

Luke responded by taking her by the shoulders and guiding her to the door.

"You're going to be nice to me, right?" Lydia said as they stepped outside. He turned down the street toward Sixth Avenue and she followed hesitantly. "Like we're gonna ease into this process?"

"Do I look like I would be mean?"

Her eyes cut to the side, flickering up and down his body. "I just want you to remember which of us is already covered in muscles and which of us doesn't even bother running to make the subway when we're late."

"I'll be nice," he promised, catching her arm gently and leading her across the street between the traffic.

"Where are we going?"

"Madison Square Park," he said. It was just two blocks east of the gym.

"And what's that about?" she asked, eyeing the papers he carried under his arm.

"This is your very own personalized training plan."

"Why do I need a plan if I have you?"

"In order to be in the best position possible to run the marathon, your training is going to extend beyond just our sessions. There will be days when you train alone. But don't worry, I'm going to give you guided workouts. That's what this first week will be about. Establishing a routine. We'll do a long run on the weekends, outdoors if we can make it happen, slowly building up the mileage. You'll have rest days Mondays and Fridays. Short runs Tuesdays and Thursdays. Cross-training on Wednesdays and Sundays."

"Cross-training?"

"Aerobic exercise that allows you to use different muscles while resting. Cycling or even walking. Those are the days you can do in the gym without me." They darted across another street. "Twenty-six miles is a lot to build up to. We have to make the most of the next twentyish weeks we have together."

"Doesn't seem so far away when you lay it out like that," Lydia mumbled under her breath as they arrived at Madison Square Park—a greenspace at the center of the city surrounded by vibrant businesses and towering skyscrapers. Like an oasis rising out of desert sands, the park was part public garden, part arboretum and part open-air museum. Lydia had spent weekends here surrounded by art installations and horticulture exhibitions.

"The park is about half a mile around," Luke said as he walked her through basic dynamic stretches to warm up.

She supposed it was to loosen her tired muscles, but a nervous tension coiled through her and when they were done stretching, Lydia felt even more stiff than before.

"I figure we'll do three miles total this morning and start your short runs off easy."

"Three?" she said, feeling overwhelmed by the thought. Long runs? Short runs? A training plan? Sure, this was what she was paying him for, but it all suddenly felt like too much. She'd barely survived the one mile on the treadmill the other day and now he just expected her to crank out three miles? "I think you skipped over two. I'd like to recommend that we try that first. Maybe even one and a half."

"Oh, c'mon," Luke said, chuckling. "You've got at least three in you."

"I think you're overestimating my abilities." He started running abruptly and she darted after him. "Okay, we're just gonna start casually like that?"

"How did you want to begin?" Luke laughed. "With a starting pistol?" She could tell he was taking things slow, because he kept up a stream of encouraging conversation as they made their first round of the park. Lydia just tried to remember to suck in oxygen as she kept track of the laps.

The park was bustling with early-morning joggers and dog walkers. She imagined they were all watching her make a fool of herself as she tried not to think of the stitch beneath her ribs that was threatening to turn into a cramp. She was suddenly very aware of the way her cheeks puffed and the way her hands cupped the air as she pumped her arms back and forth. Was she pumping them too much? Was her stride too short? Too long?

"Doing okay?" Luke asked.

"So great," she gasped.

"Try inhaling and exhaling through your nose and mouth at the same time."

"Why? Does it look like I'm about to pass out?" She wondered if he would catch her if she did. How mortifying would that be, and in front of all these people. Lydia sucked in a sharp breath through her nose.

"Try it," he said encouragingly. "It'll engage your diaphragm for maximum oxygen intake and help expel carbon dioxide more quickly."

Lydia opened her mouth as she inhaled and exhaled, focusing on her breathing as they counted down mile two. It was trickier than she expected, and part of her felt like she was about to accidentally catch some nasty flying bug in her mouth, but Luke was right about her breathing becoming easier, so she was loath to change anything, no matter how ridiculous she might look.

She glanced over at Luke, trying to emulate his form: arms bent but relaxed, gaze straight ahead, shoulders in line with his hips, leaning slightly forward. He practically glided beside her, seemingly unbothered by the heat or the beads of sweat that gathered at his neck. She'd never thought this hard about running before. Wasn't this supposed to be natural for humans?

"Almost there," Luke said as they neared the end of their final lap.

Almost there was not close enough, and the moment they passed the tree Luke had selected as the lap marker, Lydia collapsed onto the lawn, her back to the grass, face skyward. Luke walked over and knelt next to her. "How're you doing?"

Her chest heaved, and she thrusted her arm in his direction. "I think I've passed away. Check my pulse."

Luke indulged her, pressing his fingers to her wrist. "Hate to break it to you, but you are still very much alive."

"You're sure? You've got the medical training to determine that?"

"I do in fact have an official pulse-checker certificate somewhere in my office."

"The one that's conveniently under construction?"

"That's the one."

"I'll believe it when I see it." Her chest still heaved, and she didn't know if she should be embarrassed by the fact she was more breathless now than she'd been during the run.

Luke sat down on the grass next to her, checking his watch.

"What's the verdict?" she asked, glancing up at him.

"That actually wasn't bad. You averaged about twelve minutes per mile. As you build up endurance, we should be able to shave some time off that."

"Endurance," she said. "Can I buy that somewhere or—"

He smirked. "Unfortunately, you're going to have to acquire it the old-fashioned way. A lot of hard work."

"Pretty sure I could buy it in California. They probably have endurance bars. Maybe they add it to their smoothies."

"Well, until you figure out how to buy your way out of exercising, let's head back to the gym. I want to walk you through all the equipment on the floor to make sure you know how to properly use everything for the days when you're training on your own."

"Running *and* gym school in one day," Lydia complained. "Yuck. If I agree to eat really, *really* clean, can we cut out like one training session a week?"

Luke shook his head. "You already have two rest days, but that reminds me. We have to talk about protein."

"This is probably not the time to tell you that I plan to go straight to Gramercy Kitchen for a mimosa tower after this, huh?"

Luke got to his feet. "You're going to crush that by yourself, are you?"

"I like to reward my pain and suffering."

"I do foresee a lot of suffering in your future."

Luke reached down for Lydia's hand and yanked her to her feet. He might have pulled a little too hard, because she went stumbling toward him. He caught her in his arms for a brief moment before she righted herself, but that didn't stop her from flashing back to the moment she'd collided with him in the gym. She flushed, turning away as she said, "I guess I should just make a standing reservation then."

"It's the least you deserve after all this hard work."

"The fact that you think I'm kidding is cute."

"How about I let you get a coffee on the way back to the gym and we cut the difference?"

"Fine," Lydia agreed. "But I don't want to hear one word about how much sugar goes into my cup."

"Whatever you say, Cold Foam."

The Manhattan Youth Center was a large, blocky building on the corner of 53rd Street and 10th Avenue, made up of lime-stained brick and crumbling asphalt yards surrounded by rusty chain-link fencing. Beyond the worn exterior, colorful artwork had been taped to every window, staring out at the street like Picasso-approved stained glass.

Lydia liked the place immediately, and not just because the morning site visit had cut Luke's gym equipment walkthrough short. She'd absorbed about all she could handle when it came to leg presses and leg curls and leg extensions for today.

"Are you going to stand there all day?" Erik called, halfway up the front steps.

Lydia lifted her phone and snapped a picture of the front of the building from the sidewalk before hurrying after him and the rest of the group from Poletti's. She ducked past Erik where he held the front door open for her. "Thanks."

"You're supposed to be holding doors open for me."

"True. Age before beauty," Lydia teased.

"You're lucky I'm not fully caffeinated yet or my retort would probably sting."

"Please," Lydia whispered as they rejoined the group. "You've been working on the same comebacks since I was hired."

Erik made a face but said nothing as the group was greeted by a woman named Miranda. She was the volunteer coordinator and as bubbly as newly popped champagne. "I'll just ask everyone to sign in," she said, gesturing to a large binder on a desk. "Then we'll get started."

Lydia joined the line behind Erik, scribbling her name and the reason for her visit into the binder before flashing her ID at the man behind the desk.

The interior of the building reminded Lydia of elementary school. The walls were covered in peeling white paint concealed behind posters and artwork. Miranda gestured down the hall, escorting them from one end of the building to the other, giving them little facts about the building and what the kids got up to while they were here.

Lydia poked her head into every room, snapping photos. The gymnasium was old, the paint on the walls a dusty red. The colorful lines on the floor that had once demarcated free throws and half-courts had been scuffed away by sneakers. A set of rickety bleachers butted up against the wall and a pair of basketball hoops with raggedy nets were installed at either end of the gymnasium, but nothing about the space felt rundown—only well loved.

Several classrooms had been repurposed into art studios, and the small library was equipped with a few computers. There was a kitchen where the kids learned to bake, and even a small dining hall with a low-lying stage.

"The kids love performing," Miranda explained.

Lydia couldn't help but imagine a small auditorium with soft theater seating, bright red curtains and a sturdier stage for the kids to perform on.

Unsurprisingly, the center was practically empty save for the handful of employees and volunteers tidying up from the before-school crowd. That meant they had a couple of uninterrupted hours to explore and sketch and design.

"What's out there?" Lydia asked, gesturing to a closed door before Miranda set them free.

"That's the outdoor yard, though it's in rough shape. Seems to get worse after every winter, so the kids don't use it much. Sort of wasted space if you ask me." She unlocked one of the doors and swung it open. "Feel free to take a look."

Lydia poked her head out, staring across the cracked asphalt. There were some cute chalk drawings near the door, but everything past that felt like a wasteland of untapped potential.

"Want to go exploring?" she asked Erik.

He gestured to his practically bald head. "I try to keep this whole situation out of the sun, but you have fun."

While her colleagues broke off into groups, chattering and pulling out their sketchbooks, Lydia stepped through the door onto the uneven pavement. There were faded white lines painted on the ground and a weather-beaten basketball hoop at the far end of the yard. A few tiny green sprouts had forced their way through cracks in the ground and her mind started spinning.

She'd taken a lot of courses in school on sustainable building, and now she couldn't help but think about how this redesign could improve the quality of life on this block. This wasn't just a competition but also her opportunity to showcase how this building could be both environmentally responsible and resource efficient.

She walked across the yard and sat at a lonely picnic table. From her position, she had a good view of the building's exterior structure. She placed her sketchbook on the table and dug a pencil out of her shoulder bag, imagining a range of solar panels on the roof along with a rooftop garden that could harvest rainwater for irrigation. That would help reduce stormwater runoff and the urban heat island effect. Lydia scribbled the words onto the corner of her page. She might not be able to change all of Manhattan, but she could make an impact on this block, with this building.

She heard the door open and close but didn't look up. She couldn't. It had been a long time since she'd been this thrilled about a project, and her mind was so full she wanted to finish getting everything on paper before the ideas leaked out her ears. That was, until a shadow eclipsed her sketchbook, forcing her to stop.

"Hey, running buddy."

Lydia tipped her head back, squinting into the sun as her insides did a somersault. Jack had a sketchbook under his arm and a stubby pencil behind his ear. She tried to appear unaffected. "Did you realize that this is where all the cool architects come to draw?"

"Obviously." He sat down across from her, and their knees bumped together as he got comfortable. "Everyone else is in the gym. Their ideas are going to start to run together and everything's going to end up being a variation of the same design. Clearly, we're the geniuses of the group."

Lydia probably should have blushed at the compliment, or at least laughed it off as a joke, but with him sitting there, the sun behind him, his face cast in shadow, he reminded her of a charcoal sketch and she couldn't get over how handsome he was. Jack reached back to sweep the dangling hairs from his forehead and pluck the pencil from behind his ear in one smooth motion.

She blinked at him foolishly, only breaking from her trance when he leaned over to inspect her page. "What are you working on?"

"Oh!" she said, clearing her throat. She looked down to see the mess of scribbles. Jack's lips twisted as if he'd just had the same thought. "There's an idea here, I swear."

Jack picked up her sketchbook, held it out at arm's length, and squinted. Lydia tried to snatch it back. "Wait a second," Jack urged. "It's coming to me. I'm starting to see something."

Lydia giggled, taking hold of Jack's arm. The moment she realized she was touching him, her palm against his forearm, she flushed. She'd been crushing on him for so long that this unexpected attention felt strange.

"I'm only joking," Jack said, still wearing a grin as he handed her sketchbook back. "I can see you've got a lot of really good ideas." His finger dropped to the roof of Lydia's hastily sketched building. "But why not a rooftop terrace?"

"What?"

His finger drifted across her page. He double-tapped on the spot where she'd scribbled *rooftop garden*. "That way it would be pretty *and* functional. You could have seating areas up there. Maybe a gazebo…"

"Ah," Lydia said. "I was thinking less about it being functional and more about the heat island effect." She glanced up for his opinion. Jack was part of the leadership team. If there was anyone that could give her a few pointers, it was him. "A massive rooftop garden could insulate the building from the heat."

He nodded slowly.

Lydia laughed. "Silence. Is that your way of telling me it's a bad idea?"

"It's interesting."

Interesting? Lydia looked down at the design. Was it too much? Was she overcomplicating things?

"That kind of green infrastructure can be expensive, which might work against you."

Maybe it was a little complicated, but just this morning running three miles had sounded overwhelmingly complicated. Now she felt pretty great about it. Heck, if she could run three miles without puking her guts out, then she could figure out how to turn this space into an environmentally conscious, kid-friendly oasis. "I'm pretty certain I can pull it off."

A grin split Jack's face. "I do find it refreshing that your design ideas take into account the community, not just the building. And I like your confidence." He got to his feet. "I'm excited to see what the finished product looks like."

"You mean it?" Lydia said, looking up at him.

As Jack laid his hand on her shoulder, Lydia committed the warmth to memory. "In a sea of concrete," he said, "I think we could use more *interesting*."

If Luke stretched his hand out, flattening his palm in line with the street, it was like he could physically feel the stirrings of the city about to awake. As a kid, he'd thought it was his superpower.

A cab driver honked as he darted across the almost-empty road. He lifted his hand in apology, then ducked down a set of narrow stairs and into the damp subway tunnel to catch his train. He was scheduled to meet Lydia this morning for their first of many weekend long runs. Technically, it was only six miles, but considering they were building Lydia's training program from the ground up, she would likely find this run difficult. He imagined her wrinkling her nose in that way that made all the freckles on her cheeks converge. The thought made him smile as the subway doors opened and closed, people moving around him like river water around a rock.

It only took about twenty minutes for Luke to get from Hell's Kitchen to the Flatiron District. Throwing open the door to the gym, he was greeted by a cool blast of air-conditioning. The lights were dimmed everywhere but over the equipment floor. Luke wasn't the first one to arrive, but it was far too early for classes, which meant it was mostly his colleagues or very early risers that were using the facility. Luke walked past the front desk—quiet without Dara, who would be in later—and down the darkened hall of offices. The lights flickered to life, triggered by his presence, and the bright fluorescents painted him like a sunbeam. Luke popped his head into his office, finding it covered in drywall dust. He sighed grumpily—this was going to take forever to clean. He backpedaled to Jules's office to update Lydia's training plan. He'd just finished inputting her three-mile numbers from the other day when Jules herself appeared in the doorway, a pair of headphones strung around her neck, a sheen of sweat across her brow.

"You've got a client waiting. You want me to have her take a seat?"

Luke glanced at the time on the computer screen. Lydia was a few minutes early, which could only be a good sign. "That's okay, I'm heading out there now."

"Kinda early for training on a weekend," Jules commented.

"Marathon prep," Luke explained. "We're making the most of the time we have."

"First-time marathoner?"

"Oh, yeah."

Jules winced. "You're going to have so much fun on those long runs."

"Hey, we're only at six miles, we've got a ways to go."

"Well, glad it's you and not me," she said, fitting the headphones back over her ears. "I can't handle anything over ten."

Luke could understand. Not everyone liked running. But personally, once he'd settled into a long run, he'd always found it relaxing. And he'd much rather get lost in the sound of his stride than be stuck in a room on a spin bike. To each their own, he supposed. Though he hoped he could get Lydia to fall in love with running. He was usually good at getting people excited about fitness—both kids at the youth center and new adult clients. It would make this process that much easier if Lydia found some kind of enjoyment in the act, whether that be competitive, as she slowly built her miles, or meditative. He printed out a couple of her workout plans for the next week and hurried out to meet her for their run, pleased to find that she was already stretching.

"What's this?" she asked when he handed her the papers.

"Your individualized workouts for the days you're solo training."

"Burpees?" Lydia almost choked on the word as she scanned the paper.

"Yeah, you know, big jump, down to the ground for a push-up, then right back up on your feet and repeat."

"I know what it is," she said, wrinkling her nose. "Remember when you promised to be nice? To ease me into the training?"

"They're actually a great exercise for runners. They work multiple muscle groups at once and they're very similar to the short bursts of speed that we'd see in an intense interval workout on a track."

"Yeah, no thanks," Lydia said, walking away to put the workout plans in her locker. "I'm not cut out for rigorous jumping."

Luke waited for her by the door, and they headed outside to finish stretching. "Burpees are good for your muscles and your lungs, and they build aerobic capacity and endurance all at once."

"I'm invoking my trainee powers to pass on this one particular exercise," Lydia said, finishing up her leg swings and knee hugs.

"You don't get to pass."

"I do," she said as she started to run away from him. "It's in the trainee handbook."

"There is no trainee handbook."

"Clearly you've just never read it. I know my rights."

Luke lengthened his stride to catch up with her as they took a right and turned down 7th Avenue. "You sound like a lawyer. Sure you didn't take a wrong turn at the career fair?"

"That's what happens when your sister and her fiancé both went to law school," Lydia said.

"Must be hard to win an argument in that house."

"You have no idea."

Luke smiled. "Look, if I let you pass on this then it's just downhill from here."

"I like downhill," Lydia said.

"No, you don't. You'll start passing on everything that feels a little challenging. If I let you do that, you'll only be cheating yourself. And then what kind of trainer would I be?"

"The kind whose clients actually like him?" Lydia proposed. "Come on, this can be my freebie for good behavior. I've barely complained today."

"We've only been running for thirty seconds!"

"You're already making me run six miles today, which is a nauseating thought. Weekends are supposed to be for relaxing. Isn't this enough torture?"

Luke shook his head. "You're doing the burpees."

Lydia scowled. They hadn't been working together long, but Luke was already starting to pick up on some of the little tells Lydia had when she was nervous or anxious: that nose wrinkle, the self-deprecating hum in the back of her throat. This wasn't really about burpees. This was about starting something new. He could tell she hated the idea of people watching her trying and failing at something. Of making a fool of herself. Of not being good enough. "You know there's no right way to go about this? You just learn and grow and get better with every training session."

"Try telling me that on the weekend we're running ten miles," Lydia said.

"Don't think about that now. Just focus on *this* run. On the next step you have to take. And don't hold your breath," he reminded her, knowing she'd end up with a cramp before they even finished the first mile.

"Who invented burpees anyway?" she muttered.

"I don't know."

"Because they clearly didn't have a pair of these," she said, gesturing to her chest. "If I give these things too much velocity we're both gonna be in trouble."

"Let's just focus on the path ahead, okay? Focus on your breathing."

She smirked. "Why? What's wrong with our conversation?"

"Besides the fact we're emphatically talking about your breasts?" He knew she flirted when she needed a distraction, and yet his cheeks still burned as he attempted to look anywhere else.

Her delicate brow arched to a perfect point. "Do you have a problem with that?"

Luke snorted. She was being a little minx, but he wasn't going to fall for her trap. Things were different from last week when she'd crashed into him with her coffee. Now she was his client. That small concession that he'd found her attractive in their first session together was out of character for him. There was a certain amount of professional decorum he had to maintain. He didn't need to be thinking about the way her pouty lips puckered when she was annoyed with him, or how the red strands in her strawberry blond hair were more vibrant in the sunlight, or the way her activewear hugged her curves.

Lydia was a gorgeous woman. He'd be telling a bold-faced lie to deny that. *A gorgeous woman who's off-limits*, he reminded himself. Of course, he'd trained attractive people before. The gym was filled with attractive people. But there was just something about Lydia—her bold sense of humor, her constant teasing, her personality—that was drawing him in. And that was a problem. He was going to have to get that off-limits thing through his head before he let any more overt attraction slip free. "We're making a U-turn with this conversation and getting back to the workout plan."

Lydia sucked in a sharp breath. "That's no fun."

Luke slowed the pace a bit. "Inhale and exhale using your nose and mouth at the same time. Like we talked about."

"How am I supposed to tease you then?"

"You're not," he said pointedly. "You're supposed to focus more on your breathing and less on trying to annoy me."

"You were blushing. I saw you."

Rolling his eyes, Luke picked up the pace.

"Okay! Wait, wait!" Lydia called. "I'll stop. Just don't speed up!"

"And you'll do the burpees?" Luke asked.

"Well, now you're just pushing it." Luke started to speed up again, but Lydia caught him by the elbow. "Fine. I will do the burpees!"

"You can do this," Luke said. "It's new and hard and uncomfortable but you *can* do it."

"I hate you. You know that, right?"

"Oh, definitely." Luke didn't stop grinning until they

reached the end of the run. They'd finished off the last two miles with a mix of jogging and walking, but overall Luke was pleased with Lydia's attempt. He held his hand out for a high five. Lydia let her hand skim his palm then doubled over, clutching her knees as she leaned against the exterior of the gym. Luke placed a hand on her shoulder. "How're you feeling?"

"A little like Jell-O."

"As long as you can still feel all your limbs." He opened the door. "C'mon, get some water."

Lydia went straight to the fountain. While she did that, Luke stood at the front desk, reviewing her training plan. At the top of the page was a space that said Client Goal. Luke had written: *charity run for the NYC Marathon*. "Hey, what charity are you running for? I don't think you ever said."

Lydia wiped the sweat from her brow with the back of her hand. "Uh, not sure exactly which one yet. But I know they're associated with the Manhattan Youth Center."

"Oh, no way," Luke said, intrigued.

"You know it?"

"Yeah, actually. I volunteer there a couple times a week. Why the center though? Of all the charities you could have picked."

Lydia shrugged, coming to stand by the desk. "I guess it was just a spur-of-the-moment thing. My company is preparing to enter a city-run competition to redesign the building that the center operates out of. We were chatting about it right before we started talking about our outreach project. I think the two things came together organically."

"I heard about that competition," Luke said. He'd been informed that a massive construction project was coming down the pipeline. The full-time staff had already begun planning to funnel funding and activities to other parts of the city in order to support the kids while the building was being renovated. "I didn't realize that change was happening so soon."

"It's just the competition, which doesn't finish until the beginning of November. The city probably wouldn't be ready to break ground on any work until next year," Lydia said. "Some of my colleagues and I actually stopped by the center the other day to have a look around. You know, get our bearings before we actually started drawing."

"It's such a great space," Luke said. "Did you get a chance to talk to any of the kids?"

Lydia lifted her shoulder. "They were still in school. We stopped by before lunch."

"Wait, what? How can you possibly redesign a building like the youth center without talking to the people who actually use the space?"

Lydia's brows rose. "That's a good point. Usually, if we're working with a client, we get a basic brief about who they are and their vision. But with this... We kind of just had the volunteer coordinator show us around. She was great though. Very passionate."

That wasn't good enough. Walking through the center while it was empty was a completely different experience than seeing it in action. "You should meet me at the center sometime."

Lydia perked up, some of her postrun exhaustion falling away. "Really?"

"Absolutely." It might only be for a competition, but the

center was important to him. If architects from all over the city were going to be vying to create the winning design, he wanted at least one person to truly have a sense of what the center represented. "I'll give you a tour. A proper one this time. And I'll introduce you to some of the kids who actually use the center on a regular basis."

Lydia smiled. "I'd love that."

"Great," Luke said, touched by her enthusiasm but not at all surprised. From the moment he'd found her staring at the ceiling, Lydia had always struck him as the type of person willing to gain a little bit of perspective, and he was eager to show her his world. "We'll set up a time between our work schedules and training."

"Totally fine if you want to book it during training," Lydia said. "Perhaps one of my solo workout days."

"Nice try," Luke said, catching on to her plan. "You're doing the burpees."

Five

Lydia

"When are you going to let me take you to Athleta so you can get some proper activewear?" Ashley asked.

"Why?" Lydia adjusted the phone against her ear as she made her way to the subway after work. "Are you getting tired of me asking to borrow things?"

"I just think with all the running you could do with filling out your wardrobe a little."

"All I need is one good sports bra to stop my boobs from smacking me in the face when Luke tries to kill me with burpees."

"Is training really that bad?"

"No," she admitted. After some online perusing, she'd worried about things like shin splints and runner's knee and plantar fasciitis, but shockingly—to her most of all—beyond the expected sore muscles, she was actually feeling okay since she'd started running. "Luke did a good job with my training plan. It's got a balance of running and rest and cross-training."

"Who are you? And what have you done with my sister?"

"Right?" Lydia laughed. "Guess that's what I'm paying him for, but I still appreciate being able to walk into work without hobbling after a run."

"Maybe you're just a natural-born runner."

"Yeah, I don't think so. I'm more of the sit-down-at-a-bench-and-draw type." A pleasant buzz filled her chest as the memory of her and Jack at the youth center swept through her. She'd relayed the entire interaction to Ashley in explicit detail the moment she'd gotten off work that day.

"You can't still be blushing over the Jack thing," Ashley said after a moment of silence, probably sensing what Lydia was thinking about.

"It wasn't just a thing. We were definitely having a moment."

"More of a moment than when you crashed into Luke and were so dazzled by his presence that you told him he took your breath away?"

Lydia hurried across the street between traffic. "You need to let that go."

"I can't. It's burned into my memory. The way you were looking at him? I half expected you to scale the man right there in front of me."

"Oh, please. It wasn't that bad. Plus, he's my trainer now," Lydia said. "And we are both very committed to this professional partnership where I pay him to torture me with exercise multiple times a week. So stop thinking about him like that."

"Like what?"

"Like he's some sort of snack I'm going to devour." Was he attractive? Sure. Was he totally off-limits now that they were working together? Absolutely. Did that stop her from flirting with him…occasionally? No—but it probably should have.

Ashley snorted. "Says the woman overanalyzing a pat on the shoulder."

"It's not the same thing at all." Luke was a delectable distraction that caught her eye during otherwise long and sometimes torturous running sessions. But *Jack*… Jack was the kind of person she'd always imagined herself with long term. He was brilliant and focused and kind. As a fellow architect, he was someone who could understand everything she wanted from her career. He probably wanted some of those same things. They could champion each other on their way up their respective ladders, the way Kurt and Ashley had.

"I just don't want you waiting for something that might never happen. You're too good to be waiting around for any guy. You know that, right?"

Lydia could tell the human rights lawyer was coming out now and hurried to intercept Ashley. "We don't have to have a conversation about my self-worth and what I deserve. It's not like I'm sitting here rejecting every nice guy that walks by. Contrary to your belief, there isn't actually a lineup of men waiting outside my apartment door with roses."

"Well, you could try talking to some of the men you meet instead of just sleeping with them."

"What's the point when I already know who I want?"

"If you're so sure, just ask Jack out."

"Nope," Lydia said. "It's too soon."

"How can it be too soon? This has been going on for years. You're like a damn soap opera. In every episode, nothing really happens, but there's just enough of a hook at the end to get me to tune in again."

"Then call me *Days of Our Lives* because this is as good as it's getting right now."

"Wouldn't knowing how Jack feels be better than pining?"

"Pining means I get to live in ignorant bliss. If he rejected me I'd have to face that rejection every day for as long as we both work for Poletti's. I'm not making the first move. Now enough about me. Talk to me about weddings. What's going on?"

Ashley hummed. "We've finally settled on autumn of next year, so I at least have the season."

"Hey, that's progress!"

"It was almost summer but I don't want to be sweaty. Plus, Kurt said we'd be competing with people's summer plans. Would you want to skip your vacation to attend a wedding?"

"Depends how much I liked the person and if they were springing for an open bar," Lydia said as she reached the entrance to the subway station. "But hold your next thought. I'm about to get on the train."

"Okay, I'll call you later," Ashley said.

"'Bye." Lydia hung up, then made her way across town to the Manhattan Youth Center. It had taken her and Luke a couple weeks to finally nail down a time when they were both available for his promised tour. Between Poletti's, Luke's other clients, regular life stuff and training, finding a free day was harder than they'd imagined.

As Lydia approached the familiar building, kids streamed in and out the front doors like the tide on a beach, overtaking the steps and flowing down the sidewalk. The kids were so buoyant, laughing and shouting animatedly after their friends, that Lydia almost didn't notice Luke waiting for her on the steps amid all the chaos. When she spotted him, she slowed enough to drink him in.

He looked…*different*.

Not in a bad way—she didn't think the man was capable of looking bad. But of course she wasn't looking at him like *that*. She'd just never really seen him in anything other than fitted athletic wear, so obviously she'd take note of him reclining on the steps in faded blue jeans and a plain gray shirt that strained against his biceps. *Oh, for crying out loud*, Lydia thought, resisting the urge to rub the sudden heat from her cheeks. This was Ashley's fault. She'd gotten her thoughts all twisted up.

The way you were looking at him? I half expected you to scale the man right there.

Lydia's cheeks flushed even hotter and she stopped walking. That had happened before she and Luke were working together. Before they even knew each other. Now they were partners in this training journey. There would be no acting on said attractiveness—they both professionals. In fact, she'd already noticed much more than just the way he looked. There was an ease and a confidence to the way he chatted with the kids. Some gave him high fives as they passed, hurrying off to meet their parents. Others bumped his fist with their own and cracked jokes. His smile was as comfortable as the rest of him, and it became obvious to Lydia that Luke didn't just volunteer here. He was at home in the center.

"You made it!" Luke said, shooting to his feet as she approached. He dusted off his jeans.

"I did," Lydia agreed, hurrying up the steps until she stood just below him. Up close it was harder not to let her gaze drift appreciatively across his broad shoulders. She tried though, settling on his face. Lydia had quickly become familiar with those soft brown eyes leaning over her while she hyperventilated after a run. Out here in the lingering daylight, his irises were flecked with green and hazel, an earthy combination that seemed to suit him. She tilted her head, wondering if his cropped blond curls looked shorter today.

"Did you get a haircut?" she asked.

"I did." He swept his hand through his hair, disturbing the curls. "The kids were starting to say I needed a fresh cut. That's the great thing about volunteering here. I never have to wonder how I look, because the kids will call me out in front of the entire gym."

Lydia chuckled. "Ah, the good old days of saying the first thing that popped into our minds."

"It's wonderful. You get over being self-conscious very quickly."

"So you're saying I shouldn't be surprised when they call out my under-eye bags?"

"What are you talking about? You look perfectly rested," Luke said, nodding to the door.

"Very smooth," Lydia said, following him inside. "I may not look decrepit, but I sure feel it. I think I've used muscles these past few weeks that haven't been activated in the almost thirty years I've been alive."

Luke said something, his mouth moving, but Lydia didn't hear a single word. Sound crashed into her like a rogue wave. It was *loud*. Joyously so. Laughter echoed down the halls in fits and starts. Small voices yelled and cheered, demanding attention. Footsteps thundered up and down stairs. Music streamed out of classrooms, and the rubber smack of a basketball thumped out of sync with it. "Wow," she said.

When Lydia had absorbed the onslaught of noise, she signed her name into the binder and flashed her ID to the volunteer behind the check-in desk. He waved her into the building.

"Where do you want to start the tour?" Luke asked.

"Anywhere," Lydia said. "You're the subject matter expert."

"All right." Luke rubbed his hands together, setting off down the hall toward the sounds of a basketball game. They'd only gone about four feet before a tiny girl with long braided pigtails stomped her foot in front of Luke and demanded help with her shoelaces.

Luke bent down. "Double knot or single?"

"Double," the girl decided.

Lydia got the impression that this was a regular occurrence. She bit her lip to hide her amusement.

The little girl glanced up, examining Lydia through squinted eyes. "Mr. Luke, is this your girlfriend?"

"This is Lydia," he answered without missing a beat. "She's definitely my friend."

The girl smiled conspiratorially, like she'd just been given secret information. Then she raced off down the hall.

"Sorry," Luke said, getting to his feet. "Remember that zero filter thing we talked about?"

Lydia snorted. "Reminds me a bit of annoying the hell out of my sister with awkward questions when we were kids."

"You just have the one sister?"

She nodded. "Ashley. She's a couple years older. You?"

"An older brother and an older sister."

"Guess we're both the babies of the family."

"As they like to remind me," Luke agreed. They continued down the hall.

The doors to the gymnasium were wide open and Lydia saw a flash of tiny bodies as a game of basketball tore furiously across the court.

"Watch out for stray passes," Luke said as they entered. "Sometimes I have no idea what they're aiming for. Might just be my head."

Lydia chuckled, keeping her eye on the court, but there was really no need. Luke walked beside her, keeping his body between the game and her like a shield. Warmth pooled in her chest at the thought, though she chuckled to herself—she might not be athlete of the year, but she could catch a basketball if the occasion called for it.

"As you can see," Luke said—raising his voice above the din of squeaky sneakers and kids shouting *ball, ball, ball!*—"the gym is well loved by everyone. I'd say it gets the most activity of anywhere in the center. The biggest obstacle right now is that the space is limited. If a group of kids want to play a full-court basketball game, no one else can use the gym. We've gotten good at assigning time slots, but it still means a lot of kids are hanging out on the sidelines, waiting for their turn to use the space." He gestured to the bleachers, where kids sat with skipping ropes and other toys.

"What about the court outside?" Lydia asked. "Does it ever get used?"

"We had a couple injuries out there last year," Luke said, "because the asphalt is all twisted up. Since then the kids haven't really been too keen to use it."

That was similar to what Miranda had told her, and Lydia filed away the information.

"Hey, Luke!" a kid called from the other side of the court. He'd just missed a rebound and the basketball game progressed back across the gym without him. "Is that your *girl*friend?"

"Gosh," Lydia laughed. "They got right on that rumor, didn't they?"

"And what's up with your hair, man?" the kid yelled, grinning a gap-toothed smile. He was scrawny and moved like he wasn't quite used to his growing limbs yet.

Luke reached up, sweeping his hand through his curls. "This is a fresh cut, Marcus. Why are you hating on it?"

"Oh, I'm Luke, look at my hair," the kid jeered.

"You're just afraid me and my fresh cut will embarrass you on the court."

Marcus grinned, holding his arms out in challenge. "Yeah, right."

"One second," Luke whispered to her. He darted onto the court with unexpected speed, and with a delighted laugh, Marcus chased after him. Luke broke into the game and stole the ball, dribbling backwards. The teams dissolved and it became everyone versus Luke as he surged between the kids, dodging and twisting, putting on an impressive display. He waited for Marcus to deke after the ball. The moment the kid's sneakers twitched, Luke ducked past him and went straight to the basket for a layup.

"Nothing but net," Luke crowed as he sank the ball. He turned around, facing Marcus and the others. The kids laughed as he did a little victory dance. Marcus waved him off the court. Luke returned to her side a moment later. "Sorry," he said, huffing. "I had to defend my reputation as the greatest ball player this gym has ever seen."

"I'm not sure Marcus would agree with that assessment."

Luke led her up the bleachers to an empty row where they could watch the rest of the game. "I missed one free throw one time and now Marcus will never let me live it down."

"Was this supposed to be a game-winning free throw?" Lydia asked.

"Yes. Our team lost," Luke said.

"Did you miss the shot on purpose?"

Luke eyed her, his cheek twitching. "Maybe."

A cheer drew her attention. Lydia's eyes found Marcus again. He was quick, zipping up and down the court, with a pretty wicked three-pointer for a preteen.

Every time he scored, he found Luke in the crowd, grinning impossibly wide.

"The kids really seem to gravitate toward you," Lydia said.

"I've volunteered here for a long, *long* time. For some of them, I've been around as long as they've been coming to the center. I used to come here as a kid with my siblings too, so I suppose in a way, I never really left."

"This place must mean a lot to you," Lydia said, nudging him gently with her shoulder. For a second, she didn't pull away. Not until he looked at her. When he did, it wasn't Trainer Luke staring back at her. It was someone else. Someone she was just getting to know. Someone that knew nothing about her mile time or all the ways she liked to get out of doing burpees. Her heartbeat quickened as she realized how much she wanted to get to know *this* Luke.

"It does," he agreed softly. "A lot of these kids come from

complicated homes. Single parents. Low-income households. They don't always have the support they need to succeed for one reason or another. The center gives them a safe space to hang out. To play. To learn. When I was a kid here, they sometimes gave us dinner. Handed out winter clothes when we were short on hats or gloves or scarves. Although they mostly helped with homework." He gestured to Marcus on the court. "And encouraged talents."

"Do you help with homework?" Lydia said, intrigued.

"Not usually," Luke chuckled. "Though I can rock some science."

"Yeah?"

He nodded. "Throw me some biology. Some chemistry. Let me tell you about mitochondria. A little sprinkle of the Krebs cycle."

"You're just a regular old Bill Nye."

"Guess you were the math girl, huh? I can imagine little Lydia out there measuring angles with her protractor. Making sure her lines were straight."

"You're totally making fun of me! The nerds are supposed to stick together. I can't believe you."

Luke smirked. "But see, I became the sports guy. I took the science and made it cool."

"Are you saying I'm not cool?" She hopped to her feet.

"Where are you going?"

"To tell the kids you're bullying me."

Luke grabbed her by the waist, pulling her back down to the bench. They were closer now than they were before, their thighs pressed together tightly.

"I'm kidding," Luke said. "You design buildings for a living. That is *very* cool."

"You better believe it," Lydia said. Knowing they were both teasing didn't stop her heart from skipping wildly against her ribs. What the hell was wrong with her? This was Luke. Just regular old Trainer Luke who made her do burpees.

"So what do you think so far?" he asked.

Lydia had to turn away, staring out at the court to stop herself from thinking ridiculous things like how soft his lips looked. There were so many warring thoughts tumbling through her head—thoughts about Luke, thoughts about the kids—but the one thing she was certain about was how truly important this redesign competition was to the center. The city was giving them an opportunity to create something to support the children who called this place their second home. And she was starting to understand what they truly needed to grow. First of all, she would incorporate a double gymnasium. Maybe she could use the space better by including a running track around the upper level, looking down over the courts. Excitement bubbled up in her and she was suddenly itching for a drawing pencil.

"Show me more?" she asked Luke, eager to absorb as much as she could while she was here with him. He nodded and took her hand for a brief moment, helping her down the bleachers. They set off on a tour of the rest of the center, each of the spaces transformed now that they were filled with children and activities. Lydia spoke with kids in the art room, letting them drag her around from painting to painting as they told her all about their favorite things to do at the center. Then they moved on to the kitchen where the kids showed her the cookies that were baking in the ovens. Everywhere they went, Luke was hounded with conversation or handed crafts for his approval. He gushed over them, and the kids beamed. After watching him with the kids and the other staff, it was easy to see why he was so popular. Luke was a cheerleader, and she realized how lucky she was to have someone like him in her corner, helping her chase down the miles toward her marathon goal.

When they finally left the center, Lydia stepped out into the cool evening, her mind buzzing.

"Glad you came back?" Luke asked.

"Absolutely." He'd been right. She'd needed to see the youth center in use, at its busiest, to truly understand what would benefit it in a redesign. Spending the evening with the kids had invigorated her. "I feel like I'm bursting with ideas."

He chuckled, following her down the stairs. "I'm happy I could help."

Part of Lydia wanted to rush home, sit down at her desk with a pencil and some graph paper, and let the ideas run wild. But all the inspiration had left her limbs thrumming with energy, and she wasn't quite ready to end the night yet. She turned back to Luke. "Do you want to grab a drink?"

For a second, he looked surprised at the invitation, but the uncertainty melted away so quickly Lydia thought she might have imagined it. "Sure," he said. "Where do you want to go?"

"It's your neighborhood." She shrugged. "Surprise me."

Six

Luke

They went to Presto, Luke's favorite Hell's Kitchen pub. It was his favorite because it was never overly crowded, and it was close enough to his apartment to stumble home after a long night. The balanced combination of metal, leather, dark wood and exposed brick had always given Luke steampunk vibes. There were bare pipes stretched along the walls and stools with wrought iron legs that sat beneath the high-top tables. Everything was bathed in a warm amber hue from the tinted bulbs that hung above the bar.

"I am in love," Lydia said the moment they walked through the door. She'd taken his hand for a brief second, squeezing excitedly, before spinning in a circle to take it all in. He could practically feel the energy radiating from her, like electricity buzzed through her veins. It was infectious, and he found himself drawn to her, grinning so wide his cheeks hurt. "This place is fantastic! I can't believe I've never heard of it."

"You haven't even seen the best part," he said, leading her

between a menagerie of tables to reach the adjacent wall. Presto was on a corner lot, which meant it was exposed to the street from two sides. "On warm nights they open all these windows." They'd been designed like giant rolling doors, mixing the din of the pub with the night noise of the city.

Luke picked a high-top table close enough to the window that they could feel whatever there was of an early-July breeze.

"You don't have history here, do you?" Lydia asked as she climbed onto her stool.

"What do you mean by *history*?"

"If this is your regular hangout spot, I just want to make sure I'm not about to be confronted by five angry ex-girlfriends."

Luke laughed. "Is that how many ex-girlfriends you think I have?"

"Higher or lower?" Lydia asked.

Luke's lips twisted like they were holding back a secret. "I'll let you keep guessing."

Lydia leaned back on her stool, eyeing him carefully. "Hmm… I'll need a drink first." She picked up a menu from the middle of the table, doing a quick scan. There were a few interesting cocktail options on there but for the most part it was beer and deep-fried food. "You're not going to chastise me about what I eat and drink, are you? I really don't want to hear that my protein ratios aren't right."

"You're allowed to have a night off."

Lydia peeked at him over the top of her menu. "Who are you and what have you done with my trainer?"

He took the menu from her hands. "I gave you those nutrition plans to make sure you were eating enough to fuel your body for all the exercise you're now doing. A night out, eating the best nachos in Hell's Kitchen and drinking a few beers isn't going to change anything."

"Best nachos, huh?" Lydia continued to eyeball him as they ordered. She was obviously suspicious that the same man who made her do burpees and run miles had talked her into eating The Brainchild: Loaded Nachos with Everything You Want and Everything You Never Knew You Needed.

Luke smirked. "I'm not a walking, talking robot of health and fitness all the time."

"You're saying what happens in Presto, stays in Presto?" Lydia asked as their beers arrived.

Luke picked up his glass and clinked it against hers. "Trainer Luke is gone for the night."

"I do like Trainer Luke, but he's just such a mood killer, you know?"

"Oh, totally. I mean sometimes a guy just wants to crush some Oreos in peace."

Lydia giggled, and Luke didn't know why, but his heart skipped at the sound. Away from the gym, Lydia felt different. She was passionate and bubbly and scowled at him far less. Though he supposed that could have something to do with the fact that he wasn't asking her to run a mile here. Or maybe she was still just basking in the thrill she'd gotten from exploring the youth center. He was actually still thinking about the way she'd nudged his shoulder on the bleachers, softly resting against him as she waited for him to tell her how much the youth center meant to him.

"Back at the youth center you said you'd been going there since you were a kid?"

Luke nodded, pulled from his thoughts, though a lingering heat smoldered in his chest. He sipped his beer. "Yeah, I was there almost every day after school with my older brother and sister. Sometimes even before school. My dad passed away when I was eight, so we spent a lot of time at the center while my mom worked."

"I'm sorry," Lydia said. "That must have been hard."

"It was," he agreed. "But my mom was a superhero. She worked a lot to make sure we never wanted for anything. I think that's why the center is so important to me. That place took care of us so my mom could work without worrying where we were in the evenings or who was helping with our homework. She was so busy and exhausted all the time, but the volunteers at the center stepped up. Filled the void. It's also where I fell in love with sports and fitness."

Lydia leaned against her hand, smiling at him in a way that told him she was listening to his every word. Luke realized this was the first time he'd ever really told anyone outside his family about what the center meant to him. Not that it was a secret. It was sometimes just hard to dredge through the memories that ultimately connected back to his father. It was also difficult to find the exact words to explain everything the center represented. It was easier to show someone, to have them experience that part of his world, but there'd never been anyone he'd cared to show before.

"I can tell those kids really like having you there," Lydia said. "Even if it's just to trash-talk you on the basketball court."

Luke chuckled. "When you're young, exercise doesn't feel like a chore, it's just fun. So I tried to keep that in mind as I helped the center design a fitness program."

"Did you always know you wanted to get into the fitness world?"

He shook his head. "My mom always prized education. She wanted us to go to school forever it seemed, so we could do these amazing things. Both my siblings went off and did their master's degrees. My sister even got her PhD. I finished my undergrad, but I dropped out of my master's program when I realized the academic world wasn't for me."

Their nachos arrived, and Lydia took a heaping bite, closing her eyes and humming in approval. She wiped her hands on a napkin and washed everything down with a sip of beer. "There's so much stigma around dropping out, but when I hear people have done that to pursue something else, I'm always really impressed."

"Yeah?"

"How many people finish their degrees with no idea what they actually want to do with their lives? Their entire goal is just to get to the end of their program and have that piece of paper. And then what? The people who drop out to pursue their passions are the ones who've really figured out what they want out of life."

Luke nodded in agreement. "That's true. Though I think it broke my mom's heart a little."

"Hasn't she seen how much you love what you do?"

Luke shrugged, chewing tortilla chips and cheese. "My siblings are both so successful, I think my mom has always subconsciously measured my success against theirs. And at some point that started to rub off on me. I've always felt like I have to prove to them that I can make something of my life doing what I love." He didn't see his siblings often, mostly at holidays or on special occasions. It wasn't that they didn't get along, they just didn't spend time together the way they once had, and whenever they did get together, Luke got the impression that his siblings still looked at him as the baby brother who was trying to figure out his life.

"Some people would say you're already winning if you're doing what you love."

Luke took a sip of his beer, getting to the bottom of his glass. "I like those people."

"But you want to do more," she said softly. A car horn sounded, and as Lydia glanced down the street, where twilight painted the backdrop of the city in blues and grays, Luke thought that maybe she also yearned for *more*.

"What I really want to do is open a gym," he said. This was the first time he'd spoken the words into existence outside of his apartment or the bank or in whispered meetings with Jules, and it felt ridiculously good. "I'm actually working on a business plan right now. Trying to get a loan."

"A gym?" Lydia's eyes widened, not in shock, but in agreement. "That's a fantastic idea. You'd be a great business owner."

"You think so?" The funding was a hurdle he still had to jump, but it was nice to hear someone believe that he could do it. Lydia held her hand up as the waitress breezed by, asking for another beer. Luke topped up as well.

"One of my favorite things about being an architect is the moment when I reveal a design to a client. Watching their faces light up as they see the actualized version of their home or building or business. We literally draw their dreams into reality. You do the same thing with people. You take their health goals or the image they have of their future selves and create that reality. You're already in the business of making other people's dreams come true. Why not one of your own?"

The waitress returned with their beers, and Luke lifted his in a toast. Lydia was right. He shouldn't be embarrassed to chase his dream. Fact was, he wasn't really embarrassed, he was terrified. Terrified that he'd tell his mom and his siblings and they'd pat him on the head and say *nice try*. "I think I just put so much pressure on myself to succeed that I've been afraid to talk about it in case it doesn't pan out the way I hope."

Lydia stared down at the glass caught between her hands. "I can understand that. Lately I've been trying to prove myself at work, but I feel like I'm in a rut. Like people don't actually take me or my ideas seriously."

"Like they don't believe you could be great," he said.

Her green eyes sparkled as she looked up at him. "Exactly. This design competition for the youth center is the first project in a long time that I've been genuinely excited about."

"So how are you gonna prove yourself?"

She laughed, the sound so pretty he couldn't help but study her face, detail by detail. The flash of her smile. The turn of her lips. The lithe, delicate line of her neck.

"Aside from kicking ass in this design competition?" Lydia said, playing with the condensation on her glass. "I'm trying to get more involved at the firm. To impress the leadership team, I guess."

"Not just your crush?"

Her lips puckered and he thought she might roll her eyes at him. "No, not just him. The big boss also thought the marathon was a great idea, and I knew I couldn't back out with him standing there, all enthusiastic about it."

"Ah," Luke teased. "So the truth finally comes out."

Lydia bit her lip, leaving a mark that he wanted to brush away with his thumb. "I know it's ridiculous, but now I'm sort of worried that my worth at the firm is going to be measured against how well this race goes. Logically, I know that would be a stupid thing to measure someone's talent and ability against, but..." She shrugged. "I feel like I never know what their expectations are or where..."

"The finish line is drawn?" Luke suggested.

The corner of her mouth quirked. "Yeah. Am I doing too much or not enough? Is my work actually terrible? No one will give me a straight answer. But somehow I'm worried that if I mess this marathon up or fail to finish, they might judge me harder."

For the first time in his life, Luke felt like he was talking to someone who could understand that nagging fear of failure. It was a whisper in the back of his head. Something he was forever cognizant of, always measuring himself against. The air around him suddenly felt stifling and he stood with his drink, cocking his head. Lydia slipped off her stool and followed him to a small booth that was closer to the window. He sat down, and Lydia slid in beside him, close enough that her thigh pressed against his, their elbows jockeying for space. It didn't feel too close though, just comfortable. The breeze shifted across the booth, and Luke took a deep, steadying breath. "When I can't shake that fear of failure, I just run through all the things in the world that scare me more. It sort of helps put things into perspective."

"You mean like if the earth somehow shifts out of orbit and

the gravity holding us to the ground fails, sending us free-falling into the sky?"

Luke burst out laughing, mostly at the serious look on her face. He liked that she could be serious and ridiculous at the exact same time. "That is oddly specific."

"I have a list of fears." She counted off on her fingers. "Sharks. Zombies. Airplanes. The ocean. Like the deep parts that are unexplored. Spiders—"

"How long is this list?"

"It goes on for a while. What's your number one?"

He thought about it for a moment. "Definitely zombies, especially considering how densely populated the city is."

"Right? It's a valid concern!"

"I see why you've come to me now. Gotta make sure you can outrun the zombies when the time comes."

Lydia turned to look him in the eye. "You've caught me. That's the real reason I'm here."

"Aligning yourself with the people most likely to survive a zombie apocalypse is smart."

"I needed some muscle."

Luke's gaze flickered from her eyes to her lips. He couldn't help himself. Her eyelashes were dark and fluttery, her cheeks pink from the alcohol, the gloss on her lips shining in their dim little corner. "I've got muscle to spare," he said, though he couldn't for the life of him figure out what made him say it. He wasn't supposed to be flirting with her, dammit. This, the way she was looking at him, was dangerous territory.

"I've noticed," she said, the little smile at the corner of her mouth telling Luke that she knew damn well they were flirting with disaster.

"Have you?" He should put some distance between them, he thought. But he didn't. Couldn't. He wanted to be here, sharing the same breath of space, close enough to see the city lights reflected in her eyes. He wanted…

Her gaze flicked up and down, dragging along him in a way that made his entire body flush with heat. "It's kind of hard not to," she said, her voice low, filled with fire that would definitely burn him.

"What are we doing?"

"You're flirting with me."

"I think you've got that backwards," he said, but he didn't dare move, praying that the frantic beat of his heart didn't break the spell that had come over them.

To his surprise and relief, Lydia reached out, so slowly it felt like time had stopped as her hand cradled his jaw. "Is this okay?" she asked, inching closer.

Yes! he wanted to shout, even though he knew it was a bad idea. That didn't stop him from nodding. Lydia closed the distance, pressing her lips to his. The kiss was firm, assured, her tongue darting out to tease his lips. She tasted like the beer they'd been drinking and spice from the nachos.

When she pulled away, the flush in her cheeks had spread down her neck. She blinked slowly, staring at him from beneath her lashes, in a way that said maybe she wanted to kiss him again. "*Was* that okay?"

"I couldn't quite tell," he said, keeping his voice low. "I think we should try again."

Lydia snickered under her breath, shifting so close she was almost in his lap. With both her hands, she pulled him to her, her fingers feathering through the short hairs at the back of his neck. This time, Luke's shock had worn off enough to make him a more active participant. He brushed his lips against hers, holding her face steady so he could feel every delicate curve of her mouth. Sirens wailed in his head. Lydia was his client. He had to be able to work with her when she showed up at the gym for her next training session—tomorrow! But tomorrow felt worlds away, and when Lydia's hand drifted from his neck down the front of his chest, he dismissed his worries and poured all his efforts into kissing her senseless.

"You were holding out on me before," Lydia gasped as they broke apart for air, blinking like it was the first time they'd truly laid eyes on each other.

"Sorry," he whispered. "I think you sort of stunned me." Luke could feel the tension between them twisting tighter and tighter. The anticipation that beat beneath his skin was intoxicating and delicious. It felt like every moment they'd spent together had been building to this. The lingering glances. The flirty exchanges. Maybe this was inevitable. He satisfied the concerned part of his brain by telling it that Lydia had kissed him first. She'd made the first move. But what if he was reading too much into this? Maybe a kiss, however sensual it had been, was only a kiss.

As if she'd heard the thoughts in his head, she deliberately put her hand on his thigh and leaned in to peck his lips. His pulse rocketed, his heart pounding against his ribs. "I think you should close our tab now," she whispered.

"Yep," Luke agreed, sliding out the other side of the booth so quickly he almost toppled straight through the open window to the street. "I'll go do that."

He hurried to the bar, practically throwing his money down

as he settled the bill while trying not to let his thoughts drift to anything that resembled a bed. He wanted her. But until she said the words, until they both acknowledged that they wanted this despite it being so, *so* wrong, he couldn't let his thoughts linger there. When he turned around, Lydia was gone from the booth. He found her waiting outside, leaning against the building. Her eyes twinkled under the streetlights, her lips curling as she spotted him. She held her arm out and he went to her. But outside, away from the soft amber lights of the pub, hesitation crept in.

"We shouldn't be doing this," he said as Lydia pressed up on her toes, her lips running over his.

"Why not?" she whispered against his mouth.

"I don't know… You, me, the gym. It's probably a bad idea."

"I thought you weren't Trainer Luke tonight," she said.

God, she really was making this difficult. "I did say that."

"Then there's no professional boundary at stake."

"You're saying it won't affect the training?"

"I'm saying you should invite me back to your place."

Her hands were everywhere, his body burning with fiery need wherever she touched him, making it impossible to think of a coherent protest. "Are you sure?"

She threaded her arms around his neck. "Just this one time. Get it out of our systems…"

Once, Luke thought. They could do this once. Clear the distraction. Right? He tipped his head back, pulling his lips just out of reach.

"Remember when you said sometimes we have to do things that are hard," she teased. "That it can be good for us?"

Luke chuckled, the sound rattling through his chest. "You're twisting my words. You know this is not what I meant."

"You should probably be more specific when you're teaching me something then."

Well, hell. He looked down at her, felt the weight of her in his arms, and suddenly had no interest in fighting it anymore. She was right. They could get this out of their systems. If they walked away from this now, he'd only ever be able to think about this moment, and it would drive him to distraction over and over again. "One time," he whispered. "Come home with me?"

Seven

Lydia

When they stumbled into Luke's place, Lydia attempted to look around, to take stock of her surroundings, but all attempts were thwarted by the sensation of Luke's hand as it shifted up the back of her shirt. She trembled against him, shaking the last of her coherent thoughts free. She wasn't quite sure how they'd gotten here. Yes, of course, she knew how they'd gotten here, in Luke's apartment. But how had she gotten here, in his arms? Here, where his lips were like embers against her skin? Here, where she was practically begging him to take her clothes off?

It would be easy to blame Ashley for putting the thought in her head today, but the truth was, the thoughts were already there. Part of her had already acknowledged how handsome Luke was, how kind, how supportive. And seeing him tonight, in his element, surrounded by a community he cared deeply for and who appreciated him just the same hadn't dulled those feelings. If anything, seeing him at what she imagined was his best had been more attractive than anything. She'd been tiptoeing around this attraction since the moment he'd crashed into her life, but she'd thought she had it under control. Maybe if Luke hadn't so brazenly encouraged her flirting tonight... *I've got muscles to spare.*

That was the moment everything shifted. And now she was telling herself that everything would be back to normal when they woke up tomorrow. They could go back to being Trainer Luke and Trainee Lydia. It would be fine. Besides, what was Luke always saying? Just focus on *this* run, on the next step you have to take. Well, tomorrow felt a million miles away and right now, tonight, this felt like the next step.

"This is my living room," Luke said huskily against her ear as he pressed soft kisses along her neck.

Lydia found the hemline of his shirt, tugging it free of his jeans. "It's nice."

He chuckled. "I haven't even turned the lights on yet."

"Don't bother." She turned her head to capture his lips again. Exercising may have given her endorphins, but kissing Luke made her feel like she could fly. When her legs bumped up against the arm of the couch, she glanced over her shoulder to make sure there was nothing in her way, then let herself topple backward. Luke tried to grab her, to steady her, and she giggled at the brief look of panic on his face as she landed on the cushions.

Light poured in from the street, but the apartment was still dim, just Luke's silvery figure moving through the darkness. "That wasn't funny," he said, smacking her foot where it rested on the arm of the couch.

"It was kind of funny," she said, lifting her foot from his hand and placing it firmly in the center of his chest.

"I actually thought you were about to fall and smack your head on the coffee table." He huffed a laugh. "That would have permanently traumatized me. I'd never be able to have sex in my apartment again."

"I probably would have needed stitches," Lydia agreed, grinning. "I can totally see you not being able to get it up after living through that. You would have had to move. And moving is such a hassle." Luke looked like he was trying not to swear and she giggled some more.

"You're meaner than I thought."

"I'm sorry," Lydia said, stroking her foot down Luke's front, stopping above the waistline of his jeans.

"I don't think you are. I think you would have enjoyed traumatizing me."

"You're probably right."

"I think you should make it up to me," he said.

"How exactly should I do that?"

Luke walked through the living room and took a seat on the other end of the couch, forcing her to sit up and turn around in order to see him. He reclined into the corner, looking perfectly content as he studied her. "In any way you like," he said, his voice low and gravelly.

Lydia's entire body reacted to his words. She wanted to grab him by the collar and haul him down on top of her. She wanted to writhe beneath him until he gave her exactly what she wanted. But he was too far away, and judging by the smile on his lips, he knew that. So instead, she crawled toward him, putting both hands on his thighs as she leaned in for another kiss. "I'm sorry," she said.

"I don't think I believe you yet. But keep trying," Luke whispered, and the invitation in his voice was the equivalent of beckoning her with his finger. Lydia's heart skipped.

"Is this better?" she asked, straddling him, one hand on the back of the couch to steady herself, one hand on his shoulder.

His hands fell to either side of her waist and squeezed gently, those roughened palms slipping beneath her shirt. "Much better," Luke agreed as he started to rock her on his lap.

In the shadowed light bleeding in from outside, his eyes were almost black. Lydia got lost in his dark gaze, heat throbbing between her legs. She threw her head back, lost in the sensation. The tension was so tight, so delicate, she worried it would snap before she reached the pinnacle of this feeling, but some subconscious part of her trusted Luke. She trusted him with her body every single time she stepped into the gym. This was no different.

She could trust him to make her feel good.

Luke pulled her hips down with a little more force than before, grinding in all the right places. Lydia's eyelids fluttered as her jeans pressed between her legs, and a moan bled from her lips. Lydia was no stranger to the occasional hot and heavy one-night stand, but it was rare that a guy had her this turned-on before he'd even taken her clothes off.

Luke leaned forward to nip at her neck. "*That* sounded like an apology."

God, this man. Lydia bit her bottom lip, eyes closed, and moved against him, replicating what he'd done moments ago. This time they both made desperate little sounds, sucking in the same air. Tomorrow, when she looked back on this, wondering why she was so desperate, she'd blame it on all the pent-up sexual frustration born of endorphins and flirting. Then she would forget this ever happened. But tonight, she wanted to hear him. When Luke's hands began to venture up her shirt, Lydia gave in to the desperation and pulled it over her head, tossing it on the floor. Luke's hands fell back to her hips, and when she caught his eyes, she could tell he was simply drinking her in. In a moment of unfettered vulnerability, her stomach dropped like she'd just been flung over the edge of a cliff, but the butterflies in her gut caught her.

"Take your hair down," he said, and she did, loving the electric chill that surged through her at his request. She shook her head, letting her hair cascade over her shoulders.

Luke reached out to twist a few strands of hair between his fingers. Then his hand slipped over her shoulder and down her back, tracing the path of her skin to her bra clasp.

"Probably should have done this part before I took my hair down," she teased, reaching around to help him. When the bra fell away, Luke leaned forward, pressing a kiss to her neck, dragging his lips down along her sternum.

He nosed at the valley between her breasts, and she could feel how badly he wanted her, and it thrilled her. There was a desperation to their movements, but they weren't frantic yet. He was savoring her, tasting and sampling and breathing her in like a fine wine.

She arched her spine, pressing her chest to his face, and he cupped both breasts, the pads of his thumbs tracing over her nipples. Once. Twice. She sucked in a sharp breath and held incredibly still. She wanted to enjoy every second of this.

"Do you like this?" he asked.

Her gaze dropped from his eyes to his lips. She wanted to taste him but she didn't dare move. His fingers were caressing. She felt like the string of a guitar, every inch of her starting to vibrate. He pinched her nipples and she gasped, grinding down against him, searching for friction to soothe the ache.

"Do you like this?" he asked again, skimming the pads of his thumbs over the stiff buds. Sensation zipped up and down her spine. She wasn't sure which feeling she was supposed to be paying attention to, but then his fingers tightened again and the breath caught in her throat.

The pain quickly gave way to pleasure, and Lydia moaned. She dropped her head and kissed him, letting him capture the end of her moan on his tongue. "I like it."

Do it again and again, she wanted to say. She wanted to beg. But she didn't, too intoxicated by the thought of letting him take the lead. Of letting him touch her in every way he thought she might like.

Something about Luke reassured her that he would take care of her in the ways she needed most. She didn't know if it was his patience—goodness knows she'd tested him these past weeks—or if it was his sweet nature, but she just knew she wouldn't have to ask him to make her feel good. He already was.

Lydia braced herself against his shoulders, grinding down against him as his hands left her breasts, sliding around to cup her ass. He obviously liked the friction as much as she did. But that was all they were going to get out of this current arrangement. "You're wearing too many clothes."

"Sorry," he said, sitting up and catching her before she could topple backward off his lap. "I got distracted." He tugged his shirt over his head and Lydia let her hands roam the warm expanse of his chest and abdomen, playing over the defined muscle. "I'm happy to continue this here," he said. "But it might be more fun on the—"

"Bed," Lydia finished for him, letting the fog of lust clear long enough for her to get her legs under her. She stood and pulled Luke to his feet. "Which way?"

"I'll let you guess."

Lydia took him by the hand and led him down the hall. It was electric between them. She could practically feel the current zipping from his hand to hers. "Bathroom," she said, poking her head into the first room they passed. "Bedroom," she said triumphantly, shoving the other door open.

"It's like you're in a rush or something," he teased.

Lydia turned and settled him with a long, searing look. He reached out, took her by the belt loops of her jeans and kissed her. It was deliciously thorough, his tongue slipping past her lips to study every inch of her mouth. Her arms hung loose around his waist, but they soon took on a mind of their own, moving to trace the button on the front of his jeans. She popped the button and tugged the zipper down, leaving enough room for her to do her own exploring.

"Okay," he rasped, breaking the kiss and chasing her hand with his own. "Now we're both in a rush."

Lydia grinned as he walked her backward toward the bed. She unbuttoned her own jeans and tugged them down her legs with her underwear before collapsing onto the bed. Using her elbows to prop herself up, she watched Luke undress, taking in every inch of exposed skin.

Luke wrapped his hand around his cock, giving himself a few languid strokes. A desperate heat flared inside her at the sight, and she knew exactly how to extinguish it. She reached for him, yearning for the moment he covered her body with his own.

"You're sure this is okay?" he asked as his knee hit the mattress. The bed dipped and Lydia wanted nothing more than for Luke to tumble toward her.

"*Yes*. Now get up here already," she complained. His answer was a smirk. Instead of climbing toward her, he retreated and Lydia thought she would actually combust. "What are you doing?"

She heard a drawer open and close, then the crinkle of a wrapper in the dark. When Luke returned, he'd sheathed himself with a condom.

"Oh," Lydia said, glad one of them still had common sense. She didn't know what it was about Luke that was making her lose herself so much faster than with her other hookups. She was usually composed and sensible. Sensible enough to remember a condom, at least.

"Oh?"

"I meant like *oh, good idea*."

He chuckled at her, the sound vibrating across his chest and into hers as his weight settled over her. It was comforting and warm as he stretched out against her, skin brushing skin.

She caught Luke's hips in the cradle of her thighs. When the tip of his cock brushed against her clit, her eyes practically rolled back in her head. "*Oh, God*, Luke."

"Was that a good *oh, God* or—"

"How can you be fishing for compliments already?"

"Not compliments. Just feedback. I like to see how I can improve my performance in real time," he teased, the words racing across her skin. "Sort of the way I remind you to adjust your running form while we're training."

"I don't want to talk about training."

"Mood killer?"

She laughed huskily. "Trainer Luke isn't supposed to be here right now."

"You're right." He reached down and instead of joining them together, he brushed his fingers between her thighs. Lydia's hips leapt from the bed. If not for his body pinning hers down, she might have launched right across the room as she chased the friction from his fingers.

"How's this?" he asked even as she threw her head back against the comforter, her eyes pinched so tight they hurt.

"Good," she rasped.

"Like *good* good or…"

"Good enough that if you stop I'll probably have to kill you." He didn't stop, and a cry of pleasure slithered from her throat.

"So, just like this?" Luke whispered, rubbing circles around her clit.

"Just…just like that," she stuttered. It was perfect. Not too soft. Not too much pressure. And just fast enough.

"You don't want me to change a thing?"

"I swear to God, Luke—" But she didn't have time to finish her threat because the circles and the pressure and the husky whispers in her ear had been exactly the right combination to hurl her over the edge of orgasm. She wasn't expecting it to happen so quickly, and she tumbled through the torrent of sensation. She felt like a skydiver who'd jumped without their parachute. She was free-falling and there was no stopping the pleasure that rushed up to greet her as her hips bucked.

The shock was so good that Lydia actually drew a blank for a moment. When she came back into herself, she could feel Luke nudging at her entrance, and the warmth that now only simmered in her core began to boil again. *God, this man.* Instead of telling him he had the permission he was clearly waiting for, she reached down, took his length in her hand and inched him inside her, reveling in the stretch of her muscles.

He braced his forearms on either side of her head. She wanted him to move faster, to take and take from her until she shattered, but he didn't. His strokes were even and smooth and her pleasure built steadily. Still, Lydia wanted more and she wanted it now, so she canted her hips to meet his thrusts, driving him deeper.

Luke dropped his head and groaned against her ear, and she was desperate to make him feel his own mind-bending release. She rotated her hips with his thrusts, noticing as he became jerky and uncoordinated, chasing his pleasure. She wrapped her arms around his shoulders as he ground down against her, his pelvis pressed against hers, and the pressure inside her released, another orgasm rocketing free. As she convulsed, Luke grunted in her ear, shuddering all over as he came.

"I've never seen you so out of breath," she said as he rolled off her. His muscles relaxed and contracted under the streetlights. "Usually I'm the one hyperventilating."

"Maybe that's because you made me do all the work."

"You liar. That is totally not true!" Lydia said, rolling onto her side. "I know how to use these hips."

"You sure do," Luke said, turning to grin at her. It was a dopey, sleepy smile. He reached out to brush away strands of hair that had gotten stuck to the sweat on her neck and chest.

"So, does this count as my cardio for the week?" she asked him.

He snorted. "I don't think so, but nice try."

"Guess there's no point in going for round two then?"

He reached out across the bed with a suddenness that startled her, snagging her hip and hauling her close. Lydia giggled into the next kiss.

Eight

Luke

Luke woke up alone, the aftertaste of nachos on his breath and Lydia's lip gloss on his tongue. *Just this one time*, she had said. *Get it out of our systems.*

He rolled over, into the space she'd occupied on the bed, inhaling the scent of her on the pillow—soapy white florals with citrus. Waking up alone was nothing unusual for him, so he was surprised at the sudden pang in his chest. At how obviously *in* his system she still was. He opened his eyes, blinking down at the hardwood floor. It was then that he noticed Lydia's socks. If she'd taken the time to put on the rest of her clothes, why would she have left her socks? He sat up, listening for her in the apartment, but it was silent. Luke climbed out of bed and shrugged into jogging pants and a T-shirt to go investigate.

The living room was empty, but the scent of coffee lingered in the kitchen. He was a simple guy and used instant, which he suspected was not up to Lydia's fancy, overpriced sugary caffeine tastes. She'd left him a mug on the counter and coffee in the pot. It was still warm. He smiled to himself at the sweet simplicity of the gesture. When he'd poured his coffee, he sought her out in the last place she could be—the fire escape.

He popped the window open, leaning out to see her better. She was curled up in the chair he kept out there, her bare feet kicked up on the railing, a pad of paper in her lap—one of the endless memo pads he ended up bringing home from the gym. Her hair was still loose, amber under the morning sun, sparkling with shades of gold. He itched to twist it around his fingers again, to feel the strands pull taut as he tilted her head, exposing the delicate column of her neck to his lips, but he quickly willed those thoughts away and cleared his throat. "Morning."

She turned and beamed at him, catching him off guard. He'd expected awkwardness or even a level of embarrassment once the sleep fog faded and she remembered what they'd gotten up to last night. But like most days, Lydia totally surprised him.

"How's the coffee?" he asked.

"Terrible. Is this how you chase girls out in the morning?"

"Yes. One of the many tactics I employ."

Lydia hummed, taking an exaggerated sip from her mug.

Luke climbed out the window to join her. The morning was oddly cool but not cold, the early-July sun quickly chasing away any lingering chill from overnight. He sat against the railings, his back to the street, just so he could look at her. This was the last of their night together, and he wanted to drink her in, soft and unguarded and smiling. "I thought you might have done a runner."

Her gaze flickered up from her page, finding his, and for a split second Luke thought he'd made it uncomfortable, but then Lydia laughed. "An unscheduled morning run? As if."

Luke snorted, knowing just how serious she was. "What are you drawing?"

She passed over the memo pad. "I thought it was pretty, the way the sun hit the buildings this morning."

"This is amazing," he murmured, putting his coffee down so he could trace the lines of her sketch with his fingertip. It was a stunningly accurate rendition of the buildings across the street. She'd captured the hard lines of the apartments and the shadowy fire escapes and the intricate design of the bodega on the ground floor. She was talented, there was no doubt about that. Probably a superstar in that office of hers. But then he remembered what she'd said last night at the pub—*I feel like I'm in a rut. Like people don't actually take me or my ideas seriously.* How could anyone look at this and not take her seriously? He'd hire her in a heartbeat to design his gym from the ground up if he had the money.

Lydia shrugged, unimpressed by her own talent. "It's just a sketch."

"This is good enough to hang on my wall and use as a conversation piece with friends," he said. He didn't know how anyone so talented could even begin to doubt themselves.

"If you like it so much, you can keep it."

Luke passed the memo pad back to her. "You have to sign it."

Lydia indulged him, scrawling her name across the bottom of the paper. She tore it free of the memo pad and handed it to him. "You all right?" she asked.

"Just thinking."

"A dangerous pastime." She tried for a smile but when he didn't return it, a line appeared between her brows. "Are these dark, haunting thoughts or just the regular kind?"

"Maybe a bit of both."

"Well, now I'm hooked." She sat back in her chair, reaching out to nudge his knee with her foot. "Go on. Can't be any worse than us seeing each other naked."

He huffed, taking a sip of coffee. He could think of plenty of things worse than seeing Lydia naked. The image of her, touched by nothing but the streetlights, wasn't one he'd soon forget, or the fact that he'd held her soft curves in his hands, touched parts of her that had made her toes curl. And maybe that was part of the problem. Actually, that was definitely the problem. "I was just thinking about what happened last night, and how that probably wasn't my smartest idea."

"You mean sleeping with me?"

"Yeah."

"Well, I hate to break it to you, but there were two people involved in the decision-making required to get us to the morning after."

"You're right," he said. "But I am sor—"

"Don't apologize. We didn't do anything wrong." Luke frowned at that, and she continued with, "Did you have fun? Did I satisfy you to the fullest extent?"

Luke fought a horrendous blush. "I think you know the answer to that."

"Then we can chalk it up to a good time."

"It was still unprofessional of me, and for that I do want to apologize. I usually never cross workplace boundaries." If

Luke was being truthful with himself, he'd made excuses last night. He knew he'd risked their professional partnership. But part of him also felt more clearheaded about the decision this morning. Maybe it was the fresh air, maybe it was the coffee, but he knew what this was, and it sounded like she did as well. But just in case, he added, "So that can't happen again. Ever."

"Don't worry. I still plan on running this race," she said.

"And I want to help get you there," Luke assured her. "I'm not trying to shirk my responsibility as your trainer, but if you'd prefer to start fresh with someone else, I'd understand. I could recommend another trainer from the gym—"

"I don't want anyone else," Lydia said with certainty. Some ridiculous part of him roared in triumph at her declaration. "I like the partnership we have going. I like the way you've set up my training plan. I watched you with the kids yesterday, and it's no wonder they all wanted to talk to you. You're a great motivator, and I need someone like that in my corner. I don't want to start all over again with someone new."

"Does that mean you're going to stop complaining every time I ask you to do a burpee?"

"Not a chance."

Luke laughed into his mug. If Lydia was prepared to make this work, then he could too. They were both adults who'd made the adult decision to sleep together. They'd chalk it up to a night where their desires got the best of them and leave it at that. Besides, didn't Lydia have a workplace crush she was trying to impress?

That idea cooled whatever remained of last night's lingering thoughts.

"Professional?" Lydia said, thrusting out her hand for him to shake.

Luke took it. "Professional."

"Glad we're on the same page about it." She let go of his hand and thrusted her coffee cup into the air. "To getting me across that finish line."

"Starting with today's eight-mile run," Luke added, snickering as she scowled at him.

"I was hoping you forgot about that."

"The sex wasn't *that* mind-blowing."

"Hey!" Lydia said as he stood and walked back to the window.

He beckoned her with a flick of his head. See, he could do this. He could just be Trainer Luke.

"Eight miles sucks," Lydia complained for the fifth—or was it fiftieth?—time since starting the run.

"What are you talking about? You're already halfway there, and you're averaging an eleven-minute mile. At this rate we'll be done in another forty minutes."

Lydia groaned. "We've been running forever."

"That's just the way it goes in the beginning. Some runs breeze by and some drag on. One day, weeks from now, you'll look back and think about how easy eight miles is."

"Yeah, right."

"I'm serious. By the end of this training plan, you'll be running eight miles as your nice, short recovery run distance and it won't even faze you."

"I'm exhausted just thinking about it."

"C'mon—" *Where's all that energy I saw last night? Luke*

caught the words on the tip of his tongue. They'd agreed to this line. He couldn't cross it. Not again. No aimless flirting, and that included bringing up the night they'd spent together. It was both easier and harder than he'd imagined. Easier because he knew this was the right thing to do. Because he was so determined to help her complete this marathon. But it was harder, too. Harder to keep his thoughts in check, especially during a long run when his mind naturally started to wander. He wondered if Lydia was having the same problem, but judging by her clenched fists and the way her brow furrowed, he suspected she was entirely consumed with thoughts of finishing these last four miles.

"You're tensing up," Luke said, slowing the pace. Her shoulders had been creeping toward her ears for at least a mile. Lydia staggered to a walk beside him.

Lydia rolled her shoulders and unfurled her fists as she caught her breath. "I didn't even realize."

"Are you in pain?" he asked. They had a lot of miles left to go before the marathon, and the last thing they needed was an injury slowing down their progress.

"No." She gave him a wan smile. "Believe it or not, I was actually trying to up my pace a bit."

"Staying relaxed is actually the key if you want to be faster. Tension compromises your running form and naturally slows you down."

"So you're saying slow and steady really does win the race?" she teased.

He squinted against the sun. "Sort of. Most runners carry tension in their upper bodies first. Watch for it in your shoulders, your hands, even your jaw."

"How do I get rid of it?"

"Doing periodic body checks works," he said. "Mentally scroll through your form cues from top down. Is your jaw clenched? Unclench it. Have your fists curled up? Shake them out. Are your shoulders relaxed?"

"What if I do all that and it doesn't work?" she asked without looking at him.

"Distraction helps too."

She hummed softly.

"When you feel that tension creeping in, focus on your breath and your stride."

"Right," she said.

Luke could think of other forms of distraction that relieved tension. Things he wasn't supposed to be thinking about, because this partnership was strictly professional between them now. But as he studied Lydia's profile, the way she suddenly wouldn't meet his eye, the way her shoulders were creeping up again, he started to wonder if maybe she was also thinking about some alternative forms of distraction. "If you're feeling okay, I think we should start running again," he said, glancing down at his watch like he wasn't thinking about last night at all.

"Yep," Lydia said, setting off. "Totally relaxed."

But as she ran past him, her body coiled like a snake about to strike, Luke knew it was going to be a long four miles... for them both.

Nine

Lydia

Lydia had already drunk two coffees with an unmention-able amount of sugar before she even arrived at the gym. Her morning had started with hazy blueprint-like shapes after bolting awake from a dream, and she'd stumbled from her bed to her desk in search of paper and a pencil to capture the thoughts. She'd made good headway on her submission for the Manhattan Youth Center competition in the weeks since she'd visited with Luke, and if she wasn't busy dreaming up additions to her preliminary sketch, then she was writing up the benefits of an eco-friendly design to go along with the proposal. She was still so grateful that Luke had invited her back to the youth center to meet the kids, though she tried not to dwell on that invitation too much or else her thoughts went spinning in very nonwork-related directions.

Dammit, she thought, shaking images of naked Luke from her mind as she tugged the gym door open. She'd been doing so well lately, too. That first run after sleeping together had been harder than she'd expected. An awkward tension had crept into her muscles—one that had begged her to look at him, to reach for him—and she'd practically sprinted through the last four miles if only to bring an end to her torture. But the tension had eased since then, and they'd found themselves back in a comfortable routine where he kept her on track for the marathon and she complained about the number of burpees in her cross-training. It felt right. It worked for them. She wasn't about to mess that up now.

"You're early," Luke called, coming down the hall from his office.

"I couldn't sleep," she admitted. "Weird dreams."

"Oh?"

"Just work stuff," she added.

"Well, I can't help you there. But I can help you get these three miles down. Give me a second to grab my watch."

While Luke gathered his things, Lydia went to stuff her bag in a locker. She usually went right to work from the gym after her short runs, so she had to bring everything she needed to shower. Today was a short recovery run, which Lydia found herself craving if only to clear her head. Luke met her at the door, and they slipped outside into the morning heat. The sun was barely peeking between the buildings, the streets still bathed in shadow, but she could feel the heavy weight of the summer humidity already pressing down from above.

They stretched in comfortable silence, Luke leading her through the steps she'd had memorized for weeks now. Then he started his watch timer and they set off, falling into step on the sidewalk. They ran in comfortable silence for the first mile.

When they were forced to stop for a traffic light, Luke

said cautiously, "So, weird dreams? Good? Bad? Or do I not want to know?"

"They're not sex dreams," she assured him, biting her lip to keep from laughing at the way his entire body tensed for a beat. She was glad they were getting back to a place where they could make jokes again. They started running.

"Good. 'Cause we're definitely not talking about *that*. What are your weird, nonsexual work dreams?"

"Well, today I dreamed that I handed in my proposal for the Youth Center design competition and it was only half done. But even after I realized it, the leadership team wouldn't let me finish it. I woke up with all these ideas and couldn't get back to sleep."

"So it turned out to be a good dream then, because it gave you ideas?"

"No, it was terrifying! My heart was literally racing when I crawled out of bed."

He laughed as they ran through a crosswalk. "I think you and I have different definitions of terrifying."

"Oh, come on, you said you were working on a business plan. Imagine handing that in to the bank and forgetting half the plan!"

"Okay, fair point," he said. "But is your proposal only half done?"

She shrugged. "It's definitely further along than that."

"So this isn't even a valid fear. What are you really worried about?"

"I don't know," Lydia said. Maybe that was a lie. Or maybe she really didn't know what the root of her fear was. Could it be the stack of previous proposal rejections? The ongoing lack of feedback from the leadership team? Was she worried she might literally forget half the proposal on the printer when she went to hand it in? "I need one of those books that decodes dreams."

"Maybe you're just afraid I'll beat you back to the gym," Luke said.

What? had barely left her mouth when Luke flashed her a cheeky smile and darted down the sidewalk.

"Luke!" she shouted over the thumping tread of their feet as they both sped up. Luke laughed boyishly as he pulled ahead, the sound so light and carefree she thought she might be able to float away on it. He'd had the advantage of surprise, and his legs were longer, but Lydia was impressed that she remained right on his heels as they rounded the block and came within sprinting distance of the gym.

They both put on a blast of speed at the end, but Luke's hand touched the gym door first and his fists lifted in victory.

Lydia dropped her hands to her hips, sucking in air. "I didn't know sprints were on the training plan for today."

"They weren't. But you stopped worrying about your dream for a minute there, didn't you?"

"Yeah, 'cause I didn't have enough oxygen getting to my brain," she muttered, but he was right. She *had* stopped thinking about the proposal. In fact, the only thing she could think about right now was the way Luke's smile was lit up by the flash of sun that peeked between the buildings.

"Either way it worked." He checked his watch. "Plus, that's your best three-mile time so far."

"Are you looking for a pat on the back?" she quipped as he pulled the gym door open for her.

"Just the acknowledgment that I'm the best trainer ever."

"You're gonna have to work harder for that one!" she called over her shoulder as she gathered her things and headed off to the showers.

When she arrived at work an hour later, it was still early, and Lydia passed Kirsten's empty desk, hurrying down the dimmed hallway to her office. She kept the lights off and adjusted the blinds at her narrow window, wanting to maintain the illusion of early-morning tranquility she'd found after the run. The moment she sat down, she unpacked her laptop and opened her proposal file. There were about a dozen things on her to-do list today for her actual job, but she could spare an hour for her personal project. Lydia made some adjustments to her current design and hit Print. She always preferred editing on a hard copy during these early design stages.

She headed down the hall to the supply room, where she could hear the copy machine revving as it started spitting out papers. Lydia turned into the room, grabbing the still-warm designs. She examined them, smiling at her progress. Luke had been right. There really was no truth to her dream. Her proposal was in good shape. The new double gymnasium she'd envisioned now included a viewing area and an indoor track with plenty of space for the kids to spread out. Luke's comment about feeding the kids had sparked ideas for a larger industrial kitchen that could double as a classroom, with areas for learning and food prep. She knew the tiny dining hall was also currently used as the performing arts space, so Lydia had dreamed up a small auditorium with spotlights and a giant stage.

On the roof, she'd left space for the garden she envisioned, but her thoughts had halted on the outdoor yard this morning. Do they get rid of it and expand the building? It was a possibility, but that would mean there was no safe outdoor area for the kids to enjoy. Maybe she should think about adding some sort of retractable covering to save the space from the elements and provide shade?

"Morning, running buddy."

"Oh, Jack!" Lydia yelped, clutching her chest, her nails digging into her skin like she might be able to push past her ribs and squeeze her racing heart. "You scared the crap out of me."

He chuckled softly. "Figured that by how high you jumped. Gotta be careful in those heels," he said, and they both looked down at her shoes. "Don't want to break an ankle before the race."

"These are wedges, not heels," Lydia said, popping her foot up to show them off. As far as footwear went, they were comfortable enough for her to make the trek from the train to the office.

"You should try something like this," he teased, twisting his foot for her to see his black leather loafer. "Highly fashionable. Practical. I could probably even run the marathon in these if I had to."

"Okay, I'll give you that," Lydia laughed. "I'll just be glad if I manage to finish the race in my running shoes."

"Speaking of the race," he said, putting his hand on her arm. "I've got something for you." He twirled her around, and she followed him to his office, wondering if her heart was still racing from the earlier scare or because Jack had just touched her.

His office was bigger than hers, but with the same view. His desk was also far more cluttered. He had thick stacks of memos tacked to the wall and photos of previous outreach days in frames. His computer was on, and the coffee in his mug was half gone. It looked like he'd gotten here even earlier than she had. Jack reached for something in one of his desk drawers, then turned around with a beaming smile and presented her with an empty metal water bottle. Lydia twisted the bottle to read the thick lettering on the side. Under the logo for Poletti's was her own name etched in black.

"I had them made," Jack said. "What do you think? I thought we could use some matching training merch. Get everyone a little excited. I know it's still months away but—"

"This is great," she assured him. "Really. Thank you. Did you get the whole office personalized bottles?"

"No. Just us," Jack said, reaching to close the drawer. "Since we're the only ones who signed up to run in the end. Everyone else just gets one with a Poletti's logo. I got a deal, so we'll end up with extras. Figured we could hand them out to new employees or summer interns if I kept them plain."

Something in that explanation left Lydia feeling strange. Not for the first time, she wondered if there was something brewing here or if she was just reading too much into a nice gesture. She ran her fingers over the raised edge of her name. Why had he cared enough to single her out like this?

"How's your training going so far?" Jack asked.

She cleared her throat, sharing a conspiratorial smile with him. "I've called in some professional help."

"You got yourself a running coach? That's smart. I've read that it can help keep you on track." The phone on his desk started buzzing, and Lydia heard the murmur of their colleagues arriving. So much for her uninterrupted hour of focused work on her proposal. "I'll have to get those office training sessions set up so we can do some training together."

"Yeah, that sounds good," Lydia lied. The last thing she wanted Jack to see was her running anywhere. At least until marathon day.

Jack picked up the phone and held it to his ear. "I'll keep you posted," he said before answering.

Lydia lifted her hand in goodbye, then fled with her new water bottle and her proposal papers. She wanted to get back to her office, preferably behind a closed door, before she started overanalyzing their interaction. Maybe there was nothing unusual about this. Coworkers got gifts for each other all the time, right?

"Lunch?"

Lydia looked up from her desk to see Kirsten in the doorway, then checked her phone. How had the morning passed so quickly?

Kirsten walked over and snatched the water bottle from Lydia's desk. "I want a cool marathon water bottle!"

"You didn't get one?" Lydia asked.

"Yes, but apparently only Jack's *running buddies* get their names on the bottle."

"You could have been this cool," Lydia teased so she wouldn't flush at Kirsten's comment. "All you had to do was sign up for the pain and suffering with me."

"He's trying to butter you up so you don't sue him when

you pass out from dehydration halfway through the marathon," Kirsten joked.

"You know, that's actually a real possibility."

"As if. I'm obviously going to be there, throwing water and snacks at you from the sidelines."

Lydia snorted.

"So, lunch?" Kirsten asked again.

"Definitely," she said, stacking her youth center papers in a pile.

"That's coming along well," Kirsten noted.

Lydia grabbed her purse and they headed for the elevators. "Luke ended up inviting me back to the youth center because he volunteers there, and I learned so much from the kids. It was a totally different experience than visiting with the office, and the ideas just started flowing."

"Wait, Luke? Like the really hot trainer that's teaching you how to run?"

"I know how to run," Lydia said. "He's making me better. But, yeah, the youth center came up during training one day and it was kind of this *oh, small world* moment. So he invited me for another tour, and we went for nachos after…" Lydia trailed off, trying not to dwell on what came next.

"Oh my God, you slept with the really hot trainer!"

Lydia guffawed. "How the hell did you get there from what I said?"

"Am I wrong?"

She bit her lip.

Kirsten skipped out of the elevator and practically dragged Lydia down 10th Avenue toward their favorite Italian sandwich shop. "Tell me everything!"

Lydia avoided mentioning anything to Kirsten after it happened because part of her felt like the only way to keep things professional between her and Luke was not to talk about it. But then she'd slipped up and told Ashley. And, well… "Before you assume I jumped the man, let me begin by saying that it started off completely innocently."

Kirsten threw open the door to the shop. "A tour and nachos totally sounds like a date."

In the lunch line, Lydia lowered her voice. "It was not a date."

They paused the conversation long enough to order.

As they waited for their sandwiches, Kirsten needled her for more information. "Get to the good part."

"I suggested we go for a drink. He picked the place because it was his neighborhood and then I sort of kissed him."

Kirsten squealed under her breath.

"I don't know what happened."

"I do." Kirsten picked up their tray as it appeared on the counter. "You saw something you wanted and you went for it." They headed for an empty table. "So how was it?"

Lydia took a bite of her sandwich. "Good. Really good."

Kirsten sighed dreamily. "And?"

"And nothing. We talked the next morning. I think Luke wigged out a bit. Said something about finding me a new trainer."

"Right," Kirsten said. "I can see how it would make things complicated. So you're training with someone else now?"

Lydia shook her head.

"Aw, boo. You've stopped sleeping with him?"

Lydia swallowed, wiping her face with a napkin. "We

agreed it was a onetime thing and would not be happening
again. I just needed somewhere to funnel all the extra endorphins and energy, and Luke was right there. But I need
him to help me get those miles down more than I need him
in my bed." There was really no sense in getting hung up on
their night together. It was nothing serious—hookup situa-
tions never were for her. To ruin their partnership over sex
would be foolish.

Part of her still couldn't believe they'd fallen into bed together. There was something inherently unsexy about training
for a marathon. At least the way she was doing it. Muscles that
she'd never used before now ached. Her joints made strange
popping sounds, and she was pretty sure she flailed like a bird
trying to take flight while she ran. Despite all that, Luke had
still slept with her. So, either he was in a dry spell, or she was
just oozing sex appeal along with her sweat.

"You guys see each other almost every day." Kirsten's mouth
froze halfway to her sandwich. "What if there are feelings
and junk?"

Lydia laughed so hard she almost choked on a pepper.

"What?" Kirsten said. "It could happen."

"God, no," Lydia said immediately. *Feelings? Between her
and Luke?* He was a great guy, really, but they were all wrong
for each other.

"Why not?" Kirsten said.

"Luke's wonderful, but…" Lydia shrugged. She knew this
thing between them wouldn't go any further than it already
had, mostly because she was waiting on a love story like Ashley's. Until that time, everything else was just filler—fun, but
filler. She had a vision in her head of how her life was sup-

posed to turn out, and she cared about Luke too much to just let him be her filler. Despite the short six weeks they'd spent together, she already knew he deserved more than that. She fully expected to meet a colleague one day that swept her off her feet, a fellow architect who just understood her world, who could support her as she moved up the ladder in her career. *Someone like Jack*, she thought, getting butterflies. Though she wasn't about to let slip about Jack to Kirsten. "We're all wrong for each other," she finished flatly.

"Then maybe he wasn't really *that* good?"

"The bedroom situation is not the problem. Trust me. I lost track of how many times—"

Kirsten held a hand up. "I've heard enough to be thoroughly jealous. If you're not going to pursue that, then *please* send him my way."

Lydia smirked at Kirsten's enthusiasm, trying in vain not to think about Luke's muscles on display while his fingers did wicked things. About his tongue ghosting across her skin. About the way he laughed when she complained about doing burpees. Or those smiles he reserved for when she conquered miles she didn't think she could. The way his eyes lit up when he talked about his business plan and the youth center and...

Okay, maybe Kirsten is right, Lydia thought as her face burned scarlet. Maybe there was a tiny, residual feeling left over.

One flimsy little feeling that she was going to have to stomp out because she had a marathon to run.

Ten

Luke

"I think my lung collapsed. That's a real thing, right? Because I'm pretty sure it's happening right now. Either that or I'm dying."

"You'd be in a lot more pain if your lung collapsed," Luke said.

"That's not very reassuring." Lydia slowed and held her arm up, reaching around with her other hand to press against her ribs. "Right here."

Luke slowed, jogging backward down the sidewalk. It was early in the day, but the late-July sun already baked overhead, and he'd done his best to keep them in the shade for most of the ten-mile run. "Think you can push through it?"

Lydia groaned, and Luke tried not to think about how that sound made him think about other things, *other sounds*. "When you ask like that it makes me feel like I need to try harder."

She started jogging. He kept the pace deliberately slow until she fell in step beside him. "Don't hold your breath. Remember what we always talk about? Inhale through your nose and mouth at the same time."

"I'm sucking in air like a vacuum, Luke. The air's not the problem."

"Okay, *okay*," he said. "I'll only worry if you start turning blue."

She wrinkled her nose but kept moving.

They'd run just over eight miles. They were in the home stretch now, on their way back to the gym, but he could tell she was struggling with these last two miles. Luke looked down at his watch. Maybe he'd cut the run short today. Part of being a good trainer was knowing when to push your client and when to pull back. Lydia was allowed to have an off day.

He glanced over at her, studying her shortened stride, her flaring nostrils, the clenched fists as she tried to shake off the cramp. "Did you drink enough water this morning? Or is your blood purely caffeine?"

"Of course I drank water," she grumbled. "I've been drinking so much water lately that I've sprouted gills."

"The rent's probably cheaper in a fishbowl."

She muttered under her breath at him, which normally would have made him laugh, but she was clearly uncomfortable and he didn't want to push it. Instead, he came to a full stop. "All right, arms up," he said, catching her elbow. He took her hands and directed them over her head. "We'll stretch it out."

"How close are we?"

"Close enough. You did good."

"Doesn't feel good." She groaned. "Does this mean I've failed training?"

Luke smiled softly at her. "You can't fail training."

"But I didn't finish the run."

"Only by like a mile and a half."

"That feels worse than if I'd just flaked out at the beginning."

"Part of these early training sessions is getting used to listening to your body, figuring out what it needs in the moment. By the time you get to the marathon, you'll know how to run through the cramp. Right now, you're learning. Not everything has to go perfectly. We'll crush it another day." Lydia frowned as he guided her until she was leaning to the side. "Hold this position for thirty seconds."

Lydia did. When she righted herself, she was still wincing.

"Show me where it hurts again."

Lydia pushed on a spot near the bottom of her rib cage. Luke laid his hand over hers, doing everything in his power to avoid meeting her eye. They'd done so well at keeping things professional, he didn't want to ruin it with a heated look. *This is all business*, he told himself as he applied gentle pressure. "Take a deep breath."

"What do you think I've been doing?"

"I mean a proper, slow inhale. None of that shallow stuff you've been doing for the last half mile."

"If you could tell I was breathing wrong, why didn't you say anything?"

"These are things you'll have to be able to notice during the marathon. Twenty-six point two miles is a lot. The occasional cramp is the least of what you can expect on race day."

Lydia made a disgruntled face but to his surprise, didn't

complain any further. She clearly understood the concept of situational learning. "Any better?" he asked.

She nodded. "A little."

"Okay, let's start walking. We'll get the blood pumping again and hop on the subway."

Lydia kept her hand on her side, massaging away the lingering ache. "Where are we?"

"We veered off course a little," Luke said, checking his phone. The route he'd originally planned had been interrupted by construction. "Actually..." he began. "Can I show you something?"

"If it involves the word *massage*, then yes."

Luke waved her toward an alley.

Lydia followed, somewhat reluctantly. "I think this is how murder documentaries start."

"Yours or mine?" he asked, wrangling keys from his pocket. He unlocked a door on the side of a warehouse.

"True," she said, catching up. "I could take you."

Luke grinned, then inclined his head, and Lydia followed him inside.

"What is this place?"

"It used to be a shoe factory back in the day."

"And now?" Lydia asked as they passed through a hall and entered the old factory floor. The machines were long gone, leaving the space empty and echoey.

Luke didn't answer, just let Lydia do her little spin and take everything in. If anyone else could appreciate the space, it was her.

"Oh, Luke!" she gasped, and he could tell she'd finally put it together. Her head tipped back to take in the pearly sunbeams cascading down through the skylights. "This place is fantastic."

"This is where I want my gym. If I can make it happen. It's owned by an old friend of my father's. He's agreed to a great deal on the rent as long as I sort out the business loan to pay for staff and the equipment."

"Wow."

He could see her mind running a mile a minute, planning and designing. He appreciated how enthusiastic she was. He hadn't even bothered to show his family yet. He knew neither of his siblings would get this excited over an empty building the way Lydia did. But this was more than that. This space represented his future, and that's the part he was excited about.

"Are you going to show me around?" Lydia snagged him by the hand, tugging in a way that made his heart race unexpectedly.

"Um…" He glanced left and right. "This is sort of it. I mean, it's gonna be empty until I can afford to turn it into an actual gym."

She made a noise in the back of her throat like she was exasperated with him. "I know it's empty *now*, but what do you envision right here?" She waved her hands toward the wall.

Luke realized this was one of the things he liked most about Lydia—her ability to dream, to imagine. She didn't see an empty warehouse. She already saw his gym, fully functional, people sweating, hearts pounding, exercise classes in full swing.

He pointed to the floor. "I want a circular reception desk here."

"In the middle?"

He nodded. "I want potential clients to have to walk through the space, get a feel for it, see people working out. That way by the time they get to the desk, they're already imagining themselves as a member. And over there," he said, gesturing to the wall she'd originally pointed out, "I'm thinking mirrors."

"Gotta have those for the gym selfies."

Luke laughed, turning as his floor plan came to life. He walked Lydia through the space, pointing out invisible exercise machines. He opened doors to dusty, unused rooms and called them spin studios and lockers. "This hall," he continued, "will probably house staff offices, maybe a lunchroom."

"And your office?" she asked.

He turned and pointed to a set of stairs. It led to an office on the second floor with a window that looked out over the entire hypothetical gym. "Up there." Saying it all out loud made it feel real. Too real. Luke caught himself grinning from ear to ear, and quickly reeled in the smile.

"What's wrong?" she asked.

"I just don't want to get ahead of myself."

"If you want to make this a reality, then you have to put it out into the universe."

He tipped his head in her direction. "What if the universe says no?"

"What if the universe is saying ask and you shall receive?"

Luke didn't believe in manifesting his dreams, but he *did* believe in hard work. He believed in all the late nights he'd spent working on his business plan, creating spreadsheets with hypothetical budgets and employees and equipment breakdowns. He believed in talking with Mrs. Amisfield over the phone, asking her questions and clarifying his concerns. These were the things that would lead him to success. Not simply… wishing for it. If he could wish things into existence, he would have asked for someone to finish his market research. That was the last hurdle he had to tackle before he'd be ready to present his plan to Mrs. Amisfield for submission.

"Just try it," Lydia said. "Close your eyes."

"And then what?"

"Close them." She chuckled at his resistance, taking up both his hands. Her thumbs grazed his knuckles and a fiery chill shot through him. It was warm and cold all at once, kindling a fire low in his belly. "Good," she whispered. "Now picture your gym."

Luke was having trouble thinking of anything other than her hands against his skin. He had to fight with himself to pull his thoughts away from other memories of her hands ghosting over his body. *Gyms.* He was supposed to be thinking of gyms. And equipment. Dumbbells and rowing machines and resistance bands and benches.

"Can you see it?" Lydia whispered.

"Yep," he said, like there was nothing but treadmills dancing in his head. Because that's what they'd agreed on.

"What's your biggest goal for the gym?"

Her question caught him off guard. But what shocked him most was how quickly he was ready to answer. "I want to partner with the youth center to offer classes and programs."

"That's an amazing idea."

Luke's eyes popped open, finding Lydia's vibrant green ones staring back at him. Her hands suddenly fell away from his, and he missed her touch. "Yeah?"

"It's unique, and I think unique sells when it comes to businesses."

"It's not about making money," he said.

"I didn't think it was." Lydia's answering smile was soft and reassuring, and for a second Luke thought he might do something ridiculous like kiss her.

This reminded him of that night in the pub, when he'd first confided in her about the gym and she'd been so supportive. She hadn't even hesitated to tell him he'd be a great business owner, and he'd believed her. Just like he believed her now. The longer he looked at her, the harder his heart hammered in his chest. He wanted to reach for her. To be the one to make the first move this time. But this was a boundary they couldn't cross. Not again. They'd promised. To stop himself from acting on his tumbling thoughts, he stepped away, digging the warehouse key out of his pocket. "We should probably head out. Do a proper cooldown."

Something in Lydia's soft stare sharpened, and she darted forward, snagging the key from his hand. "I thought we were done for today," she said, dangling the key like bait. "You said I did good."

He tried to grab it but she slipped away, glaring at him playfully. That did nothing to help the sensations he was trying to keep at bay. "Lydia—"

"You said we should listen to my body."

Luke groaned, wishing she wouldn't take his words out of context.

"My body says no to your cooldown."

From where Luke was standing they both needed a cooldown, because everything inside him was on fire.

"You can't just break your own rules."

He surged forward and caught her by the wrist. She laughed, leaning back against the wall, tugging him closer. Luke realized the position he'd put them in, but suddenly nothing in the world was strong enough to pull him away. His hand tangled with hers, around the key, but she didn't let go and neither did he. "I don't mean to break my rules," he whispered. They were standing too close for anything else.

"Then what do you mean to do?" she asked. Was she thinking about the same thing? Was she remembering the night they'd stumbled into his apartment?

His eyes drifted down to her lips. *Don't ask me that*, he should say. But when he found her gaze again, hot and daring, it was all too much and they both closed the distance desperately. Luke wrapped his free arm around her waist, pulling her flush against him, and Lydia fisted her hand in his shirt, her lips searing against his. He savored the sensation, the risk, until his heart felt like it would pound out of his chest. Lydia tilted her head so he could run his lips along her jaw and down her neck. She moaned in a way that had his blood boiling, and it was suddenly too hot to do anything but chase relief from the heat. He leaned against her, pressing his leg between hers, and she moved against his thigh.

Lydia made a desperate noise, the sound rubbing against him like a caress, and suddenly Luke was bumping up against the wall, his hands scrambling to find purchase at her waist as their lips connected again and again. It felt like something inside him had been set free, and he was terrified that it would be locked away again.

Lydia let her hands roam up and down his chest. The sensation of her fingers dipping over his muscles drove him wild. So much so that he knew he was in danger of getting lost in this. Of making excuses like he had the night after the pub. How easy would it be to say just once more? Lydia was a tidal wave that had crashed into his self-control and despite their having agreed to boundaries, he was barely treading water around her. *What does this mean?* he wanted to ask. How had they ended up in this position again?

Something rattled in the warehouse, the sound echoing over the beat of his heart, and they both jumped. Luke forced his eyes open, forced himself to look at her. Lydia was already staring at him, the sound having startled them both back to reality.

"Pigeons," he said breathlessly.

"What?"

"They get in…" He gestured upward. "Through the skylight sometimes. There's a shattered pane of glass or something."

They both looked up for a beat, and when they looked back down, their eyes connecting again, Lydia jumped back as if his touch scalded her. He immediately missed the weight of her in his arms.

"Shit," she said, touching her fingers to her lips. She lifted her other hand and pointed at him. "Sorry. We can take it back. Five-second rule. It doesn't count."

"That's about dropping food on the floor." He wisely chose not to mention that their kiss had dragged on for a lot longer than five seconds.

"We're not doing anything," she said. "Stop looking at me like that."

He couldn't help the laugh that bubbled free. "Like what?"

"Like you've watched me undress in your apartment."

"I have," he pointed out.

"No!" She whirled around and marched toward the door. "It doesn't count!" she yelled over her shoulder. "It was just a slip. A mistake! I'm taking it back."

"Okay," he agreed, waiting for his heart to stop racing.

"Good. Wipe it from your memory. I'll see you on Monday!" She shoved her way out the warehouse door and was gone.

"See you Monday," Luke muttered, dropping his head back against the wall. *What the hell just happened?*

Eleven

Lydia

Lydia stood barefoot in front of the dramatic wall of windows in her ridiculously tiny top-floor apartment. The historic 1900s town house came with sixteen-foot ceilings, a beautiful skylight and direct views of Gramercy Park, which totally made up for the lack of square footage.

There was nothing she loved more than moments like this, standing in front of these windows, a cup of coffee in her hand, with the silk of her pajamas whispering over her skin as the August sunrise crept over Manhattan. It was almost six thirty, and though she had training this morning, she'd been drawn to her laptop like a moth to a flame to put more finishing touches on her youth center proposal before she met up with Luke.

Lydia had been playing around with her final draft for a week now, making small changes, and she'd reached the point where she was genuinely worried she was just ruining it. But every time she thought she was satisfied with the project and tried to hand it in, she panicked that something might be wrong—a typo or a crooked angle—and she would start reviewing it all over again. At this rate, she wasn't sure it was ever going to get submitted.

She sipped from her mug of overly sugary coffee. Luke would have rolled his eyes at the amount of flavored creamer she'd dumped into her cup, but she didn't care. She needed it today. And the thought of his perturbed face all wrinkled up made her chuckle, which was a nice reprieve from remembering the look of stunned disbelief on his face after she'd kissed him the other week. Lydia knew it hadn't been her finest moment. She'd just gotten caught up, again, in Luke's warmth, his passion, his excitement and let herself get carried away.

Lydia massaged the bridge of her nose. In her defense, Luke had just finished telling her to listen to her body, to figure out what it needed. Sure, he'd been talking about running at the time, but clearly there'd been a momentary lapse between her mind and body, and the next thing she knew she was kissing him like a fool. Not that Luke had helped the matter. From what she remembered, he'd responded rather enthusiastically as he deepened the kiss…

Thankfully, Luke had chosen not to mention the kiss since, and Lydia saw no reason to bring it up. But even though she wanted to lock the kiss away in a box and drop the key into the Hudson, it was almost harder to bury the moment than it had been to get over their one night together. A kiss was a prelude. It spoke of things to come, unfinished business. *But there's nothing happening between us*, she kept reminding herself. Nothing but today's short run.

If there was any plus side to the kiss, it was that Lydia and

Luke had both hyperfocused on getting her miles down to avoid making things awkward, so at least the slip hadn't derailed her training. In fact, she was feeling solid about her progress. They were building up to run twelve miles this weekend. If someone had told Lydia she'd be running anywhere but to the coffee shop down the street months ago, she would have laughed in their face. Now, it didn't sound so impossible. Now she knew it was something her body was capable of. Of course, she had more endurance and more stamina, but mentally the challenge of that many miles didn't terrify her anymore. Ask her about twenty-six miles and an uneasy feeling still ricocheted through her gut, but twelve? She was almost excited by the challenge, especially because she still wanted to make up the shortened ten-mile run.

Lydia finished her coffee, put her mug in the sink, and popped into her room to change for the gym. She stripped and walked past the full-length mirror that leaned against the wall next to the closet, doing a twirl. Lately, she'd started to notice little changes. She'd slimmed down in areas and was more toned in others. The biggest change was the definition in her legs, and feeling extra confident this morning, she chose a pair of running shorts instead of her usual leggings.

When she got to the gym, Luke was waiting for her by the front desk, like he so often was when they ran these short, early-morning runs. She stowed her things in her locker, then joined him.

"Ready?" he asked.

She nodded and followed him out the door. They stretched and set off at a steady pace. For a while there was nothing but easy breathing and the sound of footsteps between them.

Lydia looked ahead, setting her gaze on the end of the street, watching cars and cyclists flash by them.

"You look stressed," Luke said, cutting through the silence about halfway through their run.

"What do you mean?" She mentally ran through her running form, dropping her shoulders and relaxing her hands the way he had taught her.

"You have a line between your brows. It's been there since you walked in the door this morning."

Lydia laughed. "Telling a woman she has wrinkles is not a wise thing to do before she's properly caffeinated. I need at least two cups, and I've only had one."

"You're deflecting."

Lydia pursed her lips, trying to put her thoughts in order. Trying to settle on the real reason she'd been up with the sun this morning. "I'm not deflecting. I'm just worried about my youth center proposal."

"I thought you said you were almost done."

"I am. It is," she said. "At least, I think so."

"What does that mean?"

She sighed, though she felt impressed at her ability to carry on this conversation while running. Weeks ago she would have been gasping, trying to get the words out. "I just feel like I'm at the point where I keep adding to it because I'm worried it's not…the best it can be."

"And is adding to it making it better?"

"I don't know," she admitted as they turned back toward the gym. "I think I just put so much pressure on myself with this project that I'm afraid of the judgment from the leadership team and from Marco. What if they don't think it's good enough?" She knew it was a possibility, of course. She just wanted to be sure that she submitted her best work. That she was satisfied with the quality, even if it wasn't the project chosen to represent Poletti's in the end. "But now I'm also worried I'm just making it worse at this point with all these little tweaks and changes I'm doing."

"Sounds to me like you have to just let it go."

"Gee, thanks. Are you gonna charge me for that bit of wisdom?"

Luke laughed. "Sometimes you just have to jump the hurdle."

"A running metaphor. Should have seen that coming," Lydia muttered.

"Hey, I've got a running metaphor for every occasion. But seriously, when you're training hurdles, you do it over and over again until it becomes muscle memory. Until you think it's perfect, that you'll clear the hurdle every time. But the truth is, you don't know if you're gonna make it until you're in the air. Until you jump."

"So you're saying I have to jump some hurdles."

He laughed as the gym came into view. They slowed, lingering outside the door. "What I'm saying is that no amount of tweaking is going to change the brilliant design that's already there, so if you think you've thrown everything you have at the project, then you have to trust your training and your prep work, and jump, hoping everything pays off."

Lydia hummed in the back of her throat. She wasn't sure she liked the idea of just handing over her design and hoping for the best. She wanted a more concrete sign that it was ready. That it was good enough. That she was going to clear the hurdle or whatever. But maybe Luke was right, maybe there would be no concrete sign. She just had to go for it.

"Look," Luke said, placing his hand on her shoulder. "If your design is half as good as everything you've been telling me, I don't think you have anything to worry about."

Lydia nodded, a lump caught in her throat as emotion bubbled in her chest. Sometimes Luke said exactly the right thing, even if it was coated in running metaphors. Why was she so afraid? She'd done her research. She'd talked to the kids. She couldn't possibly have prepared herself any better than that. "Thanks, Luke."

He grinned. "The running metaphor strikes again."

"All right, I'll give you that one," she said, humoring him as she slipped into the building to shower and change for work.

A flutter of excitement washed through her as she got closer to Poletti's. With Luke's support, she'd come to the conclusion before she left the gym that she was going to do it—she was going to hand in her proposal. It was ready. *She* was ready. So when Lydia reached her office, the first thing she did was send the entire document to the printer.

Kirsten barged into her office a moment later, closing the door behind her. "In case anyone is wondering, you saw me going downstairs to get supplies and you have no idea when I'll return."

Lydia smirked. "Are you hiding?"

"The Marshalls just walked in."

"Ah," Lydia said. Mr. Marshall owned a string of high-end residential buildings in Midtown. He'd been working with Poletti's since before Lydia had even been employed, and was both one of their biggest and wealthiest contracts. He never stopped talking, and he also flirted openly with Kirsten despite her lack of interest and his wife's constant presence on his arm.

"Jack took them off my hands," Kirsten said.

"Jack's great like that." Lydia scanned her emails quickly. "Did you see this email from the outreach team?"

"The lovely office jog to get our blood pumping?" Kirsten asked, grimacing.

"It's marathon prep," Lydia said.

"I'm not running the marathon! I don't know why I have to get sweaty in the middle of the workday."

"Because you love me."

"I will fundraise your money, but I draw the line at needing to shower after lunch."

"Maybe we'll get a short day out of it." Lydia left Kirsten and headed down to the copy room. She found her document sitting in the paper tray and flipped through it to make sure everything had printed properly—the last thing she wanted was weird ink smudges cluttering up her design. Pride swelled in her chest like a balloon as she got to the end of the document. Dare she say that she was hopeful about her chances of being selected to represent Poletti's in the competition? Maybe Luke and his weird metaphors were paying off.

"That's the smile of someone who just figured out that the printer will also staple your pages together if you push the right buttons."

Lydia chuckled as Jack darted into the room. "Is that what *you* discovered this week?" Jack held his finger to his lips, and Lydia tried not to let herself study those lips. The fullness. The way they curved when he was teasing. How smooth they looked.

"Shh," he whispered. "Don't let Marco hear you say that. I've just convinced this place that I know what I'm doing."

He winked at her, and Lydia's fingertips suddenly felt numb where they clutched her proposal. A couple months ago, she wasn't even sure he knew who she was. Joining the marathon team had changed everything. It had made them… *Friends* might be too strong a word, but *acquaintances* wasn't right either. She didn't know the word for someone who teased her one moment and bought her gifts the next—even if it was just a training water bottle. Someone who understood how hard she had to work for this career that was both creative and specialized, that would demand her time and her passion as she competed to reach a place that satisfied her professionally. Part of her felt like she'd never have to explain that feeling to Jack, and for that reason alone, he felt familiar.

"It'll be our little secret," she said, drawing an X over her heart. "I thought you were supposed to be dealing with the Marshalls?"

Jack's nose wrinkled. "I might have given them the slip at Erik's office."

Lydia huffed. "That means Erik's going to dump them on me next."

"Not if you don't go back to your office."

Lydia raised a pointed brow at him.

"Hey, I rescued Kirsten. I think I deserve some credit."

"So, we're just playing client hot potato now?"

"Pretty much."

Lydia went to stick her head out the door to see if the hallway was clear, but Jack grabbed her at the last second, hauling her back into the room. He closed the door quickly. "What are we doing?" Lydia whispered, her pulse fluttering at the base of her throat. Jack left his arms around her and she flushed from head to toe.

Jack inclined his head, and Lydia studied the strength of his jaw until she heard the voices. One was Erik. The other had to be Mr. Marshall. "We'll just take a look and see if Marco's in yet."

"He's going to dump him on the boss. This is why Erik's smarter than all of us," Jack said, releasing her to peek out the door. Lydia didn't know if she was chilled or flushed or about to collapse. "I think we're in the clear." Jack left the door open. "If they weren't such big clients, I'm pretty sure Marco would have let Kirsten tell Mr. Marshall exactly where to shove it by now."

"She might still do that if he's not careful."

"So, what do you have there anyway?" Jack asked, nodding to the stack of papers in her hand.

Lydia remembered why she was in this room in the first place. "My proposal for the youth center. Just looking for leadership's stamp of approval and then hopefully off to Marco."

"Oh, excellent." He held his hand out for the papers. "I can pass it off to the rest of the leadership team if you want."

Lydia handed it over. He glanced through the first couple of pages, and Lydia suddenly felt like her guts had turned inside out.

"I'm really excited to get into the details," Jack said. "I'm glad you stuck with your original design."

That bead of pride bloomed in her chest once more, making her feel giddy.

"I'll talk to you later," he said, tucking her proposal under his arm.

She didn't realize she was staring until Erik appeared at her shoulder. "We love to watch them walk away, don't we?"

"Don't be ridiculous," Lydia almost snapped.

"Please, I've been at this game a lot longer than you. I can practically feel the tension."

Lydia buzzed her lips together. "You're the worst supervisor."

"I'm your favorite and you know it. That's why you agreed to come host the booth at the Future Architects of New York mixer next month."

"When did I agree to that?"

"Right now?"

Lydia threw her head back, staring at the ceiling. "Ugh, fine."

"It's okay," Erik said, flashing her a wicked grin. "I know you're only doing it to buy my silence."

"Kind of frosty in here…" Lydia said lightly, arranging cheese and crackers on a plate at Ashley's kitchen counter. When she'd arrived twenty minutes earlier, Kurt had said hello and promptly walked off to his office, claiming he had work to do. It was probably true—human rights lawyers always have work to do—but Lydia could also tell she'd arrived in the middle of a fight.

"Hmm?" Ashley said. "I can turn the AC down."

"You know I'm not talking about the AC."

"Tell me about the love triangle you're in."

"What a lawyerly deflection," Lydia replied, rolling her eyes. "I'm not in a love triangle. Luke is my trainer slash friend whom I accidentally slept with once. And Jack is my crush whom I'm definitely not sleeping with. Simple as that. Now, back to you and your drama. Why didn't you text me not to come if you guys were in the middle of something?"

"Because I hardly get to see you anymore since you started all this training. And we're not in the middle of anything," Ashley said, popping the wine cork with way more force than necessary.

Lydia scoffed. "Yeah, right. This sort of feels like the kind of thing that doesn't need an audience."

Ashley put the wine bottle down, staring at the empty glasses in front of her. She sighed. "It's just wedding stuff."

"I thought you were making progress. You know, autumn. Maybe nail down an actual date, book a venue."

"That's what I thought too, but then Kurt's parents decided they didn't like autumn, so Kurt's second-guessing. Then I called Mom to complain and she actually agreed with them."

Lydia grumbled. She was going to have to text their mother and tell her to stop interfering. "So when do *they* want to have your wedding?"

"Mom wants summer, and Kurt's parents want spring. When it's rainy and chilly and gross. And no, I don't care that rain is good luck. I just… I don't know what to do anymore or how to make everyone happy, and what little free time we have turns into arguments about it." Ashley's voice grew thick. "We've waited so long, you know. Did everything right to set ourselves up for success. And now it feels like one stupid obstacle after another. Like maybe this isn't supposed to happen for us. I feel like we're stuck, trying to make this real. And I know you don't have to be married to be a family. I *know* that. I just... I want this so much."

"Hey," Lydia said gently as Ashley wiped tears from her cheeks. She reached for her shoulder and squeezed. "Everything's gonna work out."

When Lydia looked up, Kurt was standing in the hall, his face crumpled in concern. Lydia cocked her head, putting her maid of honor skills to good use. Kurt immediately crossed the living room, pulling Ashley into his arms. "I'm sorry."

"I'm just frustrated," Ashley muttered against his chest.

Lydia stuffed cheese into her mouth. "Good. Keep it coming."

"I know we're trying to keep the families happy," Ashley said, stepping back to lean against the other counter. "I just don't know where that leaves us in the middle of everything."

"I'm sorry, babe." Kurt sighed. "I think waiting this long worked against us. My mom has all sorts of expectations that I'm trying to live up to now and your mom's basically egging her on."

"You do know that *you're* the ones making this life together?" Lydia cut in. "They might be disappointed with your decisions, but everyone will learn to live with them or they won't. I mean, in the grand scheme of things, it's one day. This feels like a lot of upset feelings between the two people who are supposed to be vowing all this lovey-dovey crap."

Kurt snorted. "'Lovey-dovey crap?'"

"You know what I mean," Lydia said, catching the cracker that flew out of her mouth.

Ashley started laughing, and once she did, she couldn't stop. Kurt did too. Lydia poured them each a glass of wine. "Leave it to the chronically single sister to sort out everyone's love life."

"You're single by choice," Ashley said. "You just like to string along your options."

"Oh, I've heard about this triangle," Kurt said, grinning.

"It's *not* a triangle," Lydia insisted. She'd know if she were in the middle of a love triangle.

Twelve

Luke

"We're done already?" Lydia asked, wiping the sweat from her brow as they circled the end of the block, the gym coming into view. "There's no way that was twelve miles. I mean, I was feeling pretty good about the run, but I also kind of thought I'd be gassed by the end. If you told me I still had another mile to go, I would have just kept running."

"See how easy it's starting to feel? How much more confidence you have in your endurance?" Luke said, grinning. "And that translates into every aspect of your life. We do the hard things here, in training, so you can be prepared to do the hard things elsewhere."

"God, please don't start with another running metaphor," Lydia said as they stopped outside Fitness Forum. "Just say good job and give me a high five."

Luke feigned disappointment. "Too bad. I had a really good one saved up. But I guess you'll have to wait until next time to enjoy it because I've gotta run—literally. I have that bank appointment."

"Oh, that's right!" Lydia said. "Go, go! You should have just canceled this morning so you could prepare!"

Luke shrugged. They'd already had to move her long run from Saturday to Thursday this week, so he wasn't about to cancel. Instead, they'd squeezed in the run before she had to go to work, in preparation for the gym being shut down all weekend so the staff could update their workplace safety certifications. "I think I'm as prepared as I can be. But some luck couldn't hurt."

To his surprise, Lydia hugged him. It was short and sweet, and a little sweaty, but it didn't fail to stir up all sorts of thoughts of steamy kisses outside pubs and in warehouses. Kisses that weren't supposed to mean anything. Kisses that he'd banished from his mind. *Poof*, gone.

If only it were that easy. Luke had been pondering that warehouse kiss every night for the last two weeks. You didn't just kiss someone for no reason after agreeing not to. So what was the reason? They'd both agreed to wipe the slate clean after the night they slept together, but the warehouse had felt different than that night. There was no pub, no alcohol, no flirty atmosphere to blame their actions on, and still they'd been drawn together. So, what did that mean? He sometimes wanted to ask her. But hell if he was going to be the one to ruin this partnership. She'd taken it back anyway—the kiss—almost immediately. That probably meant something too.

"You don't need luck," she said with a certainty he wanted to bottle for emergencies. "You've got this."

"I've got this," he repeated, flinging the door to the gym

open. He shivered as the cool AC hit him. "Do you have your workout plan for tomorrow?"

Lydia waved him off. "I have it memorized by now. Hurry up. Before you're late."

Luke rushed down the hall to his office, grabbed his change of clothes, and took the quickest shower of his life. His slacks clung to his legs as he emerged from the locker room and grabbed the thick file folder from his desk. He'd already emailed Mrs. Amisfield all the documents, he just figured bringing hard copies was a good idea. Luke touched his pockets. Phone. Wallet. Business plan. He hurried back down the hall, and was surprised to find Lydia still chatting with Jules at the desk.

"You're going to be late," Jules chided.

"I'm going!"

"You'll do great!" Lydia shouted after him.

He checked his watch. Maybe Lydia was right and he should have canceled the run. But he'd figured spending the morning with her was a good way to take his mind off the appointment and his nerves.

By the time he got off the subway, he had no choice but to run. He skipped up the station stairs two at a time, until his thighs were burning, and rushed down the street to the bank. Damn this August humidity. He wafted the file with his business plan across his face, trying to cool down. He'd needed some extra time for market research, but today, if everything looked good, Mrs. Amisfield would officially be submitting his application for a business loan. The fact that he was about to be that much closer to his goal of opening his own business felt a little surreal, and he took a second to let the thrill of anticipation settle over him.

Then he dabbed at his forehead with the back of his hand, checking his reflection against the glass door, and strode into the bank, summoning everything calm, cool, and collected in his arsenal. He crossed the lobby to check in with the front desk.

"Luke Townsend," he said. "I have an appointment with Mrs. Amisfield."

"Wait here," the clerk instructed before wandering off to inform Mrs. Amisfield of his arrival.

Luke shifted from foot to foot, a familiar bout of nerves rattling around his gut. He probably should have eaten something after the run. What if his stomach growled obnoxiously in the middle of their meeting?

"Luke?"

He turned at the sound of his name.

Mrs. Amisfield stood outside her office door. She waved him over, and Luke hurried across the bank.

"Sorry I'm late," he said, slipping into the office and sitting down. "I got caught up at work and there were a million people on the platform—"

She sat across from him and held her hand up. "Not to worry. We've all been bested by the traffic on the subway."

Luke relaxed a little. She didn't seem put off by his disheveled appearance, but when she looked up at him, he recognized something in her eyes. It was that *you-were-close* face. He'd been given that look by coaches over the years. Heck, he'd given it to his own clients time and time again when they got within reach of their goals, when the finish line just slipped through their fingers. He saw it in the pinch of her thin lips, in the tilt of her head, in that way her brows sank. This was the consolation face. He'd tried and failed.

He knew it before she even opened her mouth.

"You know, for your first crack at a business plan, this was well put together."

But? He wanted to shout the word. Or was it *however*? Maybe even a little *in spite of*. How was she planning on breaking the news to him? He felt like a fool for running all the way down here. "It didn't make the cut," he said, trying not to sound as disappointed as he felt.

He must have failed at hiding the disappointment because Mrs. Amisfield sighed. "I've been looking at the numbers and based on what you have here, I can tell you that you're not going to get approved for your funding."

Luke winced at hearing the words even though he already knew it was coming. What did she mean he wasn't going to get the funding? How could she already tell? He had the building space all worked out. He'd *just* shown it to Lydia. She'd loved it. He'd already envisioned how he would set things up. This didn't make any sense. "I just... Sorry, what?"

"I know that's not what you wanted to hear from me today," Mrs. Amisfield began, "but I believe it's better to get right to the point. I could have submitted your plan and let the rejection come back, and we could have this conversation then, but I don't like wasting my clients' time."

"I appreciate that," Luke said because he wasn't sure what else to say. Did he thank her for all her wasted time spent answering his questions? Did he walk away with his head in his hands like he wanted?

"You have the beginnings of a strong application here, but there is some concern about your revenue stream. You say here that you want to provide youth classes and programs free of charge?"

Luke met her eyes. Was that what all this was about?

"It's admirable, of course," Mrs. Amisfield said. "But for a brand-new business, just getting off the ground, without a substantial track record, saying the words *free of charge* makes banks hesitate."

"Right," he said, deflating inside. "I was planning on finding donors to support the youth programming. I think I put that in there."

"And again, a great idea in theory, but if the donors don't pull through and you're running around providing all these free youth classes, who's paying your staff? Who's paying for equipment repairs or rentals? Who's keeping the lights on?"

The more questions she asked, the more Luke started to feel like an absolute idiot. He'd basically arrived at this appointment with a lot of great ideas and not a great plan to execute those ideas.

"The concern is that by focusing on the youth, you won't have enough regular clientele to be making the money we need you to make in order to give you this loan."

Luke nodded as she closed the file on her computer screen. He picked up his folder from the desk, tucking it under his arm.

"I'm not going to submit this right now because I've been doing this job long enough to know what the answer will be," Mrs. Amisfield said. "The risk is just too great. But if you come up with a better business model and find a way to minimize that risk, I'll be happy to take another look."

"Thank you," Luke said, struggling to get the words out when all he really wanted to do was toss his business plan into the Hudson. "I really appreciate your time." He stood, shook her hand, and walked out of the bank without feeling anything. The defeat was too great to even wrap his head around it.

Nothing really sank in until he walked back into Fitness Forum, finding Dara and Jules standing at the front desk. Then the reality of the situation landed in his gut like a load of bricks.

"How'd it go?" Jules asked quietly as he approached.

He mustered something that might have looked like a smile and shrugged off her question. "I'll get it next time."

"Your girlfriend was in your office," Dara said as he shuffled past them and down the hall.

Though he knew Dara was joking, his thoughts immediately went to Lydia. When he opened his office door, on his desk was a piece of paper folded into a card with a four-leaf clover sketched on the front. He opened it and read the note inside.

I know you crushed your meeting. But here's some luck for you to keep in the bank for next time you need it. P.S. Your office is a disaster.

Lydia had signed her name with a tiny heart. Luke looked around at his office. He still hadn't bothered to hang his certificates back on the wall or organize his things after the renovations a few months ago. He'd been too busy with his clients and preparing his business plan—preparing to leave Fitness Forum altogether. He supposed he would have nothing but time now.

Luke balled up Lydia's homemade card and tossed it across the room, the force of his failure burning like acid in his chest.

Thirteen

Lydia

There were a few things Lydia was willing to be late for, and a toasted lox and cream cheese bagel was one of them. It was a farther walk than her usual lunch spot, so she hurried back into the elevator, waiting impatiently for it to spit her out in front of Poletti's. She wanted to sit for ten minutes and enjoy every last caper before she had to get ready for the firm's marathon training session. Since she'd completed her long run yesterday with Luke, and was technically doing another run today with the office, on what was usually her rest day, she'd decided to give herself the weekend off.

As she popped out of the elevator, she texted Luke to let him know her plan. I just don't want to overuse all these excellent muscles I'm building. Also, how did your appointment with the bank go?

That's probably a good idea if you're running back-to-back, Luke replied almost instantly. Maybe just do some light cross-training Monday so it's not three full rest days between now and our next short run. He said nothing about his business plan, so either he was really busy with all his recertification training, or maybe he hadn't heard anything yet. People always said no news was good news, but how long would the bank take to make a decision about his loan?

Lydia carried on to her office, staggering to a stop when she reached the doorway.

There, on her desk, sat her proposal for the Manhattan Youth Center with a bright red pen mark scratched through the front page. She dropped her tinfoil-wrapped bagel on the desk and flipped the first page of her proposal open just to be sure she wasn't seeing things. *No*, this was definitely the proposal she'd handed Jack last week.

It had taken her weeks—no, *months*—to complete. How could it possibly have passed through every member of the leadership team already?

Lydia skimmed through the pages looking for comments... for notes. Even a little frowny face would have made her feel like someone had actually taken the time to read it. There was nothing but the red pen on the front: a single, straight line, left there like the words and diagrams beneath it meant nothing. She was so shocked, all she could do was stand beside her desk, hugging her arms to her chest like that might contain the all-consuming disappointment that threatened to spill out of her. She hadn't even noticed that Jack had stopped outside her office door until he spoke.

"Hey, running buddy! You brought your running shoes, right? I know most of the office isn't looking forward to our little training session, but I'm hoping we can stir up a little excitement. Maybe I'll try bribing them with doughnuts. You know, dangle them on a little string like in those old cartoons."

His smile, which would usually be infectious, only made Lydia frown more.

"You okay?" Jack asked. "Sorta looks like someone stole your favorite drawing pencils."

Lydia pushed the proposal toward him.

He walked across the room and reached for it, his brows drawing together.

"I didn't expect to get it back so soon," she said, surprised she could force the words out at all.

"I only passed it off to the rest of the team a few days ago," Jack admitted.

"Did *you* even read it?" She hoped she didn't sound as hurt as she felt.

"Of course I did," he assured her. "I thought what you did was really inventive. Great use of the space. It really felt like you were catering to the kids' needs while also being conscious of the environment and the community."

Any other day his words would have made her beam. Now she was just confused. How could the rest of the team think so little of her design? "Did the leadership team have any notes? Maybe I can scrap a few ideas and get it to where they want or—"

"I'm really sorry, Lydia. They didn't say anything to me. I could ask for you, but it looks like the rest of the team just didn't think it was a good fit for what Marco wants to put forward from Poletti's." He laid the proposal down on the desk and reached for her, his fingers curling over her shoulder.

Despite his warmth, all Lydia wanted to do was shiver.

Maybe it was because of the soft smile he gave her—the consolation smile.

"I'd chalk this one up to a learning opportunity and move on to the next project."

"Right," Lydia said, feeling unsure of herself, of her talents, of her ideas. Of the evening spent with Luke, exploring the center, picking his brain. Everything felt like a waste. Logically, she knew that only one project was going to be selected to represent Poletti's in the competition. Even if only a third of Poletti's decided to submit something, she'd still be competing against nine or ten other proposals. She wasn't foolish or naive enough to assume her work was better than everyone else's, but Jack himself said he'd only given it to the rest of the leadership team a few days ago. Maybe they hadn't bothered to read her work before rejecting it.

That thought infuriated her, but what Lydia hated more was that she'd kind of expected Jack to go to bat for her. Had he just scribbled his thoughts on some Post-it note and tossed it onto the next person's desk? She shook her head, trying to displace some of her disappointment. If the rest of the team didn't think she'd made the cut, then why did Jack's actions matter?

"I'll see you at training," Jack said, letting his hand slide down the length of her arm to her hand. He smiled and squeezed, and Lydia felt her heart lob against her ribs. She'd always wanted Jack to smile at her like that, to look at her like that, she just sort of wished she didn't feel so wretched when it finally happened.

"See you out there," she said, trying to salvage the moment. "I'll be the one in the sneakers."

"Ah, no. That's what I was going to wear."

Lydia watched him disappear from her office, knowing that in the end, he was only one voice on the leadership team. If she was ever going to prove herself in this office, she needed more support than just Erik's and Jack's. That thought didn't make her feel any better, and by the time she'd changed into her activewear and met the rest of the office nearby at Chelsea Park, the bagel she'd scarfed down sat in her gut like a waterlogged brick.

"Running makes me want to puke," Kirsten complained as they made a slow lap of the park together. They'd quickly broken off into groups, some running, some walking and some cheering the team on from shady benches. "Maybe I should start taking private lessons from your sexy trainer."

"They do help," Lydia said, knowing her old self would have already pitched over into a bush. "At least Jack didn't make us do a long warm-up. Luke makes me do burpees."

"Ew. And you're paying him for that?"

"Yeah. I'm actually funding my own torture."

Kirsten hummed. "Well, it's working, because you're all fit and glowy lately. That's part of the reason I'm out here sweating with you instead of opting for *team bench*. I want to be fit and glowy, too."

Lydia didn't feel particularly glowy right now.

Kirsten took a gasping breath. "I figure it's either the exercise or the hot sex with your trainer."

Lydia rolled her eyes. "I'm not sleeping with Luke...anymore."

"Boo! I like it better when you're both being unprofessional," Kirsten said.

"Well too bad," Lydia said. "Though I *am* sort of in the

mood to make bad decisions with someone right now." She could use a good distraction.

"Oh? Why?"

"I got my proposal for the youth center back today—nothing but red pen."

Kirsten snorted.

"It's not funny," Lydia complained. "I'm kind of devastated here."

"Sorry, I wasn't laughing at you. I'm just not surprised to hear that. Actually, I'm a little confused as to why you are."

"What do you mean?"

Kirsten's perfectly manicured brow arched to a point. "Most of the leadership team is gunning for partner at the firm. It makes sense that they'd want *their* designs front and center for Marco to choose from."

Lydia stopped abruptly, feeling like she'd been jostled from a dream. "What?"

"Didn't you know?" Kirsten slowed, clutching her sides.

"I had no idea."

"They're probably hoping one of them gets selected and Marco will take note of it when he makes his decision. It would give them a leg up as far as the partner race goes."

"God, you really do hear everything at the front desk, don't you?"

"Kind of my job," Kirsten said. "Marco's been hinting at bringing someone on as partner for a while. Honestly, Lyds, no matter how good your proposal was, it might not have made the cut for that reason alone."

Dammit, Lydia thought. Was this why she was always struggling to have her work move up the ladder? Because the leadership team was there squashing anything that didn't directly make themselves look good? How long had this jockeying game for partner been going on? Weeks? Months? "Is Jack going out for partner too?"

"He's on the leadership team. It would be weird if he wasn't."

Lydia didn't know what to say. If Jack had known all along that she had no chance, why didn't he say something? *Maybe he doesn't realize*, she thought. He wouldn't have deliberately let her make a fool of herself, right? It wasn't like he'd sabotaged her. He'd been just as surprised when she showed him her rejected proposal. He'd even had good things to say about it.

"Are you okay?" Kirsten asked.

Lydia didn't want to be annoyed with Jack, but the fact that he was involved with the rest of the leadership team, who were all vying to impress Marco, made her feel even more defeated. If she'd understood this from the beginning, she never would have bothered entering. In fact, she'd hazard to guess most of her colleagues would have also saved themselves the trouble if they knew this was going to be a popularity contest between the leadership team. "I'm a little pissed off, actually..."

"Maybe I shouldn't have said anything."

"No, I'm glad you did. It helps put everything in perspective." They started jogging again, even slower than before. "I guess I just wish Jack would have given me a heads-up."

"Why would he?"

Lydia shrugged. Because they'd been getting closer lately. Because they had a rapport. Because he called her his *running buddy*.

"Ladies," a familiar voice said, and they both looked up as

Jack ran past them. He wore sleek shades and shook his head, dislodging the hair that stuck to the back of his neck. Every exposed muscle was coated in a thin sheen of sweat. As he coasted by them, Lydia's eyes traced the fine definition of muscle in his calves. Jack was a regular runner. She could tell by his form. Luke would be impressed if she ever managed to stride that gracefully.

"Hot damn. He's like a cover of *Men's Health*," Kirsten said.

"Yeah," Lydia sighed, cocking her head.

Kirsten nudged Lydia and they came to a stop. "What was that?"

"What was what?"

"You. Looking at Jack. All starry-eyed."

"I'm not starry-eyed. You're the one who pointed him out, talking about *Men's Health*."

"But I didn't *sigh* like that." Kirsten's entire face shifted from confusion to glee in an instant. "You have a thing for him!"

"I absolutely do not."

"Is it mutual? Did I miss an office romance developing? Is *this* why you're not getting unprofessional with Luke?"

"You didn't miss anything."

"Are you sure? Should I just go catch up with your *running buddy* and get all the hot gossip? Don't underestimate how fast I'll run for this information."

"Calm down, Sherlock. Okay," Lydia conceded. "I might have had a small office crush on Jack."

"Had? As in past tense? Because that look you gave him had present tense written all over it."

"I don't know. Present Tense Lydia is still kind of pissed about this whole proposal thing."

"Just promise to warn me if you two start banging in your office at lunch. I do not want to walk in on that."

"Oh, please. You'd be standing outside the door the moment it was over for a play-by-play."

Kirsten snorted. "Okay, yeah, true."

"It's bullshit, is what it is," Ashley said as she grabbed plates from the cupboard.

Lydia shrugged, cradling her wineglass. She'd felt like drowning her sorrows after work and had shown up on Ashley's doorstep with dinner and a frown. "I guess I have to accept the possibility that my proposal was actually terrible."

She'd spent enough time in school having her projects critiqued to know there was a possibility she'd completely missed the mark. Only Marco had never given them a brief. He'd basically handed them the task and set them free. That's what had made her so excited initially.

"It wasn't terrible," Ashley said. "You know how I know? Because it's like this everywhere. Women are consistently judged to have less leadership potential so they're less likely to be promoted. And they're held to much higher standards in the workplace. You know, it's these ingrained societal attitudes that make women undersell their work. That make them more tentative when applying for—"

"Okay, *okay*," Lydia said, holding her hand up to interrupt Ashley's rant before she started pulling out old case law to prove her point. "I believe you. And I love you for being so passionate about all this. But can you stop being a lawyer for five minutes and just be sad with me?"

Ashley sucked in a breath and let it out. "Fine."

"Good," Lydia said. "You can fight the injustices of the world later."

Ashley sat down on the couch and needled her side. "Show me the proposal."

"I don't want to look at it anymore."

"C'mon," Ashley said. "I know you worked really hard on it. You deserve to show it to someone who cares."

Lydia smiled a bit. Sometimes she liked being the younger sibling. She put her wineglass down on the coffee table and got up to retrieve her laptop from her workbag. She sat back down, turning it on. "So, how goes the wedding conversation?"

"We're reevaluating our options and finally prioritizing what we want," Ashley said.

"Are the moms going to freak out?"

Ashley grinned. "Oh, definitely."

"Why does it sound like you're keeping a secret?"

"You'll know when you're supposed to know."

"Okay, Yoda, just remember, I'm your maid of honor, so some notice would be nice if I have to have a speech ready." Lydia turned back to the computer screen, opening her proposal.

Ashely took the laptop from her. "What am I looking at?"

Lydia pouted as she pointed to the screen. "Massive double gymnasium. Industrial kitchen. New theater wing. And this was my favorite part. The rooftop garden."

"The kids would have thought that was so cool," Ashley agreed. Sitting like this reminded Lydia of when they used to play together as kids. Lydia would make intricate drawings of castles and villages, and Ashley would make up rules for their kingdom. Their parents should have known they'd have an architect and a lawyer in the family way back then.

"I worked really hard on this." Lydia leaned her head against Ashley's shoulder. "The corporate ladder sucks."

"I know you did, and it does," Ashley said softly, scrolling through Lydia's design. "More wine?"

Lydia got up to get it herself. "We're gonna need the bottle."

Fourteen

Luke

The weight of rejection worsened like a bad breakup. That's what Luke had discovered in the week since he'd failed to provide a business plan good enough to secure the funding for his gym. It hit him hardest in the quiet hours, right before getting out of bed, and all he wanted to do was drag the covers over his head and wallow. The only reason he was even moving right now was because it was time for one of his long weekend runs with Lydia. And if anything was going to get him out of bed, it was her. Not because he particularly felt like running this morning, but because he'd promised to get her across that finish line.

Luke's heart skipped at the thought. *Nope, don't go twisting things. Don't go assigning meaning where there is none.* Lydia had made it clear that reescalating things between them had been a slipup—a mistake, she'd called it. Which it was, because here he was starting to catch actual feelings when clearly Lydia wasn't. *But what if?* his mind kept whispering. Luke rubbed his hand down his face. He didn't have the energy to sort through those complicated thoughts, especially not when he was still so full of wretched disappointment over his business plan. *Keep it professional*, he told himself as he rolled out of bed to brush his teeth and throw on some shorts before heading out the door.

Yesterday, he'd sent Lydia a text telling her to meet him at Central Park. It was only a fifteen-minute walk from his place, so Luke opted not to take the train.

Luke arrived first and found a bench, then reviewed Lydia's training plan on his phone while he waited. Today was a big milestone—thirteen point one miles, to be exact. That was a half-marathon, which meant they'd reached the midpoint of her training. His plan was for them to run along the paved drive that circled the park. At six point one miles it was the longest loop, which meant they only needed to complete a little over two laps. That was going to be his selling point for this morning when Lydia inevitably wrinkled her nose at him. He spotted her strawberry blond ponytail swinging behind her from down the street.

"Morning," he called as she approached. "Happy half-marathon day."

"What?" She met his eye, curiosity flashing across her features.

"After today, you will have officially run a half-marathon."

"Thirteen point one miles?" She smiled but it didn't split her face the way he expected it to when she realized she was halfway to her goal. In fact, she looked sort of defeated. She'd been that way all week.

"You feeling okay?" he asked.

"Never better."

That was clearly a lie. She followed him through a quick warm-up routine, and though she performed the actions, her mind seemed to be elsewhere, her gaze getting lost in the distance. As they started running, Luke could tell she wasn't paying attention to her breathing or her stride, and she quickly fell out of step, with a cramp beneath her ribs.

"You want to tell me what's up?" he asked as she bent over, clutching her knees.

Lydia moved to the edge of the path and flopped down on the grass, her arms thrown over her eyes to shield them from the sun. "I'm too bummed out to run. My head's not in it."

He sat down beside her, nudging her with his elbow. Compared to her usual complaints about the number of burpees in her training plan, this one he could actually sympathize with. "Rough week?"

She snorted, lowering her arms so she could look at him. "I got my proposal for the youth center back."

"I had no idea. You never mentioned it."

She picked at a blade of grass and tore it into tiny pieces. "Because they tossed it on my desk with a red line through it, which means thanks but no thanks." Lydia scattered the tiny, shredded pieces of grass. "There wasn't even one word of feedback. There never is. How am I possibly supposed to get better or know what to change?"

"I'm sorry, Lydia." Luke felt horrible. He'd been the one to encourage her to hand the project in to the team. "I sort of feel like I pushed you to submit it with my stupid running metaphor." Maybe she hadn't been ready. He'd been trying to be supportive, but had he failed at this too? Had he screwed up his business plan *and* her proposal?

She sat up so suddenly that he almost fell over as she turned to him. "No, God. This is not on you. Please don't think that. You were right. I was ready to submit it, I just… I found out that the entire leadership team is gunning for partner at my firm. So the assumption is that they're rejecting everyone else's proposals so that only theirs end up on the boss's desk."

Oh. He studied the pink in her cheeks and the way her nostrils flared. She was filled with frustration, and rightly so. "That's a slap in the face."

"It was," she agreed.

"If it makes you feel any better, my business plan was rejected by the bank. Actually, it didn't even make it to the point of rejection. It was so bad, it never even got submitted. So no gym for me."

Lydia pouted, which drew his attention to her lips, and he realized for the first time how close they were. "Luke," she said sadly, offering condolences on the death of his dream. "Why didn't you say something before today?"

Luke shrugged. "For the same reason you didn't."

"When I texted you and asked how your appointment went, you didn't say anything, so I figured you were still waiting to hear back! If I'd known it went so poorly, I would have said something before now!"

"Hey, I brought this up to make you feel better, not to get your sympathy."

"Why would that make me feel better?"

He shrugged. "It's a my-misfortune-is-worse-than-yours kind of thing."

"I really wanted you to open your gym."

"I wanted your proposal to do well." He sighed heavily as

she plucked another blade of grass and tossed it onto the path. Now they were both sitting here, miserable. That wouldn't do. They were supposed to be training. And training was supposed to be fun and invigorating and inspiring. He climbed to his feet, reaching for her hand. "Come on."

She threw her head back. "I don't want to run."

"We're not running."

"We're not?" she said, immediately sounding suspicious.

"No. I'm gonna make brunch and we're going to eat our feelings." After that they could worry about being inspiring and getting the miles down.

That earned him a genuine smile, and Luke's heart flip-flopped in his chest. Had she felt the sudden heat? The sparks as their hands connected? He was trying to be a good friend, dammit. He didn't need these pesky feelings getting in the way. He would just bury them under eggs and bacon and stacks of pancakes until there was no room left for disappointment or these confusing tugs at his heartstrings.

By the time they got back to his apartment, Lydia was deep into her explanation of the inner workings of Poletti Architectural Studios.

"I never knew architects had this much drama going on."

"That's the problem!" Lydia said as she leaned against the kitchen counter. "Neither did I. And now I sort of feel like an idiot for spending so much time on this project. Plus, you took time out to show me around the youth center and introduce me to the kids!"

"I liked showing you around," he said, taking eggs and bacon out of the fridge. "How do you feel about mushrooms?"

"Mushrooms are good. I just feel like the leadership team should have tempered our expectations. That's all. And Jack..." She trailed off.

Lydia took a deep breath, like she was preparing to unleash fire.

"*Okay*, I get it." Luke recognized that look. "Jack is the villain in this story."

"He's not the villain," Lydia said, though she sounded like she was trying to convince herself of that. "I just don't know how I feel about him right now. I thought we were becoming friends." She scoffed, her cheeks pinking a bit. "I actually thought he liked my work."

Oh. The pieces suddenly fell together for Luke. Jack wasn't the villain. He was her crush. This was the man who had started everything. Who had been the reason Lydia walked into his gym, looking for a trainer. Luke didn't know what to think. He didn't even know what to say to that. A strange coiling tension gripped his heart. Was this jealousy? Was he jealous of this faceless man who'd disappointed Lydia? That was ridiculous.

She waved her hands. "Whatever. We don't have to talk about Jack."

Good, Luke's thoughts roared. "At least you have somewhere to direct your rage. I have no one to blame but my own foolishness."

"Chasing your dream isn't foolish," she said.

"Tell that to my bank." He dug through his frying pans for one that had a lid.

"I'll march down there and demand they give you heaps of money."

"Heaps?" He laughed as he stood up, setting a pan on the counter. "*Heaps* is good. *Heaps* should have been in my business plan from the beginning."

Lydia swatted his arm playfully. "At least you can take another shot at the business plan."

"I don't know if I'm cut out to own a business."

"Don't say that," Lydia said. "You *have* to try again. One of us needs to succeed, and I've lost out on my chance."

Luke snorted. "So all our hopes and dreams rest on me?"

"Exactly. Figure out a better business model and give it another shot. What's that they say? Aim for the moon and land among the stars."

"Maybe," Luke said, wondering if he truly had it in him to try again. How could he not, when she was looking at him like that, her green eyes all wide and sincere? But... "Today I sort of just want to be grumpy."

"That's fine. We can be grumpy and disappointed together."

"That's what we are. A couple of regular old failures having brunch."

Lydia bit her bottom lip to keep from laughing, and he watched the way it slowly slid between her teeth.

Suddenly she was leaning toward him, and Luke froze. "Lydia," he warned. "We shouldn't." Lydia knew it was wrong because he was her trainer, because they'd agreed to these professional boundaries, but for him it was so much worse. The emotional lines were getting blurry. These feelings he was having... They were starting to get dangerously tangled.

"Aren't you sick of being told what you can't have?"

"This isn't why I invited you back." He wanted to make that clear before this went any further. He'd genuinely just intended to feed her and let her vent and then figure out when to reschedule the long run. But the waters were getting muddy. Was he Trainer Luke right now or just regular Luke? And who was she? His mind flashed back to the morning in the warehouse, to her palm drifting down his chest, to the warmth of her... His body responded to the memory.

"But we're so sad," she said, stepping closer. She stretched up on her toes and closed the distance, pressing a soft kiss to the corner of his mouth. "And endorphins are good."

"They *are* good," Luke agreed, standing perfectly still.

"Plus, we should probably do some sort of physical activity today."

"Wouldn't want to ruin your training schedule," Luke said.

She blinked up at him, her dark lashes fluttering over those teasing green eyes. "So what are you waiting for?"

He let himself reach for her. The moment his hands wrapped around her waist, warring thoughts exploded to life in his mind, but the loudest of them called for him to hold her tighter. Pull her closer. So he did. He lowered his head, catching her lips, and something desperate surged through him. A fire that wanted to be stoked. She gasped against his mouth, humming at his eagerness. The kiss broke with a smacking sound.

Lydia's eyes were glassy when she finally opened them, her one hand locked around the edge of the counter, her other hand clinging to him for support. Luke understood what they were doing. This was just some mutual care and comfort between friends—something they both needed after this past week. Right now he didn't care if that's all it was, because she was right. He was sick of being told no, of being rejected. He wanted *someone* to want him. And in this moment, *she* did. She wanted him like he wanted her, so he held her and enjoyed the heat of her body as he pressed her up against the counter.

"You should put the food back in the fridge," she husked, her head thrown back so his lips could explore her jaw and dance across her neck.

"We can eat first if you want." He felt kind of bad now. He *had* promised her food.

Lydia shook her head. "I don't want to do the things we're about to do on a full stomach."

"It might be good to have some energy."

"We'll stop for snacks in between. Moderate in protein. High in complex carbs."

Luke chuckled, tugging the elastic from her hair so he could sink his hand into it. "With talk like that you're just trying to rile me up." He lifted her into his arms.

She yelped, then giggled, her arms tightening around him as he carried her down the hall to the bedroom. She ground her pelvis against him and Luke almost ran them into the door, forcing him to put her down. He hadn't bothered to make his bed before leaving this morning, and he might have been embarrassed now if it weren't for how quickly Lydia was stripping out of her clothes. Any other time he'd want to undress her slowly, to savor the moment, but he didn't have the patience for that now. His cock was straining inside his shorts, and he needed to relieve some of the aching pressure.

He pulled his shirt over his head before eagerly helping Lydia guide her shorts down her legs. He let his hands roam from her calves up to her thighs as he stood back up, enjoying the never-ending expanse of skin. Her hands darted out to his chest, exploring as his muscles flexed beneath her delicate fingers.

"Do you want me to keep going?" she asked before letting her hands drop lower.

"God, *yes*," he hissed as he shoved his shorts down his hips. Lydia's hand wrapped around his exposed cock, and she stroked him slowly from base to tip. He threw his head back and groaned at how good she made him feel.

When he twitched in her hand, he leaned down to kiss her, nudging her gently with his hips until she'd butted up against the edge of the bed. Instead of laying her down, he kissed his way across her jaw and down her neck, tonguing at the hollow that met her sternum. He let his lips ghost between the valley of her breasts and across the softness of her belly as he got on his knees, pressing a kiss to her hip bone. His hands smoothed over her flesh as he guided them up and down her legs, squeezing her thighs gently.

Lydia's hand fell to the top of his head, her fingers weaving into his hair, attempting to guide his lips to where she wanted him most. She squirmed, her legs trembling as he nibbled his way along her inner thigh. Her fingers tightened in his hair, and he smirked against her skin. "Did you want something?"

"Don't make me beg."

"I would never." He squeezed her ass and she jerked against him, desperately looking for friction as his tongue darted out to lap at her folds.

"Oh… Oh, *yes*," she said as he found her clit. She released his hair, both hands falling to the bed as she sank down, looking for support.

Luke wrapped his arms around her waist, pulling her to the very edge of the bed, giving himself room to drive her wild.

Lydia's hips jumped as his lips and tongue danced around her clit, and her moans became a frantic, unending string of profanities as she ground herself against his face. He glanced up as he continued to lap at her, stroking that tiny bud into oblivion. Maybe it was the pressure or the rhythm or the fact that she looked down just in time to catch his eye, but she snapped her head back with a shuddering cry as she trembled through her orgasm.

When it was finished, she fell back against the bed, her breasts rising and falling like twin peaks as she caught her breath. Luke climbed to his feet, retrieving a condom from the drawer next to his bed before joining her. Lydia turned to look at him, her face a mask of contentment and bliss.

"More fun than running thirteen miles?" he asked, enjoying the way the sunlight spilled across her skin.

"Much more enjoyable." She sat up on her elbows, eyeing his erection. "What are you waiting for?"

"Just wanted to give you a second to recover. I know that was probably pretty mind-blowing."

Lydia smirked, rolling their bodies until she was sitting on his hips. "I don't know if you've heard, but I've been working out a lot lately, so I'm a lean, mean endurance machine."

"Oh, really?"

Lydia bent forward, one hand on his chest, the other reaching between their bodies to guide him to her entrance. He groaned when she sank down on his length. "I could probably do this all day."

He chuckled, catching her hips before she could go any further. "Let me just set some reasonable expectations here."

Lydia laughed and that sound surged through him. These feelings he was developing...it couldn't just be him, right? They should have waited until they were no longer working together, but if Luke stripped all that away, the fact was that Lydia was here, with him. She'd chosen to confide in him, and that had to mean *something*.

What about Jack? his thoughts whispered. He reached up, letting his fingers tangle in strands of her hair. Jack was old news. He was the crush who'd disappointed her. But this, what was happening between him and Lydia, felt real.

And if Jack *wasn't* old news? If Lydia didn't feel the way he did? He'd end up getting hurt if they carried on like this. He couldn't let this happen again while they were still working together, he shouldn't, but he also had no clue how to stop.

"Don't worry," Lydia was whispering in his ear. "I'll let you break for snacks and water so you don't embarrass yourself."

He waited for her to lean down and kiss him. "That's all I ask."

Fifteen

Lydia

"I can't believe you forgot you were supposed to be here today," Erik mumbled under his breath as crowds of prospective architects wandered around the Hilton hotel reception room. "I told you, first week of September. Put it on your calendar."

"I didn't forget," Lydia said, adjusting their poster board. "I was late."

"Because you forgot."

"Maybe I got distracted again wallowing about my youth center proposal and it slipped my mind. You can't just expect me to remember to show up to these sorts of things on a random Thursday."

Erik looked at her pointedly. "I sent you an email reminder. And I also told you we could talk about the proposal if you're still upset."

"I'm not upset." Lydia smiled politely at a young woman

who stopped by their table to pick up a pamphlet. "It's been two weeks. Why would I still be upset?"

"Is this what having a daughter is like? Passive-aggressiveness? Glaring at me from across the room?"

"Yes." In truth, the rejected proposal wasn't bothering her as much as the fact that Jack had also turned up to represent Poletti's today. No offense to the Future Architects of New York, but if she'd known he would be here, she probably would have tried to get out of the mixer. She glanced across the room to where Jack was busy mingling and networking, handing out business cards and Poletti's pamphlets.

"You know I was as out of the loop on that decision as you were," Erik said.

"It's not just *this* proposal, Erik." Lydia sighed. "It's every other rejected proposal I've found on my desk lately. Is this why? Nobody gets to climb the ladder or sit center stage until the leadership is done showing off for Marco?"

"I'm gonna talk to Marco about what's been going on."

"No, don't do that," Lydia said. "I don't want to be the girl who whined to the boss because she didn't get picked."

"That's not what's happening here."

"But that's how everyone will see it. All they'll see is me. Stepping on toes." That's the last thing she wanted—to be the office tattletale. "The decision's already been made. I'll just have to do better keeping up with the office politics next time." She looked away from him, no longer capable of enduring that pitying gaze, and organized the pamphlets on their table for the fiftieth time since arriving. Someone, likely Kirsten, had gone out of their way to plaster the poster board and the pamphlets with pictures of Poletti's best contract builds. On one tiny image in the corner of the poster was an eco-friendly residential building design Lydia had helped create a couple years ago.

"Well," Erik said. "If you change your mind about that, I'll be making the rounds."

"Right," Lydia said, eyeballing the handsome architect that had just appeared on the other side of the room. "I know why you're really going over there."

"It's called networking," Erik whispered. "You should try it. Might make you feel better."

"Excuse me for bringing the vibe down." Despite her sullen mood, she conjured a smile, which Erik returned before making his way across the room. He was right. She couldn't stay frustrated and annoyed forever. She'd just have to get over it. And maybe she'd do that. Tomorrow. Today she only had to last one more hour; then she could pack up and flee this reception room. She even had the afternoon off from work as a reward. Her phone buzzed and she dug it out of her pocket. Luke had been texting her on and off all morning, keeping her entertained as she complained, first, about forgetting about the mixer, and then second, about being stuck at the mixer.

She bit her lip, wondering if she was being selfish, smiling down at his texts, indulging their conversations beyond just a trainer and a trainee. But they were friends, weren't they? *Friends don't repeatedly fall into bed together.* That day in Luke's apartment flashed back in bits and pieces. Again, she'd told herself that it hadn't counted as breaking their rule, that it didn't mean anything, because she didn't want to hurt Luke, who'd been nothing but good to her as a trainer, as a friend, and…whatever else they sometimes were.

They'd both just been so disappointed, so sad, that they'd gravitated toward each other that day like magnets. Comfort was all they were after, nothing more. Thankfully, Luke seemed to have understood that. They both knew the marathon was only two months away. They both knew where their focus needed to be, and they hadn't spoken of that day since. So she didn't know why she hadn't been able to shake the memories of what they'd gotten up to.

Training, she thought. Focus on the training. She was gearing up to run fifteen miles this weekend. Each run was getting longer and harder, requiring more of her focus and attention. She felt sort of bad because she'd been spending more time with Luke than anyone else. She wasn't seeing Ashley as much as she used to, and there was probably some maid of honor thing she was failing at, but one thing at a time. Just focus on the next step you have to take, as Luke would say.

When she looked up from her phone, a young man in a slightly oversized suit was hovering by their table. Lydia shot him what she hoped was an inviting smile. "Hey! Are there any questions I can answer about Poletti's?"

Now that she'd opened the lines of communication, the man stepped forward. "I'm actually just looking to get a feel for a few different firms."

"Are you still in school?" Lydia asked, curious.

The man nodded. "My final year. Does Poletti's do a lot with sustainability?"

"Um…" Lydia started answering. "I can't say it's a priority, but we definitely work on the occasional project." She pointed to their poster. "This one was great. We prioritized a cool roof design to deflect sunlight instead of absorbing it.

The building owner was on board with going green, so we focused on renewable energy systems and leaned heavily into solar power."

"Did you take a lot of courses on sustainable building when you were in school?"

Lydia chuckled. "Oh, so many. I remember doing this course where the professor talked about how green buildings have healthier inhabitants and that really stuck with me. I think it's part of what made me want to focus on sustainability."

The man picked up a pamphlet. "I'm glad to see you getting to put all that knowledge into a design."

The corner of Lydia's mouth quirked. If he only knew how much of that knowledge she'd poured into her youth center proposal. "Here," she said, passing him a business card. "If you have any more questions you can reach out to our admin assistant, Kirsten. She'll put you in touch with someone that can answer them."

"Awesome, thank you."

As the man wandered to the next booth, an older woman with curls upon curls of dark hair and green cat-eye glasses approached. In an odd turn of events, she held a business card out to Lydia. "I couldn't help overhearing," she said. "You sound like you know what you're talking about on the sustainability front."

"It's definitely one of my passions when it comes to new builds." Lydia glanced down at the business card. Angela Reeves. Coleman and Associates.

"Do you have a card?" Angela asked.

Lydia touched her pocket out of habit, but realizing that all she had were the generic cards for Poletti's, she picked one up and scribbled her name on the back.

"Thanks," Angela said as Lydia handed it over. "We do a lot of work in that area, and if you're ever interested, I'd be happy to sit down with you and talk about what Coleman and Associates has to offer."

Lydia opened her mouth, staring down at Angela's card again, her brows furrowed. "Oh, gosh," she said. "Thanks, but I'm not currently looking." Had she been mistaken for a new grad? "I'm actually really happy where I am."

"Offer doesn't expire," Angela said. "Just putting it out there."

Well, Erik *had* told her to network—though she didn't think this was exactly the networking he had in mind. "Thanks, Angela. It was good to meet you."

"Good to meet you too, Lydia," she said before melting back into the crowd.

Lydia stared at the card long after Angela was gone, and she didn't know why. She wasn't looking for another job. She was happy at Poletti's. Most of the time. The past few weeks had been an anomaly. Things would blow over between her and Jack and the leadership team. Still, her curiosity got the better of her. It couldn't hurt to take a peek at what the competition was doing.

She googled *Coleman & Associates* on her phone, scrolling through some of the projects listed on their website. It took all of thirty seconds for her to become completely engrossed. She'd seen some of these building designs around the city, marveled at them even. And Angela was right, this company put a big emphasis on sustainability. Lydia was drawn to their

About page, and was reading the team bios when a shadow fell across her screen.

"You look like you could use a coffee."

"Luke?" she said, surprised to find him standing there, holding out a warm paper cup. "What are you doing here?"

"I was volunteering at the youth center. You're basically down the street. I figured I'd just meet you here and we could head over to the gym together when you're finished. What time does this wrap up?"

"Supposedly after lunch," she said. "So hopefully anytime." She smiled her first real smile of the entire day. "How'd you get in without a pass?"

He lowered his voice, whispering like it was a secret. "You can get in anywhere either wearing a construction vest or carrying multiple coffees. It makes it look like you belong."

She shook her head, lifting her cup. "You didn't have to do this."

He shrugged. "You sounded like you could use a pick-me-up. So I made it extra sugary just the way you like it."

Lydia took a sip. She swore the sugar went straight to her bloodstream, and she beamed at him before narrowing her eyes. "I'm not going to hear about this during training later, am I?"

"I would never," he said.

"Mm-hmm. I'm on to you, Luke Townsend."

He did a twirl, checking out the room. "So, this is what architects get up to for fun, huh?"

"I wouldn't say fun. I'm supposed to be networking."

"And how's that going?"

"I think a woman just tried to poach me for her firm, so pretty well, I'd say."

"There you go. And you're in charge of this display thing?" he said, gesturing to the poster board.

"I am single-handedly holding this display together. My supervisor ran off to try his luck with a man at the bar," Lydia said, pointing Erik out. "And Jack is a networking machine, apparently, so I'm on my own."

Luke set his eyes on Jack and didn't look away. "So, that's Jack, huh?"

She frowned at his tone. "What?"

"Nothing. He's just handsome and very charismatic, judging by all the laughter going on over there." Luke's brow arched as he caught her eye. "Not at all the dastardly villain you made him out to be."

Lydia flushed at the mention of the other week. In between all the sweaty adult fun, she'd also inadvertently revealed to Luke that Jack was her office crush. In fact, she thought her exact words were something along the lines of *I thought he liked my work*. God, was she in middle school? It sure sounded like Jack was the boy that broke up with her at recess, stomping all over her heart. Admitting that to Luke almost felt stupider than sleeping with him again.

Groups around them started to pack up and Lydia sighed. "Finally! I didn't want to be the first to leave."

She passed Luke her coffee so she could tear down the Poletti's table display. The sooner she got everything packed up, the sooner she could get out of here.

"How'd we do, running buddy? Any takers?"

Lydia's entire being flushed as Jack appeared at her side,

grabbing the poster board from the table and folding it into sections. "Uh, maybe a few."

"I handed out so many business cards Poletti's is going to be flooded with résumés."

How strange it was to be standing here, Jack on one side and Luke on the other. Should she introduce them? Would it be weird? Jack had no concept of Luke's existence, and yet she'd already given Luke a far too detailed rundown of Jack and her work situation. What would she even say?

Before she was forced to make the decision, Jack tucked the poster board under his arm and tossed the bag full of pamphlets over his shoulder. "Gotta run," he said. "But I'll see you tomorrow."

Lydia watched him disappear into the crowd.

"I get it now," Luke said a moment later.

"Huh?"

He gestured to his face, a coffee still in either hand. "You gotta look behind the eyes. Clearly the supervillain type."

"Shut up," Lydia replied to his teasing. "It's not funny."

"Whatever you say, *running buddy*."

Lydia snatched her coffee back. She knew Luke was just messing with her, and she supposed that was better than having a serious conversation about it. Though she would have preferred if he'd simply ignored the whole damn thing. "I'm officially not talking to you." Lydia took a long drag from her cup, hoping the burn of the coffee down her throat would ease the burn in her cheeks. She was grateful when her phone started ringing.

"Hey," she said, answering Ashley's call.

"What are you doing right now?"

"Um, I'm with Luke. We were just about to leave that architect mixer I told you about and head to training."

"Could you do me the world's biggest favor first?"

"Of course," Lydia said.

"Meet me at the City Clerk's Office at two o'clock."

She frowned. "Is everything okay?"

"Everything's good. Great. Bring Luke if you want."

Lydia caught Luke's eye. He looked as concerned as she felt. "Ash, what's going on?"

"I'm getting married."

Sixteen

Luke

"Thanks for coming with me," Lydia said again as she paid for a small bouquet of flowers from a street vendor outside the City Clerk's Office. "You didn't have to, and I know it's eating into our training time. Gosh, is it weird that *I'm* nervous?"

"It's not every Thursday afternoon your sister springs a last-minute marriage on you," Luke said.

"I'm still shocked. Eloping was the last thing I expected from Ashley." Lydia thanked the vendor for the flowers before pushing through the revolving door. "My mom's going to lose it when she finds out."

They entered the lobby. The Office of the City Clerk was like any other government building Luke had ever been inside—stark, absurdly clean and quiet. It was the complete opposite of the youth center. "Manhattan Marriage Bureau," Luke said, pointing to a small gold sign on the wall. "I think we're in the right place."

Lydia headed in that direction, the first door on the right, but before she reached it, someone called her name. It was her sister, Ashley, who Luke recognized from the gym. They'd never formally been introduced, but he spotted her from time to time as he rushed off after clients and she made her way to yoga. She wore a soft white sundress, and beside her stood a tall, bookish man in a suit.

"You came!" Ashley said.

"Of course I came!" Lydia said. They hugged, then Lydia handed her the flowers. "You're eloping?"

"We're eloping."

"And this is what you both want?"

Kurt nodded. "It is. We can have the party later. We just want this moment to be for us."

Luke watched Lydia smile. "Then let's get you married." She turned suddenly. "Oh, Ash, you remember Luke, right? From the gym? And Luke, this is Kurt."

"Yeah, hi," Ashley said, reaching out to shake his hand. Luke traded her hand for Kurt's. "I don't begrudge you trying to teach my sister how to run. Maybe she'll come to yoga with me next!"

Luke laughed. "I don't know about that, but there's a marathoner in there somewhere." He was grateful for the reminder of their professional relationship, that they weren't acknowledging the less professional elements of his friendship with her sister. Not that he expected Lydia wouldn't have told her—from everything he'd heard they were especially close—but he didn't think the marriage bureau was the right place to try to sort through his feelings on the subject.

Feelings that became more complicated when he thought about Jack. He hadn't been able to put a face to Lydia's office crush until today. He could see why she'd liked him—the guy was basically perfection walking around in a suit—but he wasn't quite sure where Lydia and Jack stood. Last he'd heard, Lydia was pretty disillusioned by him. Then Jack had called Lydia his running buddy, and as much as Luke had teased her, determined not to make things weird, he'd also been caught off guard at how strange it made him feel.

But it wasn't Jack she'd asked to come witness her sister's marriage.

It was him.

"Shall we?" Kurt said, gesturing to the door, pulling Luke from his tangled thoughts.

Lydia looped her arm through his, and Luke felt some of the anxiousness inside him settle.

Kurt led them past security to the reception desk, where they all handed over their IDs. After paying, Ashley and Kurt got a numbered ticket. Kurt tapped the ticket against Ashley's nose. "Guess this is really happening now."

Lydia grabbed Ashley's hand as they all sat down on the green couches, waiting for one of the flashing TVs above the numbered stations to read out their number. Several other groups were gathered in the room as well. It was all quiet, anxious, excited whispers.

When their number was called, they all walked up to the station, then handed over their IDs again. Ashley also handed over a marriage license. Then the clerk passed them a paper. Ashley and Kurt signed first. Then Lydia and Luke signed as the witnesses. It was all very efficient. Once they were done, it was back to the green couches.

"I didn't know if I was supposed to change or if I should

bring anything," Lydia said to Ashley. "I kind of wish you'd given me more of a heads-up."

"We barely gave ourselves a heads-up," Ashley laughed. "We were playing around with the idea, more like a joke every time we sat down to try and plan things, and it just kept sounding better and better. Neither of us knew it was actually happening until we did the paperwork and got the marriage license. Then we booked an appointment and it was suddenly real. You were right, though. Why should our wedding day cater to everyone else's happiness? Seems like a disappointing start to married life. This way we have all the control."

"I'm happy for you," Lydia said.

"Good. Because you're telling Mom."

Luke grinned at the momentary look of horror on Lydia's face. "As your maid of honor, I will bear this burden. But if you don't hear from me in four to six weeks it's because she's killed me."

Their number was called again and all of their heads perked up.

The next station was a horseshoe-shaped atrium. Ashley handed the paperwork they'd all just signed to an employee, who told them to wait with the other couples in the room. There were doors on either side of the atrium, leading to rooms where the officiants were marrying other couples. Kurt pulled Ashley in for a hug, and Luke hovered close to Lydia, trying to give the couple privacy.

"How do you feel now?"

"So weird. My sister's about to be married and that means she's really gone and grown up. I wanted to be just like her, you know, when we were kids. Everything she did I had to do too. Even as we got older, that hasn't really changed. Frankly,

I'm a little surprised I didn't follow her right to law school."
Lydia shrugged. "Ashley's always seemed to be following this
perfect, traditional life plan, and now that she's deviating, I'm
a little thrown, to be honest."

"Sometimes life's more fun when things are unexpected."

"As long as it makes her happy, I suppose I can roll with
the unexpected."

"Are there going to be waterworks?" Luke whispered.
"Should I stuff my pockets with tissues?"

"I'll hold it together," Lydia promised, straightening her
shoulders. "I *am* really glad you're here."

Warmth surged through him at her words. "Putting moral
support on my résumé."

Lydia laughed.

When their group was called, she took his hand, guiding
him through the doors to their right and into a tiny room
with pale pink walls. The officiant welcomed them, standing behind a podium. Ashley and Kurt placed their rings and
Lydia's small bouquet of flowers on the podium, then, without any other pomp or circumstance, it began.

As Luke stood there, watching these almost strangers get
married, he glanced over at Lydia, her hair a little windswept,
her cheeks pink from smiling so much. Maybe it was all the
lovey-dovey newlywed vibes ricocheting around the room, but
he couldn't help thinking about how his life had changed since
meeting her. Before Lydia, he'd never given a passing glance
to the architecture in the city. Now his camera roll was filled
with old brickwork and rusty fire escapes because he knew
Lydia loved those parts of the city. He noticed the shapes of
windows and crumbling archways in gardens. He noticed the

way one block differed from another. Sometimes, he even expected to walk around a corner and find Lydia standing there, a sketchbook in her hand.

Before Lydia he might have considered letting this first rejection for his business plan end his dream. Now all he could think about was what she'd said to him the other day about trying again.

The officiant stopped talking, and Kurt and Ashley kissed. Lydia clapped, bouncing up and down on her toes. When she turned to him, her eyes were glazed. "You said you'd hold it together," he joked.

"Obviously I lied!"

Luke reached into his pocket and produced a tissue. "I figured."

Lydia took the tissue from him, laughing, and Luke rubbed errantly at his chest, wondering if she realized just how tightly she was tugging on his heartstrings.

"Are you actually going to do some work today or are you just going to keep staring at your phone?" Dara asked. It was still early for a Saturday and Luke started, not quite awake as he leaned against the front desk, waiting for Lydia to arrive for their fifteen-mile run.

"Where have you been the last few days?" Jules asked from the other side of the desk, stapling a workout plan together. "I feel like I've barely seen you."

Luke stuffed his phone back into his pocket. "I picked up a couple more clients." He figured if the bank turned him down for his business loan a second time, he was going to need to start saving more money himself. Sure, it would mean his dream of owning a gym was years away, but he wasn't giving it up that easily. "Also, I sort of ended up at a surprise wedding ceremony on Thursday, so I shifted my afternoon around."

"For who?" Dara wondered, ignoring the phones.

"You're supposed to answer those," Luke said.

"I like to screen the calls in case it's someone I don't feel like talking to."

"That's literally the definition of your job."

Dara shrugged. "Whose wedding?"

"Lydia's sister eloped."

"Ah, the *client* you spend all your time with."

"I'm training her," Luke said pointedly.

"Yeah, I can tell," Dara said, bringing up his schedule on the computer and scrolling through his appointments. Jules peered over her shoulder with interest. "Look at this. Lydia. Lydia. Lydia. Geez, do you ever give the girl a break?"

"We're building up to a marathon!" Luke said, reasonably. "That's a normal training schedule." Dara waggled her eyebrows at him. "Has anyone ever told you that you're very annoying?"

Dara beamed. "You're just mad because I uncovered your secret girlfriend."

"She's not my girlfriend," Luke said, trying not to flush. Dara was as bad as the kids at the youth center. "I don't *have* a girlfriend."

"I can see why. I don't know how your *client* puts up with you."

Luke grumbled, walking away from the front desk. "I don't have to sit here and listen to this. Come get me when Lydia arrives."

"Good!" Dara yelled. "It's easier to gossip about you when you're not around."

Luke headed back to his office. It was still a disorganized mess, which never failed to amuse Lydia. He collapsed on the leather two-seater against the wall. He needed to stop thinking about her. If Dara and Jules were starting to notice, then maybe he was being too obvious with the way he was currently feeling.

Obviously he hadn't been looking for something serious, but he'd be a fool if he didn't acknowledge all the ways they seemed to fit. And though he certainly didn't set out to fall for a client, somewhere between Lydia kissing him at the pub and running all over the city with her, things had changed. He groaned, running a hand down his face.

"Don't let her get to you," Jules said.

Luke lifted his head. Jules was leaning against the door-jamb. "Who, Dara?" He waved off the thought. "She's always like that with me."

"What *her* did you think I was talking about?"

"No one."

Jules bit her lip. She knew exactly who Luke was talking about.

"I like her," Luke confessed, staring at the ceiling. What use was there in lying? Jules and Dara could see right through him. "A lot. I think it surprised me how much we connected. It's just complicated because…"

"You're training her," Jules said.

Luke sighed. "I offered to get her another trainer early on, but she declined and we thought it would be okay. It wasn't supposed to be anything serious, but now—"

"Now you're attending wedding ceremonies with her," Jules said, finishing his thought.

"Yes, thank you!" Luke said. "What the hell does that mean?"

Jules laughed. "You could write her a note like in the first grade and ask her to check *yes* if she likes you back."

Luke huffed. "If only it were that easy. If I pull the plug as her trainer and ask for more, I'm worried I might freak her out. What if she truly doesn't feel the same? Then I've ruined our professional relationship and screwed up her training because I couldn't figure out these feelings." He didn't want Lydia to panic and stop training altogether because *he* couldn't read the signs. Maybe they'd both really just needed some comfort a couple weeks ago when she'd poured her heart out to him about work. Maybe it was a coincidence that he'd been in the right place at the right time and gotten roped into the wedding ceremony. Maybe it all meant nothing. But it was starting to feel real. And he wanted more of that.

"Look, the fact that you've fallen for a client is tricky, but you've got to figure things out one way or another. Love can be beautiful even when it's complicated, but this in-between stuff is going to get messy really fast."

"I know," Luke grumbled.

"If it helps, I've never heard you talk about anyone the way you talk about Lydia."

Luke flopped back on the couch as Jules walked away. He still had no idea what to do. Did he risk their professional relationship? Did he ask her for more? He needed a sign from the universe.

"Lucas!" Dara's voice echoed down the hall. "Lydia is here!"

Luke jumped to his feet, hurrying out to meet her before Dara could start spouting off words like *girlfriend* in front of Lydia. He smiled, perhaps too wide, but he worried she might be able to see the longing in his face if he didn't. "Ready?"

Lydia matched his smile. "Absolutely not. But let's do this."

"You're usually a little more enthusiastic," Luke said, leading her outside.

"Something about fifteen miles feels daunting," Lydia said as they warmed up.

Luke couldn't help but think that she'd found the perfect word to describe how he felt. This thing between them felt daunting. But he wasn't supposed to be thinking about that.

"I mean, I made it this far, so I can't just go back, but there's still an awfully long way to go."

Her words twisted the feelings inside him. He cleared his throat. "We don't have to think about all those miles today. We just focus on this run. On taking the next—"

"Step," Lydia cut in, rolling her eyes with a smile. "Yeah, yeah, I know. I'm gonna put that on a T-shirt for you."

"It's excellent advice." They set off together, and Luke led her toward the East River Greenway, entering at 34th Street so they could run along the waterfront. "How's your sister taking to married life?"

"Great," Lydia said. "Ash and Kurt just left on a spur-of-the-moment honeymoon and I had to call and tell my parents about it all."

"Well, you're still alive, so I take it your mother has come to terms with the decision?"

"She kept saying she was going to pass out while we were on the phone." Lydia made an amused sound. "My dad thinks it's great. Says it's gonna save him tons of money."

"I suppose that's one way to look at it," Luke said. It was a cloudless day, the sky a vivid blue, while the water of the East River sparkled under the sun's reflection. In the distance he could just make out the Williamsburg Bridge. They fell into a comfortable silence, his world narrowing to the sounds of Lydia's breathing, the length of her stride and her mile pace as they ran through the swerving, greenery-filled pathways of Stuyvesant Cove Park.

"I can't believe we haven't run through here before," Lydia said as the path widened. She'd come so far since that first run where she could barely keep her breathing under control, never mind carry on an entire conversation. They were joined by other runners and cyclists and weekend waterfront strollers as they entered the East River Promenade. It was filled with green spaces, benches and trees.

"What?" he teased. "Were you getting sick of running around the gym?"

"I mean, I think I trip over the same curb every time we circle the block. You have to admit this *is* a nice change."

"I'm just kidding," he said. "You're right. You can't beat running along the waterfront. I was actually trying to save this stretch for when the trees started to change colors. We're a little early for that still, but we'll come back another weekend."

Lydia shot him a surprised look.

"What?"

"I didn't know you put that much thought into these runs."

"What do you mean?"

"Like you considered when the leaves would change just so that we'd get to run beside all the pretty fall colors. That's really…thoughtful, I guess."

Luke didn't know if he was supposed to chuckle at that, but he couldn't help himself. "Do I not seem like the thoughtful type?"

"That's not what I meant."

"You seem to be saying a lot of *something* without knowing what you mean."

Her cheeks flushed, the rosy color of exertion darkening.

Lydia cleared her throat. "It's nice," she said finally. "That you put that much thought and time into planning these runs. That you care enough—"

"To make sure you don't die of boredom?" he suggested.

Her lips twitched. "It's nice," she said again, softer this time, and he had to look away to stop himself from staring too hard.

"Well, I'm glad you like the view, 'cause this stretch of the greenway is only about four and a half miles, so we've gotta do a few laps this morning."

Lydia hummed in approval, settling back into her form. They slowed a few times, long enough for Lydia to snap photos of various parts of the skyline that piqued her interest as they passed the Manhattan Bridge and then the Brooklyn Bridge. But all Luke could think about was the blush in Lydia's cheeks and how genuinely she'd said *it's nice*.

Jules's words from earlier rushed back so fast it almost made him breathless. If he could navigate all these complicated and messy feelings, if he could figure out what they meant, maybe this thing between them would get to be beautiful.

Seventeen

Lydia

"You're packing up?" Erik said, frowning as he poked his head into Lydia's office.

"I know you're getting older, but that's usually what the end of the day means," Lydia teased. She'd had her fill of tedious reviews and client meetings today; she was more than ready to meet with Luke and squeeze in her short run. Months ago she never would have voluntarily taken herself to the gym after work, but that's apparently who she was now.

"Watch it," Erik warned. "I'm the one who writes your year-end review."

Lydia grinned, unplugging her laptop charger from the wall. "Why? What's up?"

"Projects wants to know if you're available to stay late to finish up some work for a client," Erik said.

"Projects has an entire team to pick from. Why are they poaching from yours?"

"Jack said something about an eco-friendly design consult."

That was odd. Those things usually came across Erik's desk in a briefing, which he then delegated down to her. Why hadn't she seen a briefing on this? And why would Jack be asking for her specifically? They'd hardly spoken since Kirsten revealed that the entire leadership team was gunning to make partner.

"So, can you stay?" Erik asked.

"I can't actually," Lydia said. "I've got nine miles to run with my trainer."

"That sounds like a lot for a Tuesday."

"Believe it or not, that's a short run. They used to only be like three miles, but I'm just so amazing now," Lydia deadpanned, "that my trainer knows I can handle more."

Erik narrowed his eyes playfully. "Sounds like you're trying to tell me something."

"Only that I'm capable of learning and growing." She'd done nothing but improve her running technique, steadily closing the gap on the miles she had to run for the marathon. She wanted to be able to put the same energy into her actual career.

"And?" Erik said, waiting for her to finish.

"And maybe that would translate into my job if Poletti's would actually approve some of our project proposals." Lydia had realized that having all her proposals red-lined meant Erik was also sitting on the sidelines. They were both filling their days with the tasks other departments didn't want to do: completing feasibility studies and financial analyses, preparing bidding documents, organizing material cost breakdowns.

"You know if it was up to me—"

"This whole place would go green?" she said.

He smiled softly at her. "You've got the skills, Lydia. And a lot of potential. Never doubt that."

She rolled her eyes at him. It was nice to hear, of course, but she'd rather have a project of their own to prove that.

"I'll tell Projects that you can't stay then?" Erik confirmed.

"Do you know what client it's for?"

"Jack didn't say. He only mentioned that you should meet him in the conference room," he said as they exited into the hall. "If you can't stay, then you can't stay. I'll let him know."

"Wait," Lydia said as Erik started to text Jack. "I'll just let him know myself."

Erik put his phone away and was gone before she could reconsider. Oh, well. She was going to have to smooth things over with Jack eventually. Not that Jack even knew anything was wrong. This was entirely a one-sided disagreement, and that was almost worse because Jack had no idea how disappointed she'd been. But they were coworkers. They were running the marathon together. At some point they would be standing side by side for a sweaty photo at the finish line. She couldn't exactly ignore him for the rest of her career.

It was best to get this out of the way. Then she could spend the rest of the afternoon sweating out the awkwardness of this conversation in the gym with Luke. She walked to the end of the hall and knocked on the closed conference room door. There was no answer. For a moment, she worried she might be interrupting someone's private meeting, but she popped the door open anyway. "Hello?"

"You came!" Jack said, hurrying around the edge of the table. His shirtsleeves were rolled up, and a shock of dark hair dangled in his eyes like he'd been working furiously at something and hadn't had time to brush it back. "I didn't know if I would catch you in time. Remind me to thank Erik."

Lydia just blinked at him, confused as Jack ushered her into a seat. She spun around, watching him throw his arms out in a ta-da motion.

"Well?" he said. "What do you think?"

"What do I think about what?" Her eyes narrowed in concern. Had she missed the briefing on something important? Did this have anything to do with the marathon? Maybe she'd accidentally deleted an important email.

Jack turned and frowned at the blank projector screen. "Oh, damn. I always forget to take the cover off this thing." He walked to the projector, where he had a laptop set up, and took the cap off. A floor plan popped up on the screen.

Lydia stared at a familiar-looking image. This was *her* design. She opened her mouth, but unsure of what to say, she just pointed at the screen and blinked at Jack. He waltzed up to the screen, all suave and easygoing, wearing that charming grin of his. Lydia had seen him use that grin on rooms filled with prospective clients a dozen times. But there was no one else here. Just her and the floor plan she'd created for the Manhattan Youth Center. "What's going on?"

"This is my pitch," Jack said, beaming. He held a tiny black remote in his hand. He clicked it, and a new image filled the screen: a photo of Jack at his desk, studiously working. It was a selfie that had obviously been taken today since he was wearing the same clothes.

"Your pitch?" Lydia repeated.

"Yes. About why you, Lydia McKenzie, should choose me, Jack Carson, as your proposal partner."

Lydia rubbed her hand across her forehead. "I am *so* confused right now. My proposal was rejected."

"Right," Jack said. "But I'm proposing a new proposal. A revise, revamp and resubmit, if you will."

"As partners?" she clarified.

Jack nodded. "You didn't get a fair shot. I read your proposal and it was really good. Good enough to land on Marco's desk. We both know that."

Lydia bit her lip, refusing to let her feelings spill over.

"I haven't submitted my proposal yet," Jack explained. "And I really think if we combine your eco-friendly, urban style with my modern, cost-effective design, we could come up with the winning selection from Poletti's."

The corner of Lydia's mouth quirked.

"But hold on," he said. "Here's what I bring to the table." He clicked the remote, a new image popping up on the screen. "Today's coffee and snacks." He rushed to the other side of the room and produced two coffees and a honey cruller doughnut. "Courtesy of Charmaine's."

"That wins you some points," Lydia admitted. She reached for her coffee as Jack poured a to-go bag filled with sugar packets onto the table.

"A little birdy told me this is how you take your coffee."

He returned to his presentation, and Lydia couldn't help the smile that stretched across her face.

"I also bring a winning attitude." A photo of him in the break room with the word Winner taped to his chest.

"Nice."

"I'm team oriented." A photo of him and Kirsten engaged in a fake conversation.

"Great communication skills," Lydia teased.

"*And* I'm your running buddy." The last photo was of the finish line at the end of the New York City Marathon. "So we're kind of already in this together."

Lydia didn't know if she was more impressed or amused. "How long did this take you?"

Jack made a face. "I might have rescheduled a client meeting."

She couldn't believe he'd rearranged part of his week just to plan all this. "Why not just ask me?"

"Because I felt like we veered off on the wrong foot somewhere and I wanted to make it up to you. I realized that a lot of proposals were getting lost in the shuffle. Yours included."

"The shuffle?" Lydia said. "That's what you're calling it?"

He sighed, coming to sit on the edge of the table next to her, and she could tell that this was him attempting to apologize for the breakdown in communication from the leadership team to the rest of the firm. "It's not a perfect system. I know that. But I really think we have a shot here. If we team up, we could really make this happen. For Poletti's. For the kids. They deserve something like the center we're trying to build for them. I say we go back to the drawing board together, lean into the best parts of our ideas and make something magical." He reached for her hand and squeezed. "Sometimes you just need to get your foot in the door. It doesn't matter how you get there. So, what do you say? Are the running buddies officially becoming proposal partners?"

"All right," Lydia said, pulling her laptop from her bag. "But you're in charge of supplying *all* the coffee."

Jack grinned. "Deal."

★ ★ ★

If Lydia were ever this late for a client meeting they would have dropped her. And honestly, she wouldn't even have blamed them. But when things had run late with Jack, she'd texted Luke to let him know she was still tied up at work, and he'd told her not to worry. Then he'd shifted his schedule around to accommodate her, which was how she found herself walking into an empty gym at nine at night.

"Where is everyone?" she asked as Luke let her into the building.

"We close at eight on Tuesdays."

"Eight?" Lydia said. "Why did I think it was midnight?"

"That's Friday and Saturday."

"Clearly I don't spend enough time here," she remarked, following him down the hall. "I can't believe you waited. You should have told me to kindly fuck off."

"It's fine," he said. "I wanted to show you your updated mile times."

"You could have texted."

"It's not the same. I can't see the look on your face."

Lydia walked past him as he opened his office door for her. The fact that she was sort of excited to see her new mile times almost made her laugh. Maybe Luke had turned her into a gym girl for life. Maybe when this was all over, they'd spend weekends on the treadmills with her complaining about Poletti's and him telling her all about the progress he was making on his revamped business plan. "Are you *ever* going to clean this space up?"

"It's tidy," Luke protested, sitting down in front of his computer.

Lydia picked up a framed certificate that Luke had left leaning against the wall. "What are you talking about? You still haven't hung this. And everything from your bookshelf is sitting in that box over there. You know they finished the repairs in here months ago, right?"

He turned slowly in his chair to face her. He had a pensive look on his face. "I guess some part of me kept thinking there wasn't much point in putting everything away because I was going to get the business loan and be packing up my office soon. When it fell through, I was too disappointed to start putting things away."

"Oh," Lydia said softly, wiping dust from the glass covering Luke's certificate.

"It's silly," he said, moving a bunch of papers out of his way and pulling out the hard copy of her training plan. "You're right. I should tidy up already."

Lydia put the certificate on the sofa and walked to the desk. She didn't know what she meant to do. Hug him? Tell him everything would be okay, or that the second time's the charm? Before she could decide, she got distracted by the papers he'd moved.

"What's all this?" she asked, picking up a rough sketch.

Luke tried to nab it from her. "I was just working on some mock-up drawings for the warehouse space to add to my new business plan. They're...not very good. I know. I was hoping drawing it out would inspire a new business model."

"What are you talking about?" Lydia said, her voice pitched too high. "These are great."

"Says the *actual* architect who's clearly lying through her teeth. These are kindergarten quality."

She did her best not to laugh. "Want some advice?"

"From a professional? Sure."

"Invest in a ruler."

Luke scoffed. "I could have figured that one out."

"Hey, that's solid advice. It'll take this from a negative two to a solid four point five."

"Negative two?" he said, feigning shock. "Is this the part where you tell me not to quit my day job?"

"I think you're pretty good at your day job."

"Speaking of," he said. "Come over here."

"I want to see my numbers. But I'm trying not to think about how few weeks are left between now and the marathon and how many miles I still have to run."

He rolled his chair back so she could see the figures on the training plan. "We've got six…almost seven weeks, and you've been making great progress," he insisted. "I'm not worried."

"Says the professional," she teased, though she leaned over the training plan to indulge him.

"Look how far you've come from where you started," he said, tapping the first page. "A few months ago you could barely run a mile."

"I think barely is overstating it. I wasn't that bad," Lydia laughed, snapping her head around. He was a lot closer than she'd realized. Close enough that she could smell his shampoo and see the stubble that trailed down his jaw. Her eyes flickered to his lips. A little closer and she could lean down and kiss him. Her stomach did a somersault at the thought. What was she doing? God, this was where Luke *worked*. This was his *office*. She immediately put some space between them.

She should know better than to mess around with mixed signals.

Her thoughts skittered to Jack and the ridiculous feelings she'd been sitting with for the better part of the afternoon. Just this morning she'd been avoiding him, but then she'd learned that he'd canceled on a client to prepare that presentation for her. As they'd laid out a tentative plan for their combined proposal, some part of her had wondered if there was something more to his apology. Was it all in her head? Had she read that instance as wrong as she'd just read this moment? She hadn't expected to still be harboring a crush on Jack after everything, but his sweet gesture had caught her off guard, and that's what started her thoughts tumbling again. Maybe she *wasn't* overthinking things. Jack had asked to be her partner, so even he must have thought they'd make a good pair in some capacity. And Jack was the kind of partner she'd always imagined herself with, right? Was it really so wrong to think that maybe their miscommunication was behind them?

"Are you okay?" Luke asked.

"Yeah, good," Lydia lied, heading for the door. "We should get out there and start doing burpees or whatever."

"Burpees?" Luke said, sounding as confused as she felt.

"I'll see you on the floor." Without even a glance back, Lydia fled his office.

Eighteen

Luke

"Is it over yet?" Lydia asked, her cheeks flushed with an end-of-September chill. The shift in the weather had been a welcome treat after pushing through her training plan on the hottest days of summer. He just hoped the weather continued to cooperate a month from now when Lydia was actually running the marathon.

Luke glanced down at his watch, then looked over to see her teeth gritted. They'd only just passed seventeen miles. They had just under one more to go to round out at eighteen today. "Not quite. How're you doing? Do you need to take a break?"

He'd just started to slow when her grimace lifted into a smirk and she breezed by him. "Kidding!" she called. She glanced over her shoulder, threw her head back, and laughed at whatever look was stuck on his face. "Don't tell me you're getting tired already!"

Luke picked up his pace to catch her as she giggled. They'd run the East River Greenway again, enjoying the changing autumn leaves, just as he'd promised. After they'd reached Battery Park, they'd cut up through the city, with no exact route in mind, building up the miles as they headed in the general direction of the gym. Eventually they'd opted just to finish out the miles circling Madison Square Park.

"Race you back!" Lydia darted off the path, checking for traffic as she ran across 5th Avenue. Luke slowed, getting caught in a crowd of pedestrians. When the group cleared, he hurried after Lydia, but she'd started sprinting, and he knew then that this was a race he was about to lose.

Luke pushed himself harder, his lungs burning, the muscles in his legs aching, but the sidewalks were too congested for him to close the distance, and as he crossed 6th Avenue, he spotted Lydia slowing outside the gym. She dropped her hands to her hips, her long hair plastered to her neck and the back of her shirt, her face crumpled up in victorious pain as she sucked in air.

"Ha!" she said, her face smoothing. She threw her arms up in victory as he approached.

"You cheated," he accused her.

Her laugh was bubbly and infectious. "How?"

"I didn't even know we were racing!"

"I literally yelled 'race you' at the top of my lungs!"

"Yeah, after you'd already made sure I got caught in a giant crowd of tourists."

"It's not my fault you weren't paying attention. You've gotta be prepared for anything when running. Changes in the weather. Rogue pigeon attacks."

Luke laughed, pulling the door to the gym open. "Is that what you've been researching?"

"I'm covering my bases," Lydia said, stopping at the front desk and taking a long drag from her water bottle.

Luke couldn't resist squeezing his own water bottle in her direction. Lydia yelped, then laughed, hurrying away to the showers.

"Ew. Can you not sweat all over the desk?" Dara shooed him away, wrinkling her nose as she wiped down the counter.

Grinning, Luke headed for the showers to wash off the last eighteen miles. As he let the hot water soothe his muscles, he considered the next month of Lydia's training plan. The race was the first weekend of November, and they'd just hit eighteen miles. Luke figured he would build her up to twenty miles in a couple weeks, and then start tapering off the distance until the race to give her muscles enough time to recover.

Luke finished in the shower, changed and headed back to his office to make notes. He found the door open and Lydia sitting on his couch, her still-wet hair pulled up into a knot at the top of her head. "Hey," he said. "Thought you'd be halfway home by now. You want to see your updated mile times?"

Lydia shrugged. "Maybe later. You want to get a drink or food or something?"

Luke's immediate reaction was to say yes, but then he caught himself. He remembered an innocent invitation like this one months ago, after their evening touring the youth center. An invitation that had made everything complicated. Lydia glanced up from her phone and caught his eye. Luke looked away, worried she might be able to read the thoughts he was having.

"I've got a lot of paperwork to catch up on," he said, the excuse weak.

"Oh, come on. I know you don't have any other clients today."

He couldn't help his smile. "And how would you know that?"

"I asked Dara to check your schedule."

Luke bit the inside of his cheek. The last thing he needed was Dara meddling. Jules already knew how he felt, and he didn't need any more pushes in a dangerous direction.

"We should celebrate," Lydia said, getting to her feet.

"Celebrate what?"

"The fact that I beat you back to the gym."

"I feel like we need to look up the definition of a cheater," Luke said.

Lydia groaned playfully. "Fine. I will get you a drink for hurting your feelings by winning the race."

"Oh, well that makes me *really* want to go."

"What if I promise to let you win the next one?"

Luke glanced over at her, and Lydia made an X over her heart.

"Thanks for walking me back," Lydia said as she led Luke up the steps of her building. She shivered, that autumn chill sweeping across the city as the sun set. It wasn't actually that late, but the sky was darkening earlier and earlier, and Luke felt like things were about to change. The marathon was getting closer. Soon there would be no need for weekend long runs and friendly postrun drinks. If nothing changed between them, then soon everything would. "Want to come up for a bit?"

Luke hesitated. They'd gone out for one drink. A strictly

friendly drink. He knew he should say good night and walk back to the subway. Maybe it was all the thoughts of things changing or maybe he was just curious to see Lydia's apartment—to gain the insight that could only come from seeing where and how someone lived—but instead of walking away, he nodded.

Lydia smiled and led him upstairs. The space was tiny, but impeccably neat, just as he imagined it would be. What really caught his attention was the copious amount of indoor plants. They filled shelves and dangled from the ceiling, stretching toward the massive windows in the living room.

While Lydia secured two beers from the fridge, he crossed the room to look out the windows. The sun was setting and he could just make out the peachy bands of the sky. "Nice view."

"I know, right? It's what sold me on the place."

He turned to her desk, which was more of a drafting table. The wall above the table was filled with framed sketches. "Did you draw all these?"

She nodded. "A few of them are from college. Others are more recent, just buildings I like around the city."

"You really are fantastic at your job." He glanced over and could tell she was fighting a smile. He walked back across the room and she handed him the beer.

"To kicking your ass on that run," Lydia said, raising her bottle.

"This again? I thought we covered this when you announced it to the whole pub."

"Just be happy for me."

Luke tipped his bottle in her direction. "You're sure I didn't just let you win?"

"Now what kind of trainer would you be if you did that?" she asked pointedly, and for a moment it felt like she might be reminding herself and him of what exactly they were doing here. She was saying all the right words and he was nodding along, and maybe they both even meant them. But there was also a part of Luke that wished they didn't. That wished he could figure out how much of her saw him as a friend and how much of her might be able to see him as something else... Something more.

"How's work going?" he asked, sipping his drink and changing the subject. At the pub, she'd mostly pestered him with questions about his business plan: What are the updates? Are you still going to host youth programming? Though he hadn't had answers to everything yet, he loved how enthusiastic she was. He also loved that she let him ramble, that she'd just grinned and sipped her drink as he went on about how his gym would fare in the market if First Union Bank would just give him a chance.

"It's gotten pretty busy lately," Lydia admitted.

"New contracts?" he asked.

"No, actually, I'm getting a second shot at the Manhattan Youth Center competition."

"Wait, what?" He shook his head. "That's amazing. But how?"

"Jack actually asked me to partner up with him. He hasn't submitted his proposal yet, so there's an opportunity for me to try again."

A flash of heat shot through him. "And you're happy about that?"

"Of course." She glanced up. "What is it?"

He shook his head. "Nothing."

"No, tell me."

He didn't know how to explain the growling rage in his chest at the thought of her and Jack spending long afternoons together. Jack in his tailored suits, with his easy laugh, calling Lydia his *running buddy*. Luke felt like his skin was on fire. "I thought Jack was one of the people who keeps rejecting your work."

Lydia shrugged. "I probably blew things out of proportion. I was upset and he was an easy target. He actually thinks we have a really good shot at getting selected to represent the firm."

"Right. Well, that's really...cool." *Cool* was the last thing he meant, but he wasn't willing to ruin their evening over a guy he barely knew.

She caught his hand. "Luke? What's going on?"

"I don't want to talk about Jack, okay?"

"Okay..." she said, dragging out the word. "You're the one who brought up work."

"I know."

The question was clear in her eyes. What *do* you want to talk about then? But that was the problem. He didn't want to talk, especially now. He wanted to kiss her senseless. He wanted to know that Jack didn't mean anything, that his feelings for her weren't one-sided, that despite all the complications, this could be something.

"Luke," she whispered, the word like a beckoning finger. He put his beer down on the counter, and reached for her. Her lips parted, a soft sound escaping.

"Ask me to leave," he said, leaning so close he could feel the phantom press of her lips against his.

"I'm not going to ask you to leave."

"You know what will happen if I stay."

"I know," she said, and she leaned into him.

It was like fireworks exploded in his brain, erasing all thoughts of Jack, and he held her tighter, until they fit like mortared bricks against each other. His hands caressed her, trailing down her back to cup her ass. In one smooth motion, Luke lifted her onto the counter, swallowing Lydia's little yelp of surprise as he leaned into the space between her legs. Situated like this, she was slightly taller, and he reveled at the sensation of pushing up on his feet to catch her lips. Lydia chuckled as they bumped the beer bottles on the counter, Luke chasing them blindly with his hands to stop them from spilling. He moved the bottles out of the way before letting his cold, condensation-slick hands slip beneath her shirt, tracing her spine.

Lydia gasped and arched, pressing against him in the most intoxicating way as he pulled her shirt over her head. Her hands were everywhere then, combing through his hair, cradling his face as she tilted her head, pressing her lips to his jaw. He felt the gentle scrape of her teeth as she moved down his neck, and Luke groaned. He could feel more than hear as she laughed, her hands dropping to his shoulders and squeezing, before raking down his front. Her hands didn't stop until they were fiddling with the waistband of his pants. When she popped the button, he came haltingly to his senses and caught her wrists.

"Shit," he bit out. "I don't have any protection."

Lydia slid off the counter and left him to go flick on the bathroom light and kneel in front of the sink cabinet. She started tossing things out of the cabinet one by one. Luke followed and leaned against the doorjamb, amused.

"Looking for your *in case of emergencies* condoms?"

"Are you complaining?"

"Not at all."

Lydia grabbed something from the back of the cupboard and held the box up triumphantly. She tossed him the box.

When she stood, Luke snagged her by the waist and hauled her closer. Lydia's hand reached back to flick off the bathroom light and then the kitchen light. Without them, the apartment was bathed in nothing but the streetlights, and they gravitated toward the massive windows, caressing and touching and kissing until they were both breathless. Luke honestly didn't know how he could *not* be reading feelings into this. Not the way she was moving against him.

It wasn't just the sex. It was more than that. Everything with her was better. She gasped as he squeezed her breast, shoving her bra cup aside so he could rub at the sensitive skin until her nipple pebbled, hard and needy against his thumb.

"You should take your pants off," Lydia whispered into his mouth.

"What's the rush? Don't you want to enjoy the view a bit?" He twisted her in his arms, so she was looking out those massive widows. He nudged her forward and the streetlights spilled across her forearms as she reached out to catch herself against the glass. Luke leaned against her, pressing his hands next to hers on the chilled windowpanes. He ground his hips against her and Lydia's head rolled back against his shoulder.

He tipped his head and kissed the exposed skin of her neck, nipping gently. Then he took one hand off the window and placed it on her hip. He rocked her against his body as he kissed his way across her shoulder. Then he slipped one hand down the front of her pants.

"Luke," she husked, catching his hand before he could go any further. "What if one of the neighbors sees?"

"Do you want me to stop?" he whispered into her ear.

"God, no." She put both hands back on the windowpanes.

"Good," he said, letting his fingers brush against her folds, carefully avoiding the delicate nub of her clit. "Because I want us both to be very, *very* satisfied."

A desperate little moan fell from her mouth. "Please touch me."

Luke didn't make her beg. He ran the pads of his fingers over her clit, stroking until he found a rhythm she liked. When she started to move with him, he held that rhythm, watching the way her fingers twitched against the glass.

He imagined stripping her bare before the window, watching moonlight caress her curves. Her thighs began to tremble on either side of where he worked his hand, and the sounds that came from her turned into breathy, demanding orders. Harder. Faster. There. Right there.

"Yes," she hissed, grinding against his hand. "Yes, yes, *yes.*"

Her knees buckled and her fingers curled into fists against the glass as she came, riding his hand all the way down to the floor as they both sank to their knees. "How was the view?" he asked as she panted in his lap.

"Stunning."

"Would you like to see it again?"

Lydia turned her face up to kiss him.

Nineteen

Lydia

Whoever composed phone alarms had summoned the melodies from the pits of hell. Lydia shifted in bed, her eyes still closed, trying to figure out which direction the horrible noise was coming from. Her hands felt beneath her pillow and traced under the sheet, searching for her phone.

Her eyes shot open, the weight of the world rushing up to greet her as memories from the weekend washed over her. She groaned, pressing her face into the pillow. It was Tuesday. It had been three days since she'd fallen into bed with Luke again, and this time, she hadn't been able to shake him. That was three days of thinking about his hands everywhere. Three days of reliving the desperation she'd felt. Obviously they were doing a terrible job of keeping things professional, and her dreams since then...

Lydia finally found her phone beneath the sheets and silenced it before rolling over and blinking at the screen. There was a text from Luke.

Meet me at the youth center tonight.

Lydia climbed out of bed and responded while she brushed her teeth. Why? You want me to watch the children destroy you in basketball?

It took Luke a while to respond. She was already heading to the train for work when he did. Ouch! You wouldn't be talking such trash if you'd ever faced them on the court.

Lydia smirked, walking into the subway station. You've never seen me on a court. I could take them and you.

Those are big words coming from a woman who can barely handle a burpee.

Lydia snorted. He wasn't wrong. Sure, she might have crushed that last eighteen-mile run and beaten Luke back to the gym. Physically, she might even look like a runner now. But a couple burpees were still her Achilles' heel.

She sent him a thumbs up as she walked into the office building and rode the elevator up to Poletti's. How exactly were they going to train at the youth center? She'd been kidding about basketball. She would, in fact, probably sprain her ankle if Luke got her out on that court. Either that or she'd be trampled by preteens.

She was still mulling that over a few hours later, when Jack knocked on her door. "Hey, running buddy," she said.

"Ah, you beat me to it." Jack leaned against her door frame with all the grace of a model posing for *Vogue*, his hair brushed back, the top two buttons of his shirt undone.

"It was bound to happen one of these days."

Jack chuckled. "So I was thinking we meet up after work and keep hammering out the logistics of our proposal?"

"Oh, I can't today," Lydia said. She wasn't exactly disappointed, but part of her wished she had the time to stay back with Jack *and* meet up with Luke. "I've got training."

"Right, no worries. How about right now? We could do a working lunch."

"Sure, that works." Lydia grabbed her lunch bag and her laptop, and headed down to the empty conference room. Jack popped down to his office to retrieve his things, returning a few moments later. "Do you want to start sketching out the redesign of the first floor?" she asked.

"You know what, I think you had such a great handle on that," Jack said, sitting down. "It would make more sense just to tack my ideas onto your original sketch. Give me a second, I'll send you through my stuff."

Lydia waited for it to pop up in her email.

"Gosh," he said. "I love this rooftop garden you designed."

"Pretty sure you wanted to make it a rooftop terrace way back when you first looked at my sketches."

"Do you think we still can?" he asked, wrinkling his nose like she might reject the idea.

"Why not?" She shrugged. "We can have a little of both."

"It'll be functional and still tackle the heat island effect. The judges are going to eat that up."

"Do you want to get started on outdoor stuff?" Lydia asked. "You can tackle the roof and the outdoor yard."

"Can you send me your working file for the rooftop? I think I can just make some tweaks."

"Oh," Lydia said. "Uh, sure. One second." She'd assumed

Jack was going to build off of his own design, but she supposed this worked too. "On the way to your inbox now."

"Perfect," Jack said. His phone started to buzz on the table. "That's a client. I'll be right back."

"No problem," Lydia said as he snatched up the phone and darted from the room.

Jack had barely left when Kirsten barged in. "I see you've traded me in for a new lunch buddy."

"This is a working lunch," Lydia said. "You know I could never replace you."

Kirsten stuck her tongue out. "I know. I actually worked really hard to make this whole situation happen."

Lydia narrowed her eyes. "I knew you were meddling."

"Well, I maybe just explained how people were feeling about the leadership team handling the proposal submissions, and Jack agreed. All he needed was a little push in the right direction. Everything else was his idea. Adorable, right?"

Lydia smiled at the memory of Jack standing up at the front of the room, talking her into being his partner. "I wish he would hurry up," she said, glancing at the clock on the wall. "We've only got an hour and I can't stay tonight."

"He's talking to the Marshalls. They called for Marco but he's not here this afternoon, so I forwarded the call to Jack."

"Never mind then," Lydia said. Jack would probably be tied up for a while, knowing Mr. Marshall.

"Sorry," Kirsten said. "I didn't know you guys were doing this right now or I would have sent the call to voicemail."

"It's fine," Lydia said. And it was. They still had close to a month to combine their proposals. That was plenty of time.

They'd just have to squeeze in a few more of these working lunches.

Lydia opened the file she'd just sent Jack and started working on the rooftop redesign.

Twenty

Luke

The moment Luke spotted Lydia hurrying down the sidewalk toward the youth center, he stood up from the steps and dusted off his pants, feeling oddly nervous as she drew closer.

These past few days had cemented things in his mind that he'd been wondering about. After the night in her apartment, he knew, at least as far as he was concerned, that this was more than just accidentally falling into bed together. It was more than just reaching out for comfort after a bad day. What existed between him and Lydia went beyond physical. There was a strength in the way they understood and supported each other, and real genuine concern for one another. He cared about her goals, her dreams, her desires. He wanted to see her succeed and be happy. He wanted more than casual let's-never-mention-it-again sex. He wanted something real with Lydia, and judging by the way she was smiling at him, maybe if he ever came clean about the way he felt, Lydia would laugh and tell him she felt that way too.

He stuffed his hands in his pockets as she jogged up the steps toward him. The best thing to do right now was just focus on the running. Everything else would sort itself out.

"Hope you came prepared to sweat."

She patted the bag strung over her shoulder. "Of course I did. But you still haven't told me what we're doing here."

"What? You're *not* ready to show me your moves on the basketball court?" Luke said, waving her up the steps.

"You and I both know how badly that'll end."

He flashed her a smile. "I know. I forgot I actually promised to run youth fitness night. Since we also had training booked, I figured I could combine the two."

"You're saying you want me to embarrass myself in front of the children." Inside, Lydia showed her ID and got her visitor's badge. She strung it around her neck.

"Just try not to fall down too much," Luke said.

"What the hell is that supposed to mean?"

Luke turned around, shooting her a grin. "It'll be fun. I promise."

"I don't know if I trust your idea of fun."

"Oh, come on," he said. "I'm not even gonna make you do any burpees."

He led her into the gym, where the kids were already assembled. According to Miranda, fitness nights had been a big draw since he started organizing them. He always took that as a huge compliment. If only redoing his business plan could be as easy as coming up with fitness programming at the center or plotting out a training plan.

Most of the kids were seated in the bleachers, but a group

of middle schoolers had gotten ahold of the bucket of palm-sized beanbags and started hurling them at each other.

Luke picked up the whistle around his neck and gave it a short, sharp trill. Kids laughed and groaned, plugging their ears. "Drop the beanbags," he called, and the kids took off running up the bleachers.

He turned around. Lydia was frozen on the edge of the gym floor, staring out at the massive obstacle course he'd spent the last two hours constructing. "What do you think?"

"I thought there was going to be more...running."

"Oh, trust me, you'll be running."

"With Hula-Hoops and beanbags balanced on my head. Do you want me to break my leg right before the marathon?"

"Go get changed already before the kids mutiny." While she hurried off to the changeroom, Luke addressed the room. "All right. Welcome to Fitness Night. Who's excited to be here?" A bunch of kids drummed their feet against the bleachers. Some teasingly booed him. Luke pointed in their direction, locking eyes with Marcus, who'd shown up with a bunch of his friends. "I'm not above making you run laps."

The kids laughed.

"What you see behind me is the Super Mega Obstacle Course Extreme. The first team to get all their members through the course together will be crowned the winners." He picked up a clipboard. "I've got you divided into teams here."

"We want to pick our own teams!" Marcus called.

"You're not picking your own teams," Luke called back. "Or else it won't be fair."

The kids fell silent, eagerly awaiting their names to be called. "When you hear your name, line up in front of one of the colored flags taped to the wall." He gestured to the far wall where he'd taped up blue, red, yellow and green flags.

"Those are supposed to be flags?" Marcus jeered. "They're just cardboard rectangles."

"Do I look like an artist?" Luke said, lifting the clipboard to read off the first name. "Kinsley. Team red." A little girl popped up from the crowd and ran over to the wall. "Jerome. Team yellow."

Lydia joined him about halfway through reading off the names, smiling as the kids ran to their positions.

"Okay," Luke announced. "That's everyone."

"We're short one person!" Marcus called, having taken charge of the red team.

"So are we!" said the blues.

Luke checked his list. "Just have one person run twice."

"That's not fair!" Marcus shouted. "They'll be tired. We get Lydia!"

"No, we get Lydia!" said the kids from the blue team.

"No one gets Lydia," Luke explained. "Because Lydia is on my team."

Marcus did the math quickly. "That means you both have to run the course like five times."

"Bingo."

"Oh, come on," Lydia said under her breath.

"Did you forget this was a training session?" he laughed. "Better go get on that starting line."

Lydia waltzed over to join the kids, who giggled at her antics.

"Remember to tag out the next person on your team," Luke said. "Runners take your marks. On my whistle. Three. Two.

One!" He blew the whistle and the kids erupted in screams and cheers.

Luke turned on some music, then raced over to the starting line, taking his position. As Lydia made her way through the obstacle course, he could tell she was pacing herself, matching her speed to the younger kids participating. That was good, because after three laps of this, she was going to need that energy. She ran back the length of the gym, tagging him out.

"Go, go, go!" the kids screamed the moment he set foot on the course. They clearly no longer cared about beating each other, only him and Lydia. He hurried through the obstacles, whipping a Hula-Hoop around his waist, then ran back to tag out Lydia. She set off, faster this time as some of the older kids set foot on the floor.

Marcus's team started throwing the extra beanbags at Luke as he waited for Lydia to return. "Interference!" Luke shouted. "You're going down!"

Lydia was back faster than he'd expected, and they traded out another round. By the time Luke returned from his third lap, Lydia was laughing so hard at Marcus's taunting that she had to wipe tears from her eyes for her entire lap, repeatedly dropping the Hula-Hoop at the end.

"Get it together," Luke said as she tagged him out.

"Um, I think we're winning, and I'm totally carrying this team."

"Only because I let you," Luke said, jogging backward to prove his point. By the time he'd almost completed his lap, he realized they *were* winning. Well, he was going to have to do something to even out the race. As he returned from his lap, he reached out to tag Lydia, but instead of high-fiving, he caught her hand, tugging her back as she tried to bolt.

"Luke!" she yelped, giggling as he caught her around the waist, lifting her off her feet. "What are you doing?" She twisted in his arms. "You're sabotaging your own team!"

"We have to let them win," he mumbled under his breath, watching her eyes dart out to track the other teams. The kids laughed and cheered, using the advantage to pull ahead. "Build their confidence and all that."

"And what about my confidence?" she teased, her hands pressing against his chest. "Don't you think they've beaten us badly enough yet?"

"Almost," he said, keeping a firm grip around her waist. He was loath to let her go, even to finish the race. A desperate thrill ran through him like a shiver. The way she looked at him, Lydia must have been able to feel it too. When she didn't push him away, his pulse jumped in his chest.

A thunderous cheer erupted through the gym. Luke finally released Lydia and looked up to see Marcus's team celebrating.

"Cheaters!" some of the kids shouted. "We want a redo."

Lydia plucked the whistle from where it rested on Luke's chest and blew it so loud his ears rang. "Everybody versus Luke!" she announced.

The kids cheered, scrambling back into their lines.

By the end of the night, Luke was exhausted from chasing kids all over the gym. "You had fun?" he asked as Lydia helped him clean up the equipment.

She rolled a Hula-Hoop in his direction. "So much fun," she said. "But why do I feel like these kids could run the marathon better than I could with no training?"

Luke laughed. "Because they have boundless energy."

"You're really good at it, you know."

"What?"

"Encouraging them. Making things fun. Maybe if I'd had an influence in my life like that I wouldn't have to learn how to run at almost thirty."

"Then we never would have met." And what a tragedy that would have been. Silence eclipsed them, and Luke cleared his throat. "Hey, so our last big training session is coming up."

"Wait, already?" she said, frowning and staring off at the wall like she was doing mental math.

"In a couple weeks," he clarified. "Twenty miles. After that, every run will be shorter, building up to a series of rest days before the marathon."

She looked perplexed. "So twenty miles and then—"

"I'll have taught you everything I know. If you can run twenty miles, then you have the endurance and stamina and skills to get you through twenty-six."

"Oh, right," she said, her brows drawing together. "Wow. Who'd have thought I'd get here, huh?"

"I did," he said.

"Yeah, sure."

"No, really," he said. "You were so determined during that first meeting. I could tell you had the work ethic, you just needed the encouragement, the push to take the running seriously, to build up your confidence."

Standing there in this place he'd grown up, watching the flush in her cheeks and the soft, pleased twist of her lips, his heart pounding like a fourteen-year-old who'd newly discovered hormones, Luke realized how far gone he was for Lydia.

He knew he had to tell her how he felt. Not now. Not yet. The marathon was close, but until her last training session, until he'd given her all the tools she needed to cross the finish line, Luke knew he'd have to wait. He'd have to be satisfied with returning her brilliant smiles, with assuming they were moving in the same direction. But the moment she crossed that finish line, he would tell her. And if she wanted him the way he wanted her… He couldn't even find the words.

And if she didn't… He'd shove his feelings aside, knowing that he'd at least carried her through to the end of her training without completely screwing this up.

Twenty-One

Lydia

Waking up with the knowledge that she had to run twenty miles on a Sunday would've made old Lydia want to puke. But soon-to-be marathoner Lydia got out of bed and immediately started hydrating. Wouldn't Luke just be so proud of her? Part of her couldn't actually believe she'd made it this far. This was the longest run she would have to do until the marathon. Everything in terms of training was, metaphorically and practically, downhill from here.

She couldn't stop smiling as she texted Ashley. Twenty miles today! Wish me luck.

That's a massive number. Kind of amazing.

I know! Luke said we'll taper off until the race, so this is my last big training milestone.

Sorta like the day you become a Jedi!

I should totally get a lightsaber out of this!

Lydia laughed to herself. It wasn't like she'd run the marathon yet, but she was still a little proud of herself. Okay, *very* proud.

Her phone started to buzz in her hand. She looked down to see a call coming through. The number looked...familiar? Since when did work call her on the weekend? Had Kirsten gone into the office for some reason? She answered. "Hello?"

"Hey there, running buddy."

"Jack? Hi," she said. He'd never called her before.

"Sorry, I'm calling from the office. I grabbed your number from the personal directory. Got a minute?"

"That's fine, yeah..." She glanced at the stove clock. She could spare a minute before she had to leave to meet Luke. "What's up?"

"I just... I'm working on the write-up for our proposal. I thought having a second pair of eyes on it would be helpful."

"I thought you were going to finish the write-up last week..." Lydia said. The deadline was tomorrow—the last Monday of October. If the proposal didn't get finished by to-night, they weren't going to make it at all. Jack had said he'd take care of the write-up. She hadn't even thought to ask about it, just completely put it out of her mind, trusting that he would get it done and pass it off to leadership. She smoothed a hand over her hair, grabbing her ponytail and giving it a soft tug out of frustration.

"I was," Jack said. "The days totally got away from me. I had to finish up the Carpelli sketches and the Madisyn port-folio came due. And Marco's got the leadership team chasing new clients."

"Oh, Jack." The twenty miles she had to run suddenly felt like one hundred.

"I'm really sorry. I know I dropped the ball. That's on me. And you've probably got other commitments. I totally get it. Don't worry. I'll get it done."

"Wait," she said, scrunching her nose up. She sort of wished she'd never answered the phone. She was supposed to be meeting Luke, but if she went on this run first, she'd be too exhausted to focus on the proposal. At this point in her training, her runs weren't twenty-minute events. Running twenty miles would take her and Luke a few hours at least. That's why they'd already had to swap the run from Saturday to Sunday, to accommodate his other clients. This run needed to happen today to keep her on target for her training plan. But the proposal was *both* of their responsibility now. That's what it meant to be partners. If she and Jack worked quickly, maybe she could just push the run back an hour or two. Luke had been great about rearranging things before. Hopefully he wouldn't mind doing it again. "I can make time," she said. "I'll meet you at the office."

"Great," Jack said, sounding relieved. "See you soon."

Lydia grabbed her workbag with her laptop and headed out to catch the train. On the way, she texted Luke an apology. I am the absolute worst, she said, knowing he would already be at the gym, preparing. But a work thing came up and I've got to run into the office for a couple hours.

He answered almost immediately. Do you want to push our run to later this morning?

Yes! Thank you! That would be perfect. She sent a flurry of emojis. When Lydia arrived at Poletti's, she hurried past her office and into the conference room, where Jack was already set up. She dumped everything on the table, pulling out her laptop.

"Hey, I really appreciate you coming in like this. You didn't run here, did you?"

"I, oh…" She looked down at her outfit. She'd already been dressed for her run. "No, I was on my way to a training thing. Didn't even think about changing."

"Good. I thought we were saving the sprinting for the last leg of the marathon."

She chuckled, but it was a hollow sound. "Okay, want to show me what we're working with?" He sent her through his working copy of the proposal and she scanned it quickly, her heart sinking. It had been over a week since she'd looked at their file, and in that time, she realized Jack hadn't finished *any* of the things he said he was going to. It wasn't just the write-up, it was so much more.

"Okay," Jack said. "To save us time, I think we should re-purpose some of your original write-up and tweak it a bit to fit our new design."

"I guess that would work," Lydia said.

"While you track down the file, I'm gonna pop downstairs and grab us some coffee from Charmaine's. I'll be right back." He disappeared before Lydia could protest. Her foot bounced against the floor as frustration flooded her veins. She tried to shake it off. There was no use in being annoyed. This was how partnerships went sometimes. And if she didn't help Jack now, it might not get done at all.

It was almost ten minutes before he returned.

"Here you go," he said, hurrying back into the room. He put the coffee down next to her, looking over her shoulder before pointing to the laptop screen. "We should probably tweak that part there."

The frustration she thought she'd stifled flamed to life, so she took a sip of her coffee. Why hadn't he done any of the things he said he would do? She was also busy juggling work and training and life, but if she'd promised to finish something on the proposal, it would have been done. She shoved those thoughts away again since they were *not* helping. They would finish this proposal today, Jack could submit it tomorrow, and she could stop stressing.

After an hour passed without much progress, she realized this wasn't going to be a simple or quick finish. Meeting Luke for a morning run was looking like less and less of a possibility. Lydia rubbed the bridge of her nose. If she genuinely wanted to put the effort in, she needed at least a couple of hours to finish the design properly. She picked up her phone, already feeling wretched.

I'm so sorry, she texted Luke. I'm not gonna make it this morning. I'm in a bit of a mess here.

Are you okay?

Yeah. And I'm definitely not canceling. I know this is an important one for the race prep. Any chance you can do this afternoon? Do you have other clients?

I'll move some things around.

Lydia bit her lip, feeling even worse. She hated to think that she was ruining Luke's Sunday, or that she was forcing him to cancel on other clients. The fact that he would do that for her in the first place wasn't even something she wanted to think about right now.

She put her phone away in her bag. She knew Luke wouldn't hold it against her in the end, but she also hated the thought of bailing on her commitments, especially when she'd been prepared.

But this was her shot to impress Marco and the leadership team. They worked for the next couple of hours, and when Lydia realized that there wasn't going to be time to do both her long run and finish the proposal, she sent Luke one more text before her phone could die. In her haste, she'd left her apartment without grabbing her charger, but maybe that was for the best. She wasn't sure she wanted to see Luke's answering text after canceling on him for the third time today.

"This really looks amazing," Jack said, scrolling through their file. "Your work is incredible."

His tone was so sincere and reassuring that some of her sharp edges started to soften. She could choose to be mad that she'd been dragged into work on a Sunday and missed her training time with Luke. Or she could chalk it up to getting to spend some extra time with Jack—something she'd only ever thought about in her wildest dreams—and finally getting recognized for the work she was capable of. "You think the rest of the leadership team will agree?" she asked.

"Oh, it's going to make it to Marco, don't you worry."

Lydia smiled, and Jack's words were enough to soothe the ache of annoyance in her chest and carry her through the rest of the day with the two of them tucked away in their own little world. Jack ordered them a late lunch, and they cleared out Kirsten's desk of the best snacks. Kirsten would be furious with her for letting Jack in on the secret snack stash, but that was a Monday problem. Right now, she just wanted to finish the proposal with the knowledge that it was their best work, and shortly past five, she closed her laptop. Today might have started off rocky, but they'd done it. They'd built something together that was good enough to land on Marco's desk. Maybe good enough to represent Poletti's in the competition.

"Hey, you wanna grab a drink? Celebrate finishing?" Jack asked. "My treat as a thank-you for all your help. You definitely rescued us here."

Lydia blinked at him in surprise. Aside from Kirsten, and the occasional lunch with Erik, she'd never been out with any of her colleagues after work hours before. But *damn* had she been imagining this moment for years. Her stomach twisted, doing a flip. Had Jack just asked her out?

Even if it was only to celebrate a job well done, she still couldn't believe it. After all this time, her little fantasy was coming true. But the truth was, now that the adrenaline of the project and all the caffeine had worn off, she was tired and still a little frustrated with herself for bailing on Luke. The last thing she felt like doing was celebrating.

"C'mon," Jack said. "Don't make me drink alone." He tilted his head, his hair falling across his eyes. He looked so eager and hopeful, and he obviously hadn't meant for the proposal to get away from him. Lydia had worked her own fair share of tight deadlines before. She didn't want Jack to think she wasn't grateful for the opportunity he gave her to resubmit. Plus, she'd already missed her training. She was supposed to be celebrating completing twenty miles right about now. And if she couldn't do that, she deserved to celebrate something.

"Sure," she said, finally relenting. "A drink would be nice."

Luke

"You staying to lock up?" Jules asked, leaning against the door to Luke's office, backpack strung over her shoulder.

"Yeah, I'll do it," Luke said, hanging his certificate on the wall. He'd spent the better part of his day in the gym, waiting on Lydia. He'd made use of his time, of course, most notably putting his office back together. But even after she'd officially canceled on him, he'd hung around on the off chance she finished up with work early. Now though, he probably had to accept the fact that she'd bailed. It was too late to be starting a long run anyhow. At this rate they'd be running well past midnight.

"She didn't make it?" Jules said, her eyes meeting his briefly before he turned away.

Luke shook his head. Would Jules think him ridiculous for waiting on Lydia this long? For rearranging his whole day? "A work thing came up. And then she had to cancel and I haven't heard from her for hours."

"Is that normal?"

"Not really," Luke admitted. During the day, they usually replied to each other almost instantly.

She'd said work was a mess, and he'd spent the better part of the afternoon running through increasingly ridiculous scenarios. She'd been so enthusiastic about this run, and she hadn't said anything to him during the training sessions leading up to it about a developing work situation. Even her last text, where she'd canceled, had been sort of vague and unlike her, and the follow-up texts he'd sent over the course of the afternoon had gone unanswered. The sudden radio silence had struck him as odd, and now that Jules had brought it up too, the hairs on the back of his neck stood on end.

"I'm sure you guys will reschedule," Jules said, hiking her bag up her shoulder. "See you tomorrow."

Luke waved and the moment Jules left, he tried calling Lydia, but it went straight to voicemail. "Hey, it's me," he said. "Do me a favor and call me when you get this. I just want to make sure you're okay. Thanks, 'bye."

Luke hung up and pocketed his phone. He cleared up his office and gathered his things slowly, giving Lydia time to return his call. Five hours between texts might be normal for some people, but it wasn't for them, and when Luke locked up, he didn't bother heading for the train, instead walking in the direction of Lydia's apartment. He didn't even know if Lydia would be home when he got there, but she lived close enough that it wasn't really an inconvenience to swing by. All he wanted to know was that she was okay.

Was that weird of him? It's not like he was her boyfriend. Maybe she'd fallen asleep. Or her phone had died. He stopped in the middle of the sidewalk. This was ridiculous. He should just go home and go to bed. He'd probably wake up to a text from her.

Luke turned around, toward the subway. But what if he didn't hear from her, and he found out something had happened? That she'd needed help or support and he'd opted to just go to sleep. *Wouldn't she ask for help if she needed it?* he argued with himself. Unless she didn't think he'd want to help her after she'd bailed on him today. Maybe she thought she'd burned that bridge. Luke turned around again, heading toward Gramercy Park.

If he was weird, so be it. Despite whatever feelings he was harboring, he was also her friend, and he was concerned. Even if he made an utter fool of himself by turning up on the doorstep of her building, at least he'd be able to stop the uncomfortable gnawing feeling in his stomach.

Luke hurried down the sidewalk, his hands in his pockets. The entire city was bathed in sunset colors, and he couldn't help but think that Lydia would enjoy the way the light clung to the buildings as he made his way down her street.

As her building came into view, he picked up his pace, eager to put all his fears to bed. He skidded to a hard stop on the sidewalk, his stomach plummeting to his feet. Lydia stood at the top of the stairs with Jack, and Luke had the uneasy sensation that he was intruding. A flare of jealousy shot through him, but it was quickly replaced by something else, something sharper, more brittle.

"I really do appreciate you spending the day with me," he could hear Jack saying. "You really came through for us."

"Well, it's not like I was going to leave you high and dry."

"No, you're reliable that way. I think I made a great decision when I asked you to be my partner."

Luke couldn't be sure because it was getting dark, but in the soft glow of the porch light, he thought maybe Lydia flushed at Jack's compliment.

"You know," Jack was saying, "I've got more project proposals coming up. If you're interested, I'd love to have you take a look at them, get your opinion."

"For a sustainability review? Those usually go through Erik."

"I was thinking more in general," he whispered, reaching out to tuck a piece of hair behind her ear. "You're full of good ideas."

Jack leaned forward slowly, his head tilted slightly, his fingers still tangled in that lock of hair he'd smoothed behind Lydia's ear. And then, like some sort of nightmare come true, Lydia pressed up on her toes, meeting him halfway, and kissed him. She pulled away after a moment, but that was all Luke needed to see to make his stomach feel like it was free-falling through the sky. More than he needed to see, actually. He'd intruded on a moment that would surely haunt his dreams for the foreseeable future.

Lydia hadn't had some sort of desperate emergency. She wasn't in trouble. She'd just blown him off to spend the day with Jack—the guy she really had feelings for.

"Luke?"

His head snapped up, meeting Lydia's eyes through those sunset shadows. He turned on his heel. This wasn't any of his business. He'd stupidly thought that there was more between them, but this was obviously why she'd always said it was a mistake. The sex was just sex. He was never anything more than a good time. *God*, he was an idiot, catching feelings when she'd never been anything but honest about their hookups being one-offs, holding a space for another guy to sweep her off her feet. He'd seen the way she and Jack had looked at each other. He knew about all the time she'd spent working on her proposal with him. Of course, this was inevitable. Luke had just been standing in the way, reading emotions into something that never really existed.

"Luke!" Lydia called, but he was walking a mile a minute, practically jogging to the subway. Racing away from her. She wouldn't catch him unless she ran, and she'd already bailed on that today.

Twenty-Two

Lydia

Lydia threw her phone down on her bed as Luke's number went to voicemail again. How in the hell had everything gone sideways in one day? She'd missed her run, finished the proposal by the skin of her teeth, kissed Jack, and then whatever the hell that was with Luke. She flopped onto her bed. She was trying not to let the overwhelming torrent of emotion free, wanting to get her thoughts straight, but she didn't know what else to do. It had been almost two hours since Luke had stumbled upon her and Jack, and she'd lost count of how many calls she'd made since. All she wanted to do was explain that she hadn't blown off their run for a night on the town with Jack, which was probably what it looked like, but besides showing up to Luke's apartment and banging on the door until he answered, she didn't know what else to do.

She couldn't even imagine what he thought of her right now. She hadn't realized he was trying to get ahold of her until she'd walked upstairs and charged her phone enough for his voicemail to come through. If only she'd heard that voicemail before letting Jack walk her home, this all could have been prevented. She didn't want Luke to think she'd purposely been wasting his time today. Why wouldn't he just answer his phone?

She scrubbed at her face. What made everything worse was the fact he'd probably seen her kiss Jack, and to Luke's eyes, that had turned the day—the evening—from an averted work crisis to something romantic. But it wasn't that... At least, it hadn't started like that.

Lydia didn't even know why she'd kissed Jack when he leaned in.

Well, that wasn't exactly true. Some small part of her had wanted to know, once and for all, if there was anything between them. And to her surprise, she'd felt nothing. No spark. No overwhelming sense of desire. After the shock of it, the realization that this paltry crush she'd been harboring meant nothing had come as sort of a...relief, and she'd broken off the kiss as quickly as it had started. But what did that mean for everything else? For her life's plan? When she dreamed of her future, when she thought about how she wanted her life to turn out, wasn't Jack the one standing there, smiling back at her? Lydia replayed the evening in her head. The celebratory drink, the awkward, stilted conversation.

By the time they'd sat down in the pub, Lydia had run out of things to talk about. It was harder to feel connected out in the real world and the conversation lagged. She didn't know why. So, she'd politely sipped her beer and peppered Jack with questions about work to keep the awkwardness at bay.

She was frustrated with herself, partly because she'd bailed on Luke and wasted his time today, only to have him turn up and see her on something that likely looked like the tail end of a date, and partly because in that hazy image of her future, Jack had disappeared. Or been replaced. Or... She didn't know. Was the middle of the night really the right time to be having an existential crisis? And how was she supposed to sort things out with Luke if he refused to answer her calls? Lydia stripped out of her clothes and took the quickest shower of her life, popping the curtain open every ten seconds to see if she could hear her phone ringing.

She changed into her pajamas and got into bed, but anxiety filled her as she lay down, and when she closed her eyes all she could think about was the phone call that had started it all. The call where Jack had admitted the proposal wasn't ready to be submitted. A stab of anger surged through her and all her frustrations surfaced at once—Luke ignoring her, Jack flaking out on the proposal and making her do most of the work—and the anxious beat in her heart was almost enough to make her nauseous.

Eventually, she picked up her phone and dialed.

"You know it's midnight, right?" Ashley croaked after the second ring. "You better be dying because I just fell asleep."

"My life is a mess," Lydia said, her voice small and pathetic as she stared at her popcorn ceiling.

"On a scale of one to Armageddon?" Ashley asked immediately. Lydia could hear her getting out of bed.

"Definitely the apocalypse," Lydia said.

Ashley snorted. "Tell me what happened."

Lydia huffed. Ashley always wanted the facts. The problem was, Lydia didn't know where to start, so she blubbered her way through everything, ending with that stupid kiss and Luke running down the street.

When she finished talking, Ashley was quiet for a long moment. Then she said, "Do you want comfort or do you want the truth?"

Lydia already felt like crap so Ashley might as well keep piling it on. "The truth."

"Jack used you for your work. That's why you feel so...unsettled. I think some part of you knows that."

"What are you talking about?"

"Think about it. You team up to create a partnered proposal and once again you're there doing twice the work to get noticed. You're rescheduling your commitments outside of work hours. You're bailing on Luke. I know things come up at work, trust me. I know that sometimes you get surprised with new information or tasks and you just have to power through it. But that's not what this situation was. You both knew what you committed to, and you both knew when the deadline was."

The confusion in Lydia's chest began to uncoil, only to be replaced with the dreaded feeling that Ashley was right. Why were older sisters always right?

"It sounds like Jack slapped his name on a dressed-up version of your original design. Which means your design would have stood on its own merits if the leadership team had given it a proper chance. Whether he meant to or not, Jack used you. And it sounds like you've been letting your desire to prove yourself get confused with how you really feel about him."

Ashley's words stung, meaning she'd struck at some spark of truth. Lydia's clear vision of her future dissolved a little more.

"I think you need to figure out if you ever really liked Jack, or if you just liked the idea of him."

Lydia swallowed hard. Was that the root of her confusion? Had she only ever liked Jack in theory? Had she really let Jack use her work because of some misguided belief that they were supposed to be partners? It was too embarrassing to think about, never mind admit out loud.

"Lydia?"

"I guess I just always wanted something like what you and Kurt had," she whispered.

Ashley spluttered. "Me and Kurt?"

"Yeah." It felt strange saying the words, but she'd always looked up to Ashley in everything. "You two just fit from the start. You went to school together. You're partners in work. In life. Now you're married. It's all worked out sort of perfectly."

"We're far from perfect, Lyds."

"Please. I used to listen to the two of you sit around and discuss case law for hours." Lydia shoved down the glob of emotion that had lodged in her throat. "I guess I put all this pressure on myself to find something like that. Someone who worked in my field. That was chasing the same career path, the same dreams. That would support me and listen to me ramble about projects for hours."

"And you thought that person was Jack?" Ashley said.

Lydia hummed. "It sounds ridiculous now."

"It's not ridiculous, you're just... I don't know. Remember when I told you that you sometimes rush into things without thinking them all the way through?"

Lydia shook her head, the corner of her mouth twitching. "Yeah."

"Well, I think that sort of applies here," Ashley said. "I think you have to ask yourself what you really want out of this."

"What do you mean?"

"Jack. The proposal. Poletti's. It sounds like you've been struggling for a while with figuring out your place there. Even before this whole youth center thing. What do you want?"

Lydia didn't have to think about it long. She'd wanted to be given a fair shot at the youth center competition, but that opportunity had come and gone. The only thing she could do now was talk to Jack about it, because what she wanted more than that was a job that truly recognized her ability. Ashley was right. She'd forced herself to jump through hoops—the marathon, the partnership with Jack—just for a chance at being noticed. She'd let herself deviate too far from believing in herself and fighting for what she deserved. It was time to fix that.

Lydia had slept restlessly, her phone clutched in her hand, still hoping Luke would call or text and let her explain that she hadn't bailed on their training schedule just to spend the evening with Jack. She'd woken to no new texts, no sign that Luke had even received her calls, and it had taken everything inside her not to bombard him with another series of messages.

If he didn't want to talk to her now, that was fine, but he couldn't avoid her forever. She might not have slept well, but at least she'd had time to figure out what she wanted to do about Jack and Poletti's.

On the subway to work, she tried to build herself up for the conversation she was about to have. She might have re-solved to have this talk with Jack, but that didn't make it easy. It was one thing to think she deserved more but it was an entirely different thing to say it out loud. By the time she walked into the office, it felt like there were hot stones rattling between her ribs.

She stopped by Kirsten's desk. "Hey, if you see Jack, could you send him my way?"

"Sure," Kirsten said. "You okay? Sorta looks like you want to throw up."

"I'm fine. I just didn't get much sleep last night."

"Doesn't sound like it was for a fun reason."

Lydia mustered a smile. "Definitely not."

"Well, I'm here if you want to talk."

"Later," she promised, then headed straight to her office and sat down. Since her conversation with Ashley, there was a measure of clarity to her thoughts that she hadn't had before, but now everything felt sort of surreal. Almost like she was a visitor, peeking in at her life, waiting to see how the ending played out. Lydia busied herself with checking her emails, trying to distract herself until a knock drew her attention to the doorway.

Jack stood there, a sheepish smile on his face. "I was informed that I'd been summoned?"

A flutter of nerves kicked off in her gut, lodging themselves in her throat. "Yeah, come in," she said. "Mind getting the door?"

Jack closed it softly behind him. When he turned around, he started talking before she could even ask if he wanted to sit down. "I sort of figured this is about what happened last night. And I just wanted to say that I really hope I didn't cause you any problems. That was never my intention."

Lydia nodded. "I didn't think—"

"I didn't want you to be confused," he cut in, rocking up and down on his heels. "I know we sort of left things in an awkward spot last night after we were interrupted, and I know we've been working together recently, but that's not why I kissed you. My feelings were real, so I acted on them."

"Jack," Lydia said, before he could cut her off again. "I... think it might have been a good thing that we were interrupted."

"Oh?" His brow furrowed for a beat. "Oh. You didn't feel—"

"No," she said gently. "Which is why that won't happen again."

"Right. I didn't mean to assume—"

"I also don't think we should be partners on the youth center proposal," she blurted out. She didn't know how to smoothly drop it into the conversation. How to say that she wanted her work back. "I know you probably already gave it to the rest of the leadership team, but we're going to have to pull the proposal." She swallowed hard. "I *want* to pull the proposal."

"Because of the kiss?"

"No, Jack," she said, wishing she'd never mixed work and romance. Wishing she'd realized that her crush on Jack had... disappeared before she'd ever kissed him. She hated that he assumed she was asking to pull the project because she didn't like him like that. "That's not why. I need to do this because it matters to me how I get my foot in the door. I want to walk through it on my own merit, because my work is good enough. I don't want to be dragged through it on someone else's coattails."

"Lydia," he started, looking a bit bewildered. "That's not what I was doing. Or, at least, I wasn't trying to."

"You were though, Jack," she said softly but firmly. He might have been her way through the door, but in order to make that happen, she also had to be his stepping stone. Even if his intentions had never been malicious, she could see it now: Jack was still out to impress Marco to secure his spot as partner. Everything had been to win points. Running the marathon. Selecting the youth center as their charity. And now they were just repackaging her proposal and slapping his name on it—exactly what Ashley had said. "You might not have seen it that way, but some part of you recognized the opportunity to use my work and took it."

The corner of her mouth quirked despite her words as all Ashley's ranting about women in the workplace came rushing back. Even now she was working twice as hard to make sure that Jack understood her position. That he didn't begrudge her for it.

Jack just looked at her, at a loss for words. Finally he said, "I'm sorry for everything."

Lydia nodded. It felt like too soon to truly accept his apology, but what use was there in dragging this out? "I'm sorry things didn't work out differently."

"Me too," he said. "I'll go pull the proposal right now."

Jack slipped out the door, and as he did, it felt like that faded image of her future, all the expectations she had for herself, was disappearing with him. She was letting go of what she'd thought her life was supposed to be, and as scary as that was, it was also sort of freeing. The coiled tension in her chest unwound bit by bit. There was only one thing left to deal with now—the marathon.

After work, she made her way across town. Luke still hadn't responded to any of her messages, so she did the only thing she could do, the only thing she'd been doing for the past five months, and went to the gym.

It was Monday, technically a rest day, which was probably why Luke looked so surprised to see her when she walked into his office. "Hi."

"Hi," he said, turning away from his computer. "I didn't expect to see you today."

"I know. That's why I came. Since you won't respond to my calls." She wasn't harsh with her words, but she wasn't going to try to pretend he hadn't been ignoring her. And sure, maybe she deserved it after stringing him along all day yesterday before canceling, but soon he wasn't going to have to worry about any of this.

"I've been busy."

"All day?"

He cleared his throat. "Since you're here," he said, handing her a stack of papers.

"What's this?"

"The rest of your training plan."

Lydia looked down at the papers. Except for her missed twenty-mile run, each run was shorter than the last, building up to race day. "I don't need this," she said, trying to hand the training plan back, but he wouldn't take it. "Look, about yesterday—"

"What do you mean you don't need it?"

"I'm not doing the marathon. There's no point."

Luke blinked at her, like he was trying to decipher the words. "You can't just…not do the marathon…"

"Yes, I can." Once again she tried to give him back the training plan.

"After all the work you've already put in? Why?"

"Because I realized I've been tripping over myself to impress people at work who aren't interested in being impressed by me. I asked Jack to pull our proposal, and leadership won't notice whether I run the marathon or not."

"Is that really what you think this has all been about? You really think you've dragged yourself here for the last five months to impress your firm?"

"That's always been the case."

"So you see absolutely no benefit to all the obstacles you've overcome, all the miles you've put in? Not one part of you thinks you should run this race for more than just your firm?" He was clearly frustrated, which was making her frustrated too.

"I know it's for charity," Lydia said, rolling her eyes and crumpling the papers in her hand. "This won't affect the firm's donation."

"I'm not talking about the charity here!"

"Then what are we arguing about?"

He stood. "I guess I just expected more from you. I never would have put all this extra time in if I didn't think you were serious about your goal."

"Look at it this way, your schedule has just opened up a lot, and now you have more time to work on your business plan."

"That's not what I was getting at."

"Then I don't get why you care so much! I hired you to help me with the marathon, the marathon is now off the table. So we can just...let it go."

"And that's it?"

"Yeah. That's it. Everything goes back to normal."

"Normal?" Luke shook his head. "You're quitting because of Jack. You think you're sticking it to the firm or reclaiming control or whatever, but you're not. You're letting him influence you. Again."

"I don't know what your hang-up is with Jack, but you need to get over it. Yesterday—"

"I don't care about Jack."

"You're sure? Because you sound kind of jealous every time his name comes up," she said without thinking. She wasn't even sure what she was saying or why she was snapping; she just hadn't expected Luke to question her decision like this, especially after ignoring her the way he had.

"Well, can you blame me?" he said, surging to the door and closing it as his voice pitched. When he turned back to her, his brow was furrowed, his chest heaving. "I have...feelings for you, Lydia. More than just sometimes-friends, casual-sex kind of feelings. I was trying to make it through to the end of the marathon before I said anything, to make sure I fulfilled my obligations to you as your trainer, but seeing as you think quitting is the answer to all your problems—"

"What?" she breathed as his confession sent her pulse racing. Everything inside her warred, somehow both hot and cold at once, making her shiver. "But we agreed..."

"When did we once follow the rules?" he asked.

"Luke—"

"I thought…maybe…but then I saw you with him."

Lydia didn't look at him, she couldn't. That's why he'd been so hurt. That's why he'd practically run down the street, away from her, avoiding her texts, her calls. She hadn't just bailed on training and wasted his entire day, she'd broken his heart. All for a kiss that meant nothing. Those coils of tension tightened in her chest once again. "Yesterday with Jack wasn't anything. It was a mistake."

"Sounds familiar," Luke said under his breath.

She winced at that. Ashley's words echoed in her head. She jumped into things, and that hurt people. She didn't want to do that to Luke, or to herself. "This was supposed to be casual," she found herself saying. This wasn't what they were supposed to be talking about today. This was supposed to be about the marathon. "There were never supposed to be these kinds of feelings between us."

Because these kinds of feelings would ruin this. Ruin them.

"What the hell did you think?" Luke continued. "That we kept stumbling into bed just because we couldn't control ourselves? That this was only about sex?"

"Yes," she said before she let herself think too hard about it. That's what this was supposed to be, how it had started. To get it out of their systems. But had it worked? Her heart thundered in her chest. She didn't know what she thought. It was all still such a mess in her mind: Jack, Luke, Poletti's, the race. She was a mess! A mess who had just realized that everything she believed she wanted out of life was a lie. She couldn't do this right now. She couldn't think about what this all meant. What months of sleeping with Luke, and *only* Luke, meant. What her frigid reaction to Jack's kiss meant. What the uneven, desperate beating of her heart meant. "I thought you understood what we agreed to…" Her voice trailed off.

"I know," he said. "I never should have let myself catch feelings. I knew better. And I can handle that if that's how you really feel. If you never once thought of wanting something more between us."

She swallowed hard. Had she? Did she?

"I can walk myself back across that boundary line." Luke's voice grew softer. "But I can't in good conscience let you quit this race without you really considering what you're giving up."

Lydia didn't say anything, his words gnawing at her.

"Don't run away from this because you're scared."

Now what was he talking about? The race or them?

"You've conquered this one mile at a time—"

"And I'm sick of focusing on the next mile," she snapped before his words could pierce any deeper. Besides pulling the proposal and backing out of the race, she hadn't even begun to figure out what she was supposed to do next. "I don't want to run."

"Then as your trainer, I can't help but be disappointed that you're giving up on yourself, because I really believed there was some part of you that was doing this for you."

She looked at him then, meeting his gaze with the same steely determination she'd felt during their very first meeting in this office. "Well, get used to it. I quit."

Twenty-Three

Lydia

Lydia woke up Tuesday before her alarm, her body still in training mode, still prepared for what would usually be a short run day. She flopped back on her pillow, trying to find sleep again, but the routine was so ingrained in her body, it practically begged her to get out of bed. To stretch and hydrate and meet Luke at the gym.

The fact that there would be no more meetings with Luke, that she'd never turn up to find him waiting for her at the front desk, slammed into her like a pallet of bricks, and she rolled out of bed to stop herself from being crushed by the weight of the thought.

Instead, she puttered around her bedroom, dressing slowly, gathering her work things, but even with taking her time and savoring her coffee, it was still too soon to leave for work. She suspected it was going to take weeks to break out of the habit of getting up this early, and the last thing she wanted to do was spend more time at the office.

Her thoughts drifted to the gym again. She had no reason to go there. No reason to walk through those doors.

Well, maybe, one reason—she still had to clean out her locker. She thought about texting Ashley and asking her to do it, but then she'd have to admit to her sister that she'd quit the race. She didn't know what Ashley would think and she couldn't bear another reaction like Luke's. Disappointment was the kind of thing that sat uncomfortably between her shoulder blades. She didn't need anything else weighing her down.

But she should at least go back to collect her spare clothes and water bottles and whatever else she'd accumulated these last five months. Lydia grabbed her laptop bag and the rest of her work things and headed out the door. She was at the gym less than twenty minutes later.

When she walked through the door, Dara waved, giving no indication that Luke had told her Lydia was quitting the race. "Morning."

"Hey." Lydia swung by the desk. "Is Luke in?" she asked, wanting the answer to be yes and no at the same time.

Dara shook her head. "No, I think he's taking some vacation or something." Her brow furrowed. "Didn't he... He didn't tell you?"

"Oh, right," Lydia said. "No, yeah, he did tell me. I just popped by to grab something from my locker." She tapped the desk in farewell. "Talk to you later."

She turned away before Dara could see the thoughts spinning through her eyes. Luke on vacation? Maybe it wasn't connected to their fight, or maybe he'd needed some space afterwards, the same way she wished she could get space from Jack and Poletti's. But never setting foot in the conference room again wasn't an option for her, and as much as Luke might try to avoid this place, at some point he'd have to return to his clients.

Well, Lydia could certainly make it easier on him by not being here when he did.

She hurried to her locker, throwing it open. She pulled out numerous reusable water bottles, making room in her workbag to accommodate them. She jammed the water bottle Jack had given her at the bottom, trying not to think about how giddy she'd been when he gave it to her. That felt like a different lifetime entirely. A different Lydia. She pulled out her spare socks and sports bras and shoved them down the sides, her workbag now threatening to burst. As Lydia smoothed her hand along the side of the bag, it caught on a paper. She pulled it out, realizing it was the training plan Luke had given her yesterday—a series of short runs and rest days, except for her missed twenty miles.

Lydia sat down against the bank of lockers. She'd gotten awfully close to the end. What a shame. Her eyes drifted down to her watch. She was still too early for work. And she had no desire to aimlessly wander the city. Her eyes drifted across the gym to the room that housed the treadmills. What she really wanted was a run. Just a couple miles. Luke wasn't here, so it wasn't like she had to worry about bumping into him, and she had time to spare.

Decided, Lydia stood, put her bag in her locker, and took her activewear to the bathroom to change.

When she was ready, Lydia walked into the room with the treadmills and climbed onto one. She started a slow jog, letting her thoughts get swallowed up by the sound of her breathing and the thump of her feet as she counted down the miles. One, then two, then three.

What she wanted more than anything was for this run to clear her head. She wanted to shake free her frantic thoughts, but with every step they grew more jumbled. Jack. Luke. Poletti's. Proposals. It was like cutlery rattling around inside her, knives scraping and forks prodding at the tender thoughts.

She reached five miles and knew it wasn't enough. Everything was still a mess.

She'd quit the marathon. Jack had taken advantage of her desire to prove herself. Poletti's was feeling less and less like home. And the idea of never talking to Luke again made her want to be sick. She took a deep breath, focusing on her form, relaxing her shoulders, and settled into her stride for miles six and seven. But what the hell was she really doing here?

Why had she even come back?

She wasn't a runner.

This was the biggest farce of her life. Lydia slowed, her heart pounding, and grabbed her phone from the cupholder on the treadmill. She texted Erik: I'm taking a personal day.

Everything okay? came his reply.

Yes, she texted back despite wanting to say no.

She'd quit the race. She'd ruined things with Luke by practically throwing his feelings back in his face. Lydia started jogging again, trying to shake his words from her memory.

Mostly, she tried to rid herself of the memory of her own reaction. *I thought you understood what we agreed to.*

But did *she* even understand? She'd fallen into bed with him over and over again. Part of her had known it was breaking the boundaries they'd set, but a bigger part hadn't cared. Why not? Because she wanted him? Because things between them were shifting and changing without her realizing? Maybe she'd been ignoring it. Purposely trying to avoid acknowledging that she and Luke had become more than casual bedfellows or training partners. More than friends.

In her head, Jack had been the perfect crush. In reality, he wasn't who she wanted. She'd been clinging too tightly to a dream, to a fantasy version of her life, and Luke had snuck up on her. He'd crashed into her world, quite literally, but she'd been too attached to this idea of her life to notice that he'd become her person. He was the one helping her chase her dreams. Cheering her on from the sidelines. Listening to her ramble about work. He'd helped make her youth center design a reality. He was constantly going out of his way for her. And though they might not be chasing the same dreams, maybe it was better that way?

But if that was the truth, why had she worked so hard to push him away? She reached mile ten before she had an answer.

You jump into things without thinking them through, Ashley's voice echoed in her head. Ashley was right, she did jump into things. This marathon. Being Jack's proposal partner. And look how those things had ended. Maybe she'd been working so hard not to catch feelings for Luke because she was trying not to let this be one of those things she jumped into and ruined. She hadn't wanted to hurt him. She'd admitted that. Acting like it was never real, like Luke never meant anything to her, was supposed to stop this from happening. But she'd still ruined it and now Luke thought she didn't care...that she didn't return his feelings.

Lydia's chest constricted.

She *did* share his feelings. She had for a long time. Pretending that things between them were a mistake was supposed to prevent her from losing him. It hadn't worked out that way. And the truth was, she wanted a future with him in it.

She wanted to see where these feelings might lead if given the chance, because she deserved someone like Luke. She'd just had to get out of her own head and let go of all the expectations she'd set for herself long enough to realize that. She had to figure out a way to tell him, to apologize, to thank him for helping her realize that in order to run toward something, she had to let go of the things holding her back.

Even if that was the old version of herself.

Yesterday, she'd been ready to quit this marathon knowing that no one at Poletti's was ever going to take her more seriously for running it. But here she was today, almost twelve miles in, sweat dripping down her back. She might have jumped into this marathon without thinking, but remembering all the training hours, the early mornings, the muscle aches, made her think she was doing the right thing now. Sure, the race was for charity, but she'd also changed these past five months, and that wasn't because she was trying to impress someone at work. So, she would finish what she started, not for Jack or Luke or even the youth center, but to prove to herself that she could do it. Luke had given her the rest of her training plan. She had all the tools she needed to complete this: the stamina, the knowledge, the drive. Luke had made sure of that. Just focus on the next step. The next mile.

Nothing existed beyond that.

She'd finish this twenty-mile makeup run today. Then she'd work on crossing that finish line. And hopefully, somewhere along the way, Luke would forgive her for almost giving up on herself.

Twenty-Four

Luke

The problem with taking time to clear his head was that there was really nothing to distract him from the things he was trying to clear from his head. Or the one thing, the one person, he was trying to rid from his mind.

Lydia.

Should he actually be surprised by that fact? They'd slept together that first night, promising to get each other out of their systems, and though she clearly had, Luke had simply fallen harder.

He knew better; she'd told him not to, but he'd let himself anyway. And that kind of fall was going to take time to recover from. More than just a few days away from the gym at the very least. Did running from the gym and all his other clients the moment he could arrange some vacation time make him a coward? Maybe. But it was a hell of a lot easier than facing that rejection head on. He'd thought he'd be able to handle it with grace, but the truth was, he didn't think he could stand being in the one place that reminded him so much of her, pretending like nothing happened. That his feelings didn't matter. Holding it all in would have been enough to make his heart stop. He just needed a few days to get his thoughts in order.

He almost couldn't believe that things with Lydia had ended the way he'd feared they would—sure, he'd worried about it. But not only had she made it clear that she did not return his feelings, she'd also quit the race. Quit her training. Luke had always worried that it would be his admission that would chase her away, but in the end it had been her own decision, and that felt even worse. It felt like he'd failed her somewhere between that first mile and now. Like he hadn't made her believe in herself enough, in her skills, in her abilities.

He thought he'd taught her more, that she'd realized she was worth more. That she knew this race wasn't just about work. Lydia had started something that a lot of people only ever dream of, but she'd tossed everything aside like the last five months had meant nothing, and Luke had been too shocked, too embarrassed to do anything about it.

He'd failed her, and then he'd lost her.

It was no wonder he was having trouble clearing his head.

As a distraction, he'd throw himself into revising and researching a new model for his business plan. Something that would allow him to keep offering youth programming without the bank worrying that he'd have trouble making his loan payments.

But as he sat at his kitchen table, his laptop open to a dozen different tabs, his thoughts kept drifting back to Lydia. He wondered what she was doing with her time now that they weren't training. He wondered if any part of her missed running. If he'd done any part of his job right, maybe she'd still find enjoyment in it.

Mostly he wondered if he'd ever talk to her again.

As far as he knew, Ashley still went to yoga, so maybe he'd see Lydia on occasion as she dropped her sister off in the morning. Or maybe she'd avoid the gym and him entirely now.

What Luke should have done was keep his feelings to himself. He rubbed at his forehead. Without adding that weight to her shoulders, he might have been able to talk her into coming back to finish her training. Now he couldn't help thinking that he'd only chased her further away. Further away from her goal, from that finish line.

He thought about his own finish line. About what would happen if he couldn't figure this out. He'd still be a personal trainer, he'd still have Fitness Forum and his role at the youth center. He thought of the kids. Thought about how it was kismet that Lydia's firm had entered the proposal competition, that she'd been running for a charity that supported the youth center, that she'd entered his world at all.

Luke sat up straighter, thinking about the charity. Poletti's was raising money and in return, the charity had sponsored Lydia's place in the marathon. What if... He snatched a piece of paper, then scribbled down his thoughts.

What if he based his business model on something similar? He wanted to offer youth classes but the bank was worried about him funding the programming. So why not a sponsorship? What if he adjusted his pricing model so that each adult membership sponsored a youth membership? That could be a unique hook to attract clients to his gym. And uniqueness would set him apart from everyone else when he presented the market research. People loved donating to a good cause. This way they could do that monthly just by working out.

His plan fell together in his mind so quickly that Luke jumped up from his chair and paced back and forth. This was the breakthrough he'd been hoping for, something concrete. Something that he'd be proud to take back to Mrs. Amisfield.

He nearly reached for his phone, giddy with adrenaline, to text Lydia about his big idea, but he left it on the table where it sat, remembering the line that had been drawn.

He'd told her how he felt and she hadn't felt the same.

That was a hard boundary line. One he couldn't cross.

So, he sat back down, opened a new document and started typing up his sponsorship plan.

Lydia

As Lydia rode the elevator up to Poletti's on Thursday morning following her short run, she willed the elevator to spit her out on any other floor. A sort of melancholy had settled over her at work in the days since confronting Jack and asking him to pull their proposal. Kirsten had done her best to cheer her up once Lydia had explained what happened; she'd kept up a running commentary at lunch and left overly sugary coffee and pastries on her desk, but the truth was, Lydia didn't really want to be there.

The worst of it wasn't even awkwardly trying to avoid Jack in the break room or pretending to feign interest in projects she had no desire to be working on, but realizing that Kirsten had been right about what she said that day when the office went running. Lydia could draw a thousand blueprints, work on hundreds of projects, but she was never going to get a fair shot at Poletti's. Not with the current leadership team in place. She slumped back in her chair, letting it twist toward her slim window, staring out at the LEGO-stacked buildings.

Was she always going to feel this way coming into work now? Unimpassioned. Indifferent. *Bored*. What did that mean for her place here at Poletti's? Her role on Erik's team? The idea of considering other options flitted through her mind, but what options, and where? Poletti's was home. This was where she wanted to be. Right?

Lydia turned on her laptop and checked her email, hoping Erik had something to take her mind off her current train of thought. *A thousand blueprints*. If she really got around to drawing up a thousand blueprints before the leadership team took notice, then she'd be a fool.

She deleted spam emails. *A thousand blueprints*. Blueprints…

She suddenly remembered the very amateur sketches Luke had done of his gym. The ones she'd found that day in his office that he hoped to incorporate into his business plan. They'd joked about how bad those drawings were, but maybe that's how she could make this up to him—apologize for dragging him into her confusion, thank him for his support, tell him he was right and that her feelings were just as strong. This could be the olive branch she'd been looking for, and with any luck, it would help him get his loan approved.

Lydia might not know what to do about her work situation, but at least she could do something to try to fill the hole in her chest that had been created by Luke's sudden absence from her life. Spurred on by the idea, Lydia opened and closed drawers in her desk, looking for a clean roll of drafting paper.

She didn't know how much time she had before he'd be submitting his business plan again, so the quicker she got it done, the better. She cleared off her desk and unfurled a length of paper across the surface. As the paper settled, out fell a small, rectangular card.

Lydia picked it up and flipped it over. It was the business card she'd gotten from Angela Reeves at the mixer—the architect from Coleman & Associates. Lydia hadn't thought much of the interaction at the time. In fact, she was pretty sure she'd told Angela she was happy at Poletti's, scrounging around for meaningful work. What a lie that had turned out to be. Lydia flicked the card against her palm. Angela had said to call her if she was interested in talking about what her firm had to offer. Lydia had only looked at their website for a brief minute that day, but she'd been intrigued by what she saw.

Her eyes danced across the desk, landing on her phone. Was this a foolish idea? Was she being reckless with her career? Jumping ship would mean starting from scratch somewhere new. Lydia would be the odd person out. She'd have to make new work friends. Learn the structure of a new firm. Figure out which rung of the ladder she was on. That sounded daunting and terrifying, but what was the alternative? Stay and let things carry on exactly as they were?

Lydia picked up her phone. What was the harm in a call? She could just see what Angela had to say. It didn't mean she was committing to anything. Lydia dialed before she could second-guess herself anymore. A surprising bout of nerves flared in her chest, drumming against her ribs. Angela had said the offer didn't expire, but would she even remember who

Lydia was? Or had she handed out a dozen business cards at that mixer?

Oh God, maybe she was about to make a fool of herself.

"This is Angela Reeves."

"Yes, hello," Lydia stammered. She'd sort of been hoping the call would go to voicemail. "I, uh, don't know if you'll remember me, but my name's Lydia McKenzie. We met at the—"

"Future Architects of New York mixer," Angela said. "Of course, how are you?"

"I'm…" Good? Confused? Freaking out about what she was supposed to be doing with her life? "Doing well, thanks," Lydia said after a beat, pleased to note that some of her nerves had vanished upon realizing that Angela remembered her. "The reason for my call… Well, I guess I'm calling…" Lydia trailed off.

"To talk about what we do here at Coleman and Associates?"

"Yes. Exactly that." Lydia let out a relieved breath.

"Good. I was hoping you would."

"You were?"

"I have a feeling we might share a creative vision. Now, before I tell you about our mission statement and our team, are you familiar with the Bosco Verticale buildings in Milan?"

Lydia's interest immediately piqued. Bosco Verticale literally translated into *vertical forest*. She'd studied those skyscrapers in school, the building facades covered in over two thousand tree species. "You're talking about metropolitan reforestation," she said.

"Exactly. Now imagine that in Manhattan, and I think you're really going to like what we have planned."

Lydia sat back in her chair, engrossed, excitement bubbling free the longer they talked. She had the same feeling she'd gotten when Luke had taken her back to the youth center and showed her around. This was the passion she'd been missing in her career lately, the enthusiasm, and as Angela continued to talk, Lydia realized that maybe this was what she'd been looking for.

A place that valued sustainability, where leaders weren't going to hold her back for the sake of their own careers. A place that believed in her, that wanted to watch her soar. A work environment that treated her the way Luke always had.

Twenty-Five

Luke

Trekking into Fitness Forum early on a Sunday morning was usually a quiet affair, but he'd walked onto the subway to find it crawling with runners and supporters carrying giant, handwritten neon signs. It was the first Sunday of November—marathon day. Part of him had thought about turning around and marching straight back to bed until all the chaos died down, but he had training plans to go over and clients to call, and he'd already wallowed enough. Avoiding the city today because it reminded him of Lydia was ridiculous and would do absolutely nothing to help him get over the hollow feeling in his chest. He had to start moving on. He could handle a little marathon madness.

He threw the gym door open, nodding to Dara at the front desk.

"Wow," Dara said. "You look rough."

"Do you ever say anything nice?" Luke muttered.

"I try not to make a habit of it."

"What are you doing here?" Jules called, coming down the hall toward them. "I thought it was race day."

Dara chimed in from behind the desk. "Oh, yeah, aren't you supposed to be at the marathon with Lydia?"

A bead of guilt caught in his gut. He'd promised to get her across that finish line, but in the end, neither of them were going to be there. "Change of plans. She decided not to run."

"What?" Jules asked. "Are you sure?"

"Pretty sure that's what yelling 'I quit' and storming off means." Luke avoided looking at Jules. Could she see right through him? Part of him wanted to turn and run the way he had the night he saw Lydia with Jack.

Jules still wore a look of confusion. "I thought I saw her here last night, outside your office."

That was odd. "You're sure it was her?"

"I thought maybe you'd told her to pick something up for the marathon. But if it wasn't for the race..." She trailed off.

Luke immediately headed down the hall. His office door was already open. He flipped on the lights, finding it empty inside, but there was a folder on his desk, addressed to him. He crossed the room and put his bag down on a chair, picking up the folder.

He flipped it open, confused at first by the stack of colored sketches. He twisted the folder, reading off the tiny descriptors until he recognized the layout of the warehouse. This was *his* gym. A note fell out of the pile of paperwork. He caught it. Opened it. It was filled with Lydia's loopy handwriting. *Luke*, it read.

I'm sorry about the way things ended between us.

I never meant to hurt you. When you confessed how you felt, I panicked. I wasn't ready to admit to my feelings. That I liked you too. More than I should have. More than a trainer or a friend. And I'm sorry I let you think that your feelings were one-sided.

His heart thundered as he stopped reading. Did this say what he thought it said? Had Lydia just admitted that this was real between them? He found his place in the note again.

You were right about a lot of things the day we fought. But mostly that I was giving up on myself. So I've decided to run.

Wait, what?

I don't know if I'm ready... I think I am. I finished the training.

Luke shook his head. If he'd known that she wanted to... If he'd had any inkling that she still planned to run...he would have been there with her. He would have finished this, regardless of how he felt. Luke scrubbed a hand through his hair, letting out a desperate little laugh. Why was he even shocked? Lydia had been surprising him since the moment they met.

I don't know if any of this makes things okay between us, but I just wanted you to know that I'm grateful for everything you taught me. And I hope you get to have your gym one day and that it's everything you could imagine. Maybe these sketches will help with your business plan.

There were pages of designs. The gym floor. His office. The break room. The changerooms. He brushed his thumb over the circular reception desk in the middle of the floor plan mock-up. She'd done all this for him?

His chest tightened, the emotion threatening to burst between his ribs.

She'd remembered everything he'd said that day in the warehouse and she'd brought his dream to life.

He had to talk to her. To see her. But, God, she was at the

race—the race that had already started—and on the day she needed him most, he was here. He grabbed his backpack, stuffed the folder inside and raced from the room.

"Now where are you going?" Dara said as he ran past.

"To meet Lydia at the finish line," he called over his shoulder. "Cancel the rest of my day!"

Lydia

"Okay, good news," Ashley said into the phone. "Mile two is going to be almost entirely downhill."

Lydia snorted, turning from her view of the Verrazzano-Narrows Bridge, munching on her prerace granola bar. It had been an early morning. She'd taken a ferry and then a bus to Fort Wadsworth in Staten Island to check into her starting village for the marathon. She was scheduled to start at 10:25 a.m. with the fourth wave of runners, and though she'd been so nervous this morning she could hardly stand still, Ashley had talked her out of her jitters. Now she was mostly excited. "So, what you're really saying is my first mile is all uphill?"

Ashley laughed. Lydia smoothed her hand along the race number pinned to the front of her long-sleeve shirt. It was a cool, overcast day, and they'd lucked out with mild temperatures for race day, especially considering it was the beginning of November.

"Remember, don't start too fast. You're going to push it uphill that first mile and then come off this first bridge revved up, so make sure you settle back into your pace."

Lydia snorted. "Any other last-minute google tips?"

"I've got a whole list here. Remember pacing and fueling, especially around the hills. Kirsten and I are gonna be in the crowd somewhere in Brooklyn."

A flash of disappointment washed through her, and Lydia was almost ashamed. Of course, she was thrilled that Ashley and Kirsten had come out to support her in all of this, but a small part of her still couldn't kick the thought that Luke was supposed to be here. He was supposed to help her get across the finish line today. That's what they'd agreed to when this started. But heck, she'd blown everything up so badly she couldn't blame him. She just hoped he knew how sorry she was.

"Hey," Ashley said. "You've got this. We'll see you soon."

"Yeah," she said, getting nervous again. "See you." They hung up, and Lydia took a deep breath, reminding herself that she deserved this. She'd worked hard for this moment, now she was going to see it through and enjoy it—as much as anyone could enjoy running twenty-six miles.

She tucked her phone into the zippered pocket of her leggings, then waited for the announcement to line up. It was about a twenty-minute wait as her corral filled, and Lydia found herself jammed in amongst a bunch of other runners, bumping elbows and exchanging smiles. The energy was infectious, and she stepped from foot to foot to get some of the jitters out. She'd already decided she wasn't going to track her run on her phone. There would be plenty of markers on the route to count down the miles. Attempting to figure out her mile time versus how far she still had to go would only stress her out and ruin her pacing.

The blast of an air horn initiated their start, and the entire crowd moved as one. Lydia felt like she'd been sucked into a school of fish as the group moved up the bridge. She focused on her breathing and her pacing as they climbed uphill. She didn't try to dart or weave around slower runners, remembering something Luke had told her in training. Honestly, she was too busy taking in the view from the middle of the Verrazzano-Narrows Bridge to be bothered with trying to get ahead: the tall, spiked buildings of the New York City skyline, the harbor and the Statue of Liberty. Lydia felt the sudden dip as the route turned downhill, and she naturally picked up her pace.

Coming off the bridge, Lydia was hit with her first wave of crowd support and she couldn't help but smile at the cheering and signage as the race route took her through Brooklyn. Lydia found her pace, careful not to overexert herself coming off the downhill like Ashley had warned. She didn't know what the next mile had in store for her, but she was never going to get there unless she put one foot in front of the other. Lydia thought about the conversations she'd had with Angela, about the job that had been tentatively offered at Coleman & Associates, one that she was eager to accept once Angela and Erik had a chance to talk. She never would have gotten to this point unless she'd picked up the phone and made that call. Every success, every win, started with something small. Something as simple as taking the next step.

Around mile twelve, while running up Bedford Avenue in Williamsburg, she heard her name being screamed. It pulled her out of her head, and she automatically slowed, looking around until she spotted Kirsten and Ashley jumping up and down on the sidewalk with a neon-pink sign.

Lydia laughed, hurrying over to them. She threw herself into their arms for a sweaty hug.

"Gross," Ashley complained, laughing as she shoved a banana into Lydia's hand.

"Thanks," Lydia gasped, taking two bites before handing it back to her. She didn't want to end up with a cramp, plus she planned to stop at the next fluid station.

"You're doing so well!" Kirsten cheered, snapping a selfie of the group.

Lydia's phone started buzzing. She dug it out of her pocket. Erik's name flashed across the screen. "I've gotta go," she said.

"We're gonna try to meet you at 5th Avenue!" Ashley called after her.

"I'll be the one sweating," Lydia shouted, blowing them a kiss. She answered the phone as she began a brisk walk.

"You sound like you're dying," Erik said.

"I'm at mile twelve, give me a break."

"I was just going to leave you a voicemail."

"You talked to Angela? How did it go?" Lydia knew that Angela had been planning to reach out to Erik. She'd given him a heads-up earlier in the week, but the nerves had been eating at her, which was partly why she'd answered her phone in the middle of the race.

"We had a nice chat," Erik confirmed.

Lydia swallowed hard. "I hope you said nice things about me."

"Funny. Only the worst things came to mind."

Lydia smirked.

"You're sure about this?" Erik asked.

"I am," Lydia said. If she only ever settled for what she was familiar with, what she was comfortable with, then she was never going to move forward. If prepping for this marathon had taught her anything, it was that she was more than capable of taking this next step. "I'll give Poletti's until the end of the month just so I can hand over any projects I'm attached to, but yeah, it's time."

In a weird sort of way, Jack asking to partner with her on the proposal had confirmed how talented she was. It also made her acknowledge that Poletti's was only ever going to hold her back.

"You're gonna do great things, Lydia. I already know that."

"That means a lot, Erik."

"Well, go knock 'em dead or whatever it is you do in a marathon."

"I think the main goal is to just keep breathing."

"Text me when you get to the end and let me know how it goes."

"I will," Lydia said. "Thanks, Erik." She hung up, the rush of nerves feeding her adrenaline as she settled back into her stride. Things had gone better than she could have hoped. Erik was happy for her. Honestly, she never should have expected anything less. He'd always been supportive. They'd both just been bumping their heads against the glass ceiling that was the leadership team. *Well, no more of that*, she thought. Like Erik said, she was gonna do great things.

She hit the official halfway point on the Pulaski Bridge, but she knew some of the hardest miles were about to start. Luke had told her there'd be a point where she hit a wall and wanted to quit. The Queensboro Bridge was that point. As she struggled through the climb, there was no crowd support, the only sounds were the pounding footsteps of other runners and their heavy, panting breaths. But she was almost at mile eighteen. If she quit now, the finish line would have been within reach, and she'd be even more disappointed in herself than when her youth center proposal had first been rejected. She wiped at the sweat that was dripping behind her ears and down her neck, focusing on nothing but her next breath.

The race took a ninety-degree turn off the bridge into Manhattan. Setting foot on 1st Avenue while being hit by the roar of the crowd reinvigorated her, and Lydia smashed through the wall that had threatened to derail her run. She stopped at a hydration station, then reset her pace as she headed all the way to the Bronx, where she was greeted by bands and dancers. Her legs were starting to ache, and the beginnings of a stitch flared just below her ribs. Lydia slowed, power walking along the edge of the street, out of the way of the other runners. She stopped at the next hydration station to fuel up again, stretch and apply pressure to the cramp, the same way Luke had shown her. By the time she had finished her cup of water, the pain had lessened, and she eased back into a jog.

At mile twenty-three, the route started uphill again, leading her down 5th Avenue toward Central Park. There was no way she was going to find Ashley or Kirsten in these crowds—there were thousands of screaming spectators with signs and the neon started to blur. *You can do this*, she reminded herself as her calves burned, her muscles starting to rebel. She'd run the outskirts of Central Park with Luke. She could do this. One foot in front of the other.

The route curved behind the Metropolitan Museum of Art and it felt like the skyline was beckoning her home, to her shower and her bed. She wanted to sleep for a year, maybe even never move again. She approached mile twenty-five, hissing through her teeth. She was so close she could hear the roar of the finish line like thunder as she approached Columbus Circle. Every single part of her body ached; she felt like a scarecrow, made of straw and held up by nothing but a flimsy stake of wood. Her legs shook, her bones were grinding in their joints, and she staggered to a painful walk. The finish line was so close, but that last mile stretched out before her like a mountain. Even if she got down on her hands and knees and crawled, she didn't know if she'd be able to cross that line.

She threw her head back, hands clutching the cramps in both her sides, wondering why she'd put herself through this hell. Her lungs burned. Her muscles screamed to end the torture. And Lydia considered it. She could sit down right here and be done with everything. Why did people do this to themselves?

Her phone buzzed, and she reached into her pocket expecting to find Ashley wondering if she'd finished the race. How would she tell her sister she'd flaked out right at the end? But the voice note wasn't from Ashley. Lydia's entire chest constricted as she pressed Play, lifting the phone closer to her ear.

"Hey, Lydia." A sob rushed up her throat as she heard Luke's voice. Maybe it was because she hadn't thought he would ever talk to her again. Or maybe it was just the pent-up race emotions. "If I've been timing you right these last five months, you're probably approaching mile twenty-five, and you probably want nothing more than to quit right about now." She laughed at the absurdity of it. At how well he knew her. "But this is it. This is the last push. So you've gotta dig deep. You've gotta keep going. I've watched you crush run after run for months. This is no different. Just keep putting one foot in front of the other."

Lydia stumbled forward, her shins complaining with every step.

"I know we both said some things, and I'm…sorry. I'm sorry I wasn't there to start this day with you. But I'm here now. Waiting on the other side of the finish line. All you have to do is meet me in a mile."

The voice note ended and Lydia wanted to burst into tears, but there were no tears left after all the sweating she'd done. She'd just have to get to that finish line and tell Luke she was sorry too.

She forced herself to keep moving. To keep breathing. Then she spotted the finish line, the route bordered on either side by dozens of international flags and crowds of cheering fans. Lydia practically hobbled, her stride sloppy, but she kept moving and moving and moving until there was nowhere left to run.

She'd done it.

She'd finished.

She was too exhausted to do anything but snap a sweaty postrace picture to prove she'd survived. Then she was ushered along by volunteers, congratulated, and escorted to an area where she received a medal and a recovery bag. She went straight for the bottle of Gatorade, doing her best not to guzzle it down and make herself sick.

She had to exit the park at 77th Street, so she headed in that direction, practically limping on her way out. She approached the American Museum of Natural History and that's where she saw him. Luke. Holding what looked to be a hastily drawn sign on the back of some dingy cardboard. She laughed, wondering if he'd plucked the cardboard out of someone's recycling. As she drew closer, she could read the sign: I KNEW YOU COULD DO IT. She thought about closing the distance by running and jumping into his arms, but she didn't have one ounce of energy left for running.

Instead, he came to her, opening his arms wide.

"Congratulations," he said as she collapsed against him. "You did it!"

She didn't care if they both tumbled to the ground. She let all her weight sag against the strength of his hug.

"Just under four and a half hours. That's an amazing time for your first marathon."

"First and only," Lydia laughed. "Let's just get that straight."

"Never say never," Luke said, lifting his hand to wipe the sweaty hairs from her face. "How do you feel?"

"Terrible," she said, grinning. "But also sort of amazing." The intense adrenaline and the thrill of accomplishment had yet to fade. More than that, she'd found this sense of freedom during the race—instead of running away from something, it felt like she'd been running toward something new and exciting. "I got your voice note."

"I was hoping to catch you before you finished the race."

"You did. Perfect timing too. I needed a bit of cheering to get me across the finish line."

"I promised I would get you there." He tilted his head as he looked at her. "Why didn't you tell me you were still going to run? I would have followed through with your training."

Lydia squeezed his free hand, the one that wasn't holding onto the sign. "I know you would have. And I couldn't have done it without all your support and everything that you'd taught me, but I also realized that I needed to do that last part by myself. To prove to myself—"

"That you were capable of great things?" Luke nodded, like he understood. "I got your drawings," he said, reaching into his bag to pull out the folder. "I just… I can't believe you did all this. Spent all this time…"

She bit her lip. "I thought maybe they could help."

"They're amazing. You don't know how much this means to me."

"I wanted to do something," she said. She caught his eye and couldn't look away. "I wanted…"

"What?" He was almost as breathless as she still felt.

"I just wanted you to know that you were right about a lot of things during our fight. I was giving up on myself, pushing you away because I was chasing a future I thought I needed, not the one I actually wanted. And when I finally figured that out, I didn't want there to be any more blurred lines between our training and our feelings for each other. I wanted you to know how much you mean to me. That this—" she gestured between them "—was something serious…something real."

"Well, that's good," Luke said softly, quietly, shuffling to flip that crappy cardboard sign over. On the back he'd written: I LIKE YOU AS MORE THAN A TRAINER. MORE THAN A FRIEND. They were the same words she'd written in her note to him. Butterflies exploded in her chest.

"After everything?" she said just as softly. "You still want this?"

"Yes," he said without hesitation.

She surged forward and he wrapped his arms around her,

sweeping her up in a kiss. It was hot and desperate and a little bit out of control as she clung to him. Her arms locked around his neck, her lips like fire against his. A fire she wanted to stoke until they were both burning. But that would have to wait until they weren't standing in the middle of the street. Until she felt like she could stand on her own two feet without crumbling into an exhausted puddle.

"It is good timing," she said when they finally broke apart.

"Hmm?"

"Since you can officially sign off as my trainer."

Luke frowned. "You're not gonna miss Trainer Luke? Even a little?"

She laughed and kissed him again. "Don't you think it's time we replace him? Boyfriend Luke has a nice ring to it."

He smiled down at her, stroking her sweaty cheek. "Boyfriend it is."

Three Months Later

Lydia

Lydia hurried down the alley and threw the door to the warehouse open, almost colliding with a burly man carrying a ladder.

"Watch yourself," he grumbled as she ducked under the ladder and carefully stepped over a bunch of electrical cords that raced into the building.

She'd just come from lunch with Ashley and Kirsten, but couldn't resist dropping in on Luke's renovations since she was in the neighborhood. After he'd revised his business plan to include her designs and the new sponsorship structure, Mrs. Amisfield had signed off on submitting his plan with much more optimism. It had taken close to a month for the bank to approve the application, but Luke had started construction the moment the funds became available.

"Hey, you," Luke called when he spotted her.

Lydia had half a mind to throw herself into his arms, but she was distracted by a text from Angela. Things are officially a go for the MYC! Contract's in your inbox. It was followed by a flurry of confetti emojis. Lydia immediately returned them, swelling with excitement. "Guess what?"

"What?"

"Angela just confirmed. I'm officially on the project for the Manhattan Youth Center!" Lydia did throw herself into his arms then. Luke caught her easily, and they bumped up against the side of the brand-new reception desk.

"That's the best news," Luke said.

"The very best," Lydia said, smiling so hard it hurt. Shortly after making the move to Coleman & Associates, Lydia learned that the firm had won the design competition. The best part was that when she'd pitched them some of her old design ideas, giving them a whole spiel about the center and the kids and things like double gymnasiums to go along with the sustainable changes, the firm had asked her to join the project team.

"You know how you should celebrate?" Luke said.

"How?"

"By coming to the inaugural test class for my new fitness program."

"Does this new fitness program involve a lot of burpees? Because I've gone strictly burpee free."

"Oh, come on. If you ask nicely I might even take off my shirt and give you a bit of a show."

"You know you could probably add a hefty upcharge to those classes. People would pay good money to see that. I should know. I *am* people."

Luke hummed in agreement. "Too bad it's only offered with my private training package."

"Private training," Lydia said. "I like the sound of that. What's involved?"

Luke let his lips skim her jaw. "We start with a nice, easy run."

"Mmm," Lydia said as his lips trailed down her neck. "My specialty. How far are we going?"

"Well, about two point three miles if we're headed to my place. But if we're going to yours—" he said, a teasing grin flashing across his face "—we only have to run a mile."

"A mile, huh?" She smiled right back. "I think I can handle that."

★ ★ ★ ★ ★